Thirteen Stepping Stones

Margarite St. John

Published & distributed by:

Bauer Communications
Fort Wayne, IN
www.amauth.com

Copyright © 2014 by Margarite St. John, LLC
ALL RIGHTS RESERVED. No part of this book may be reproduced without the express written consent of the publisher. All inquiries should be made to Amauth at patrick@amauth.com.

ISBN-13: 978-1500471408
First Edition

This book is a work of fiction. The characters, names, places, incidents, and events are either the product of the author's imagination or used fictitiously. Any similarity to real persons, living or dead, events or locales is entirely coincidental and not intended by the author.

Cover design by Angie Underwood, BookCoverPro.com.

Coding and page layout by Sara Norwood, www.norwoodarts.com

In Chapter 14, Bridget and Justin quote from the poem The Walrus and The Carpenter, which appears in Lewis Carroll's *Through the Looking-Glass and What Alice Found There*, 1872. Jabberwocky, the title of Chapter 14, is taken from the title of Lewis Carroll's nonsense poem of the same name, which also appears in *Looking-Glass*.

Printed in the United States of America.

Books by Margarite St. John

The Florida Murder Mysteries
Face Off
Monuments to Murder

The Fort Wayne Murder Mysteries
Murder for Old Times' Sake
The Girl with a Curl
Hot as a Firecracker
Agenda for Murder
The Art of Death
Thirteen Stepping Stones

The Christmas Novel
Postcards from a Tuscan Christmas (illustrated)

Non-Fiction
Finding Mrs. Hyde: Writing Your First Popular Novel

Our Loyal Readers Say About:

Face Off

"I really enjoyed Face Off. It is far better than James Patterson, Patricia Cornwell & Stuart Woods I also read over the past few months. I have recommended it to friends!"
- Jamie

"Easy and enjoyable reading.... The pace compelled me to read just one more chapter.... explosive beginning and end."
- A fan, Marco Island

"Well-written and fast-paced....characters are thoroughly fleshed out... surprising and very exciting."
- Anne-Marie

"Interesting characters... compelling story line... easy comfortable writing style keeps you involved and draws you on... I'm left wishing for more!"
- pageturner

"Couldn't put the book down! Extremely well-written ... suspenseful plot ... interesting characters. Each chapter ended with a hook, so I couldn't wait to start the next one!"
- Heather

Monuments to Murder

"This is the second book from this author that I have read and I absolutely loved it!! Suspenseful, interesting characters with whom it was easy to identify, and a plot that was both intriguing and yet easy to follow. I literally could not put down my Kindle for 2 days until I finished it! I would say that this author has exactly what it takes to please the suspense novel fan and keep them coming back for more! Can't wait to read her next novel."
- Heather

Murder for Old Times' Sake

"Of the dozens of mysteries I've read this summer, Murder for Old Times' Sake merits recommendation. The collection of characters runs the gamut from good to bad to downright ugly, as well as a couple who are an intriguing combination of those. Just as intriguing are the complicated business, family, illicit, platonic, and romantic relationships that weave the characters together in a story that begins with a sinister undercurrent and gradually builds to a nightmarish conclusion. Multiple doses of the unexpected and an interesting story within the story kept me off balance and eager to read more, my definition of a great find. Fans of Mary Higgins Clark, Diane Mott Davidson, Karen MacInerney, and the like won't be disappointed."
- Bridget

The Girl with a Curl

"A fantastic fifth murder mystery by this author. I could not put this down and I had no idea who the murderer was until the very end. I found the business with the tarot cards fascinating . . . A lot of great research. . . . There were laugh out loud parts. . . . I highly recommend this book."
-Anne-Marie

Hot as a Firecracker

"A fantastic fifth murder mystery by this author. I could not put this down and I had no idea who the murderer was until the very end. I found the business with the tarot cards fascinating . . . A lot of great research. . . . There were laugh out loud parts. . . . I highly recommend this book."
-Anne-Marie

Postcards from a Tuscan Christmas

"I loved this Christmas story, its romance, intrigue, and beautiful Tuscan setting. Tales of redemption . . . illustrate the meaning of Christmas."
- Anne-Marie

Agenda for Murder

"Another great mystery from Margarite St. John! I loved this one, and found it similar to this author's others in that each chapter ended with a hook, keeping me from being able to put it down. The characters were interesting, the plot was exciting, and the story included interesting pieces of information that the author's background in law really made vivid for the reader. I enjoyed it immensely and can't wait for the next book to become available!"
- Heather

The Art of Death

"Another great mystery by this author. It is creepy, funny, and a thorough mystery all the way to the end. The characters are interesting and the story line is mesmerizing. Introductions of new technologies integral to the story are instructional and fascinating. Only recently have some of them been discussed in the media. I have enjoyed all of Margarite St. John's books and I am looking forward to the next book."
- Anne-Marie

Cast of Characters

The Bristolls and Tilleys
Congressman Theodore "Tad" M. Bristoll, U.S. Representative from Indiana's third congressional district
Cordelia Tilley Bristoll, Tad's wife, a member of the Founders Board of Summit Academy
Porter Bristoll, the Bristolls' youngest child, a student at Summit Academy
Sebastian A. and Millicent Peabody Tilley, Cordelia's late father and aged mother

The Bristolls' Employees
Chase Sumner, Tad's press aide
Mimi, Tad's secretary
Tarik, Tad's driver and bodyguard
Mrs. Brighton, Porter's nanny
Mrs. Tooley, the Bristolls' Fort Wayne housekeeper

The Bristolls' Most Ardent Supporters
Maria and Sheldon Steinmacher, the Bristolls' old friends

The Jespersons
Kayla Jesperson, Tad's special assistant and Bridget's roommate
Dr. Ed Jesperson, Kayla's father, an anesthesiologist
Janice Jesperson, Kayla's mother, a medical technician

Kayla's Circle
Asher Stroheim, Kayla's ex-boyfriend
Mac Bevan, Kayla and Bridget's landlord

Bridget and Her Family
Bridget Deel, a teacher at Summit Academy, Kayla's roommate
Kate Deel, Bridget's older sister, Lexie's junior assistant
Peter Deel, Bridget's older brother

Summit Academy
Alexandra "Lexie" Royce Wright, entrepreneur, investor, and founder of Summit Academy
Sheila Powers, Lexie's old friend and President of Summit Academy
Mrs. Rudall, Sheila's secretary
Justin Creed, the Director of Security at Summit Academy
Suze and Buck, Bridget's friend, the Academy's art teacher, and her husband

The Inquirers
Walter Richardson, private (ex-CIA) investigator first hired by Tad Bristoll

Josh Rosen, Kate Deel's fiancé, a freelance writer
Sly Poolow, private investigator favored by D.C. insiders
Mama Bee, a psychic

Table of Contents

Part One

Prologue – The Athenian – Wednesday, April 20, 2013
Chapter 1 – Summit Academy – Monday, July 22, 2013
Chapter 2 – Not for Public Consumption – Monday, July 29, 2013
Chapter 3 – The New Amorous Problem – Monday, July 29, 2013
Chapter 4 – Kayla's Diary – Monday, July 29, 2013
Chapter 5 – Bridget's Journal – Wednesday, July 31, 2013
Chapter 6 – Mac – Thursday, August 1, 2013
Chapter 7 – Party Planning – Saturday, August 24, 2013
Chapter 8 – Advice from a Warrior – Saturday, August 24, 2013
Chapter 9 – Anything You want – Saturday, August 31, 2013
Chapter 10 – Prince Harry – Saturday, August 31, 2013
Chapter 11 – Surprise Surprise – Saturday, August 31, 2013
Chapter 12 – Kayla's Diary – Saturday, August 31, 2013
Chapter 13 – Icarus – Friday, September 6, 2013
Chapter 14 – Jabberwocky – Friday, September 6, 2013
Chapter 15 – Bridget's Journal – Friday, September 6, 2013
Chapter 16 – Asher – Friday, September 13, 2013
Chapter 17 – Mugged – Friday, September 13, 2013
Chapter 18 – *SEAL Breeze* – Sunday, September 15, 2013
Chapter 19 – Nerves of Steel – Sunday, September 15, 2013
Chapter 20 – Bridget's Journal – Sunday, September 15, 2013
Chapter 21 – All Gone – Sunday, September 15, 2013
Chapter 22 – Ending the Game – Monday, September 16, 2013
Chapter 23 – Much to Fear – Wednesday, September 18, 2013
Chapter 24 – Kayla's Diary – Wednesday, September 18, 2013
Chapter 25 – ISS – Friday, October 18, 2013
Chapter 26 – Pig at a Trough – Monday, October 21, 2013
Chapter 27 – Grave Robber – Saturday, October 26, 2013

Part Two

Chapter 28 – Outrunning a Demon – Saturday, October 26, 2013
Chapter 29 – Oak Tree – Saturday, October 26, 2013
Chapter 30 – Bridget's Journal – Sunday, October 27, 2013
Chapter 31 – Sunday Breakfast – Sunday, October 27, 2013
Chapter 32 – Sunday Cleanup – Sunday, October 27, 2013
Chapter 33 – emails – Sunday, October 27, 2013
Chapter 34 – Whose Call? – Monday, October 28, 2013
Chapter 35 – The Heir – Monday, October 28, 2013
Chapter 36 – Guilt – Monday, October 28, 2013
Chapter 37 – Bridget's Journal – Monday, October 28, 2013
Chapter 38 – Weird Game – Tuesday, October 29, 2013
Chapter 39 – Dr. Jesperson – Tuesday, October 29, 2013
Chapter 40 – Say a Prayer – Tuesday, October 29, 2013
Chapter 41 – Suspicions – Wednesday, October 30, 2013

Chapter 42 – Lock the Door – Wednesday, October 30, 2013
Chapter 43 – Halloween – Friday, November 1, 2013
Chapter 44 – The Cottage – Saturday, November 2, 2013
Chapter 45 – Gossip – Monday, November 4, 2013
Chapter 46 – Headline – Monday, November 4, 2013
Chapter 47 – Deep Throat – Monday, November 4, 2013
Chapter 48 – Assumptions – Monday, November 4, 2013
Chapter 49 – Bridget's Journal – Monday, November 4, 2013
Chapter 50 – Wolverine Mother – Tuesday, November 5, 2013
Chapter 51 – A New Friend – Wednesday, November 6, 2013
Chapter 52 – Tabloids – Monday, November 11, 2013
Chapter 53 – Bridget's Journal – Monday, November 13, 2013
Chapter 54 – Vigil – Wednesday, November 13, 2013
Chapter 55 – Bridget's Journal – Wednesday, November 13, 2013
Chapter 56 – Last Call – Wednesday, November 13, 2013

Part Three

Chapter 57 – Revenge of a Sort – Wednesday, November 13, 2013
Chapter 58 – The Note – Wednesday, November 13, 2013
Chapter 59 – Whirlwind – Monday, November 18, 2013
Chapter 60 – Keepsakes – Monday, November 18, 2013
Chapter 61 – Bridget's Journal – Monday, November 18, 2013
Chapter 62 – Style – Tuesday, November 19, 2013
Chapter 63 – The Riddler – Thursday, November 21, 2013
Chapter 64 – Motive – Thursday, November 21, 2013
Chapter 65 – Bridget's Journal – Thursday, November 21, 2013
Chapter 66 – The Human Heart – Sunday, November 24, 2013
Chapter 67 – Good Instincts – Tuesday, November 26, 2013
Chapter 68 – Timeline – Tuesday, November 26, 2013
Chapter 69 – Apparition – Tuesday, November 26, 2013
Chapter 70 – Stones – Wednesday, November 27, 2013
Chapter 71 – Wake Up Call – Wednesday, November 27, 2013
Chapter 72 – Sixth Sense – Wednesday, November 27, 2013
Chapter 73 – Secrets – Wednesday, November 27, 2013
Chapter 74 – Closure – Wednesday, November 27, 2013
Epilogue – Survival – Monday, December 30, 2013

About the Author

Part One

"There is no distinctly native American criminal class except Congress."

Mark Twain

"My sole purpose in life is to help other Americans."

Congressman Theodore M. Bristoll

Prologue
The Athenian
Wednesday, April 10, 2013

Cordelia Bristoll, née Tilley of the Mayflower Tilleys, emerged from the ladies' lounge of The Athenian, her new Valentino suit buttoned up and vintage Hermès scarf arranged just so. She was ready for a good lunch -- the chef's signature split pea soup with a croissant and two small glasses of the finest Spanish sherry.

She was also ready for the awkward meeting that lay ahead of her. Awkward meetings with young women no longer worried her. In her thirty-one years as Tad Bristoll's wife, she'd had to endure four other such meetings. All four times she walked away, head high and flag flying.

"Good morning, Mrs. Bristoll," Marcus Parces said, sketching a half bow. As always, he was immaculate in his tuxedo, his smile as unchanging as his tan. "Your table is ready. Aren't the cherry blossoms beautiful today?"

"Thank you, Marcus. Indeed they are. I love this time of year in Washington. How have things worked out with your brother? Franco, is it?"

"*Sí*, Franco. His papers are being processed." Another half bow. "Give my thanks to your husband, the good Congressman. Without him . . . ."

"Without me, you mean," Cordelia said with a little laugh and a dismissive wave of the hand. "But, yes, Tad helped. What else is a political husband good for?"

Marcus's head dip and slight smile delicately conveyed two

opposite responses: his appreciation for the grand dame's little jest and his respect for the good Congressman. It was a joke among the members that had Marcus been born in Cleveland rather than Caracas, he'd have become a diplomat, perhaps the U.S. ambassador to a particularly cantankerous remnant of the Spanish empire.

As the two walked down the hall to the dining room, Cordelia uttered her usual sentiment. "Aren't you lucky, Marcus, to work in this magnificent building." It was a statement, not a question, and as usual Marcus murmured his agreement.

Taking the chair in the corner facing the room, Cordelia signaled "one more thing" with her hand before Marcus stepped away. "My guest today is a young woman named -- oh, gosh, what is it?" She unbuckled her black alligator Birkin, removed a pair of reading glasses which she held to her eyes without slipping them on, and read from a slip of paper. "Madison Alley. Or is it Alley Madison? The names these young women have these days, you don't know whether they're a man or a woman or even an address." She smiled. "Anyway, she's in her twenties, blond, probably wearing a dark suit. She'll be here in ten minutes if she's on time. Meanwhile, I'd like a glass of that Spanish sherry you recommended last week. And another for my guest."

Absentmindedly repositioning the little bud vase holding a cherry blossom stem, she looked around with satisfaction at the fluted columns and arched floor-to-ceiling windows, the marble statue of Athena in the center of the room. Every table bore a starched white tablecloth. The Whistler on the north wall was a gift from her own family, the Tilleys. Such simple but imposing décor! So comforting to belong to this exclusive club!

Now called The Athenian, the gray brick townhouse was built in the late 1800s in the Beaux-Arts style. Originally a private residence, it was acquired in the 1920s as an exclusive club for women from families distinguished by lineage, money, or political power. Thanks to the Mayflower, centuries of wise family investments in shipping, oil, and gas, and her male ancestors' penchant for what they called public service -- never politics -- Cordelia possessed all three criteria for membership.

Like her mother and grandmother, she very much admired the Greek goddess for whom the club was named. All the women who rightfully entered through the door reserved for members -- and there were never more than sixty at any one time -- aspired to Athena's wisdom, courage, and strength. They also shared her patronage of the arts. To that end, they arranged erudite lectures, private museum tours led by the best docents, and the occasional public service project involving American art or history.

Cordelia's husband, Representative Theodore M. Bristoll, now the Chairman of the powerful Ways and Means Committee, was less distinguished and much less rich than her own family, but he was handsome and ambitious, a politician so skillful his enemies never saw the knife until it was much too late. She alone had seen the dark side of him at once. But it hadn't put her off. She was drawn to his dark side. Her own father was powerful and distinguished but a bit blasé, the scion of too many generations of inherited status.

Tad wasn't lazy. Even at nineteen, she saw that. She liked the Midwestern hardness of Tad, both his tall, lean body as he held her close at a college dance and his wit as he whispered heartless observations about the other dancers. He was brash and exciting, with just enough polish to pass for sophisticated. She'd never met anybody like him.

For her, it was love at first sight. A cliché, but true nevertheless. That night after the dance she told Betsy Hardwick, her best friend, that she would marry Tad Bristoll.

"You can't know that," Betsy said.

"But I do."

"He has a bad reputation."

"For what?"

"Girls and bourbon."

"Good," Cordelia said, feeling deliciously rebellious.

And despite Tad's drinking and womanizing, two years later she did marry him, in a dazzling ceremony attended by five hundred of her parents' closest friends in Washington's National Cathedral. To her parents' pre-wedding protests, she answered that life with Tad

Bristoll would never be dull and she had enough ambition for both of them. She then moved to Fort Wayne with him, certain that one day she would return to the nation's capital in a more exalted role.

The marriage would never have worked had she not held so many aces. Without her father's counsel, Tad would have lost his third race for the House and would never have known how to maneuver for real power once he was in office. And without her money and social connections, Tad would not be a popular guest at the Georgetown cocktail parties where the most lucrative coalitions were formed. Eventually, Tad could poach her social connections, but he could never poach her money, which was held in a family trust administered by high-priced attorneys wearing razor wire. Without her, he'd be reduced to living on his salary, generous though it was. With his taste in bespoke suits, fine bourbons, and imported cigars, he could never do that.

Cordelia did not rise as she watched Marcus escort Tad's latest fling to her table. The young woman was pretty, almost a dead ringer for herself at that age but without the sophistication that comes from generations of good breeding. The girl's eyes were glued to her iPhone.

Cordelia instinctively squared her shoulders as the woman approached. With a kind smile that masked her disdain, she took in the long straight hair, the navy pantsuit with the cheap buttons, the Nine West handbag in industrial tan -- the uniform of the ambitious legislative aide. The pretty face was so tight with self-importance and ambition, its freshness, Cordelia thought with satisfaction, would fade before its owner was forty.

After taking a final look at her iPhone and laying it on the table, the young woman held out her hand as if this were a business meeting. "Mrs. Bristoll?"

Cordelia politely held out her hand in response but folded so only her fingertips made contact. "Please, no formality. Call me Cordelia. Take this chair to my left. And, please, do put that thing away. Alley, is it?"

"Madison," she said, blushing a little as she turned the iPhone over. "Alley's my last name. Confusing, I know, but -- ."

"Forgive me for getting it wrong. Madison it is. And thank you for coming. You have pretty eyes. Very pretty."

"Thank you," Madison said.

"I've ordered split pea soup for both of us. It's the chef's specialty. And sherry for both."

"Oh, no, ma'am, thank you but I don't drink. And if I could just have a salad, dressing on the side, I'd prefer that to soup."

"The soup here is much better than the chopped salad. And please accept the sherry." She pushed the glass nearer the girl. "At least taste it before you reject it. It's a Palo Cortado, very rare, quite dry. Perhaps your palate isn't ready for it, but you can practice. Now, is that a southern accent I hear?"

"Yes, ma'am -- Cor -- Cordelia, I mean." She ducked in embarrassment. "So awkward for me to use your name. I'm from Charleston, you see."

"Which Charleston -- West Virginia or South Carolina -- and what does that have to do with anything?"

"The Queen of the South, the only Charleston that counts." Madison laughed as if only joking. "Manners were very important to my mother. Among other things, I was taught never to call older women by their first name."

Amused, Cordelia cocked her head. "What about keeping that thing" -- glancing at the turned-over iPhone -- "on a lunch table?"

"Just part of my work but I won't look at it unless it's an emergency."

"What about referring to me as an older woman?"

"Oh!" Madison said, her cheeks reddening. "Sorry, I didn't mean it that way. Just being polite. It's a habit."

"Ah, a habit. Is it polite to be sleeping with my husband?"

Madison jerked in shock. "What?"

"You heard me," Cordelia said in her kindest voice. "And you know what I'm talking about."

"I'm just his aide."

Cordelia pursed her lips. "And your specialty is?" *Other than seduction.*

"Revenue enhancement. I have a bachelor's in political science with a minor in economics and a master's in tax accounting."

"Impressive."

Madison shrugged as if ashamed of bragging. "Mr. Bristoll has a lot of creative ideas for raising revenue without raising taxes. That's the theme of the day for both political parties, and I'm very good at that kind of thing. So Tad -- Mr. Bristoll values that."

"And much else about you, I believe."

Madison's chin rose a fraction. "I . . . I don't have anything to apologize for."

"Oh, I think you do. But now that I see you up close, I understand why Tad hired you. You wouldn't know this, but you look just like me when I was young. If I view the situation from a certain angle, it's flattering. Really it is. If I could stay twenty-five forever, he'd never stray." She nodded at the untouched glass sitting in front of Madison. "Taste that sherry first."

Her hand shaking, Madison lifted the glass to her lips and took a little sip. "I thought you invited me here to talk about . . . about work, perhaps something about Mr. Parces."

"No."

"Well, then, maybe we should talk about . . . about all this . . . woman to woman. Put our emotions aside. Work something out that makes all of us happy."

"No, I don't think there is such a thing. And I'll do the talking, not you. Hard for your generation to keep silent, I know, having been taught that self-expression is your right. How old are you?"

"Twenty-six."

"Of course. Twenty-six. I know how attractive men with power are to women your age, but when they're married, you really need to lay off." Cordelia's laugh was sharp. "*Lay off.* That's a slip of the tongue if there ever was one. Oh, here's our soup. The croissants are delicious, so be sure to try one."

Madison stared at the soup and the croissant. She placed her napkin on her lap but did not touch the silverware. "I didn't expect this. I want . . . I think I should go now."

Cordelia grabbed the girl's wrist. "You will not embarrass me, Madison, by slinking away. Now pick up your spoon -- the one on the far right -- and start eating. If you grew up in Charleston, as you claim, then you know how to eat soup like a lady. Am I right?"

Madison nodded, a watery film forming in her eyes. "I *did* grow up in Charleston. I know table settings. I know how to eat soup."

"Good for you. Now, while you eat that delicious soup, hear me out. And then you can slip away before dessert, though the prune whip is to die for. As my husband's agent, I invited you here."

"What do you mean, his *agent*?" Madison asked in a strangled voice.

"My dear, did you think I was acting on my own? Oh, no. Tad's tired of you but he hates giving bad news to lovers. He always has me do it. It's time to end the affair. And you must leave his office."

"He never said a word!"

"Of course not."

"And I like my job. I need it to pay the bills. I don't deserve to be fired because I'm good at what I do!"

"Oh, I'm sure of that. You're good at what you do. Too good. But we've arranged another job for you. One of Indiana's junior Congressmen needs an aide and he likes your résumé, so starting tomorrow you'll work for him. A little reduction in salary, I understand, and you'll find Mickey Tull *very* loyal to his wife, so it won't be the same but it'll pay the rent and you'll leave not only with a new job but a fine letter of recommendation from Tad."

"Tad promised . . . ," Madison whispered.

"Tad promised what? That someday you two would be married? He's a romantic, poor man, so much softer inside than he appears. He's a turtle, a hard shell protecting a lusty heart. Sometimes he moves so slowly he forgets where he was going. As you've surely learned, he makes a lot of promises he never intends to keep. I suppose he told you that we're married in name only, or it's a marriage of convenience, or we're separated. Or perhaps he claims I'm cold and distant. Something like that."

"He said you're an alcoholic." For a second, Madison's face

was ugly with scorn.

Cordelia laughed. "Hardly that, but who would blame me if I were? Speaking of alcohol, I think I'll have another sherry. Will you join me?"

Madison shook her head. "How did you find out about -- ?"

"About the affair? You think Tad confessed? Oh, he did, but not in words. I've been married to the man for thirty-one years. He's passionate, always in love with somebody -- though never so much as with himself. Because of his carnal passions, he's not subtle about women. Every time he starts another affair, his interest in the House gym is suddenly renewed. He buys new underwear he thinks I don't notice and brings home too many flowers. If you ever marry, you'll catch on to all the signs, believe me."

"He doesn't have affairs. . . . Well, except -- ."

"Except you? Oh, Madison. How naïve. Did you think you were the first? Or would be the last?"

"He told me he's never done this before. I don't understand."

"Of course you don't because he's a practiced liar. I don't hold it against him. A politician who isn't skilled in deception is a loser. He thinks his lies give you hope and protect me from pain."

Contempt crept back into Madison's eyes. "If he's as bad as you say, why do you stay with him? For the money? The status? What?"

Cordelia chuckled. "Because I love him. And just so you know, I didn't get my money or status from him. Quite the reverse. But I suspect you just named your own motives for the affair, so that look of contempt you just gave me should be a look of shame. You do have a conscience, don't you?" Without waiting for an answer, she removed an envelope from her Birkin and laid it beside Madison's soup bowl. "Now here's some money for a taxi. Go home now and get ready for tomorrow. I understand you share a little townhouse on G Street with another legislative aide."

"You've been spying on me?"

"Let me see. You drink Diet Coke with no ice, read Talli Roland romances, and on the weekends jog along the Potomac in boy shorts. Your favorite color is yellow and you collect campaign buttons. Do you want me to continue?"

Madison looked at her with fear. "You knew my name all along, didn't you?"

Cordelia took a deep breath. "No worries. I'm not a stalker, but it's my duty to know things. Your desk is being cleared out as we speak and your possessions will be sent to Tull's office, so there's nothing for you to do but take the rest of the day off. Go shopping." She tapped the envelope she had laid on the table. "There's some real money in here. All cash, of course, in twenties. I'm generous that way. My advice is this: splurge on a good bag and shoes." She pretended to sniff the air. "And better perfume, less fruity. If you must buy a cheap suit, then have it altered to fit and replace the buttons with good ones. Nothing like the right accessories to let people know you're a woman to be reckoned with."

Madison shot her a final look of contempt. "I'm not that shallow."

Cordelia was unfazed. "Of course not. But you're smart. And it's smart to dress for the position you want, not the one you have."

As Madison turned away and pushed her chair back, Cordelia tapped the table. "Look at me, Madison."

Madison reluctantly complied, her lovely gray eyes red with suppressed tears.

"I don't have to remind you to keep your silence, do I? Not a word to anyone. No further communication with Tad either -- not a text, an email, or a tweet. If I hear even the slightest rumor of anything I don't like, I'll . . . ."

"You'll do what?" Madison asked after a long pause. Her voice contained the merest hint of defiance.

Cordelia smiled and softened her voice to a purr. "I never finish that sentence, Madison."

1

Summit Academy
Monday, July 22, 2013

Bridget Deel was excited. Nervous too. She was meeting Sheila Powers, the President of Summit Academy, for lunch. Alexandra "Lexie" Wright, the founder of the academy, had arranged everything as a favor to her assistant, Kate Deel, Bridget's older sister.

The academy was a college preparatory school for the children of parents who were unhappy with the public schools. Bridget was a newly minted graduate of Indiana University, eager to find a job in Fort Wayne. Teaching in a private school was her dream.

Kate told her a lot about Sheila and Lexie. The two women were old friends from Carroll High School. Sheila was African-American, married to a police detective, the daughter of a judge, formerly a middle-school teacher. Lexie was a self-made entrepreneur and investor worth millions, married to a local developer. Both had one child. Despite their illustrious career credentials, they unashamedly gloried in all the fripperies of womanhood -- designer clothes, fine houses, and glamorous vacations. They were dreamers who knew how to make a profit from their dreams.

"Let this be lesson number one," Kate said. "The best way to find your dream job is to know someone. The right someone. Social connections count."

"I think I see where this is going," Bridget said drily. "If I get the job, I'll be indebted to you forever."

Kate's smile was mischievous. "I'm counting on it. Now let me give you three hints about how to impress Sheila and Lexie. The meeting is going to feel casual, like just a social occasion, but believe me this is a serious interview I've arranged."

"Should I take notes on your hints?" Bridget asked.

Kate smiled. "Not a bad idea. First, be likable, smile, and look everybody in the eye."

"Is that one hint or all three?"

"Just one. A collective hint I'll call demeanor."

"I *am* likable and I always look people in the eye."

"Sometimes you forget to smile. All I'm saying is bring your best game. Second, listen to them. Listen hard. Let them do the talking."

"Of course."

Kate glanced at Bridget's notes. "Underscore the word 'listen.' I know you're brimful of ideas for teaching techniques and textbooks, but mention them only if invited to do so. They're the experts, not you, so don't be a know-it-all."

"Kate, you're making me sound like something I'm not."

"Sometimes you're a little over-enthusiastic, Bridget. That's all I'm saying."

"What's the third hint?"

"Don't ask about hours or benefits or chances for advancement or anything suggesting you're more interested in your own welfare than the students'."

"Don't I have a right to know those things? And won't I look weak if I don't ask?"

"No. I've been present at meetings between Sheila and Lexie before, so I know all about the academy. Believe me, you'll like what you discover -- if you get the nod. And getting the nod isn't a sure thing. Eleven other candidates are interviewing too. Four are experienced teachers and two have a Master's degree. You're interviewing for the best job in town for a woman in your position. Just go with it. And I'm going to be there to keep an eye on you.

I'll kick you under the table if you get off course."

"Just remember, Kate, I bruise easily. So do you. So perhaps we should agree on gentle nudges."

Kate laughed.

Bridget didn't laugh. "My college advisor said the most important thing in an interview is to be yourself. But you never mentioned that."

"Terrible advice unless you're likable."

"Which I am."

"Which you are. Which is why I didn't have to mention it."

It was exactly 11:30 when Bridget parked behind the school. She didn't see her sister's car. Should she wait so she wouldn't have to walk in alone? No, she decided. Be brave.

Even from the back the H-shaped building was impressive. Constructed to resemble an old English citadel of learning, its brick walls sported ivy and espaliered pear trees. The courtyard was enclosed with colonnades and slate walkways, rather like a medieval monastery. A fountain featuring a giant bronze globe graced the center of the courtyard. The oak door to the back entrance was massive -- and locked. But within seconds, before she could even decide how to signal her presence, it swung open, leading to a marble-floored hallway smelling faintly of -- could it be? -- freshly baked bread. A handsome young man whom she later learned was in charge of security greeted her.

"Bridget Deel to see Mrs. Powers."

"Welcome. I'm Justin Creed." He led her down a long hall to the front of the building, where he took a seat at an elaborate console and consulted his computer. "You're early, so have a seat. Mrs. Powers' secretary will come get you in a few minutes."

"Thanks. May I ask you a question?"

"Sure," he said, his eyes on his computer monitor.

"How did you know I was outside?"

He turned to look at her. She couldn't help but notice his buzz cut, his penetrating dark eyes, his strong chin. She wondered how old he was and whether he'd been in the military. "The building looks old-fashioned, I know," he said, "but electronically it's state of the art. The doors are always locked. Given the dangers in the outside world, it has to be that way."

"What dangers?"

"Mostly the lone nutcase who wants to shoot up a school. From this station, I keep track of everything, inside and out -- but as unobtrusively as possible. Nothing too obvious."

"Is this a good place to work?"

"You're interviewing for a job, are you?"

"I am. I want to teach high school history."

"I love history myself.... Do you like a tight ship or a relaxed one?"

Bridget was startled. "I don't understand."

"Okay. Picture this. You're in the middle of the ocean in a hurricane. The ship is yawing and pitching like crazy. What kind of captain do you hope is on the bridge?"

"Well, a live person to start with."

He laughed. "Good one."

"A smart captain," Bridget continued. "Experienced. On the ball. In command."

"I'm with you on that. And that's what we've got here."

"What's all that about a hurricane at sea? You make the atmosphere sound . . . turbulent."

"Not in here, but it is in the big world, isn't it? Thank goodness for Mrs. Powers. She's as nice a captain as you'll ever meet, but believe me, she knows how to run a ship. She tells you what she expects, she lets you figure out how to deliver the goods. If you deliver the goods, you're a very happy crew member."

"And if you don't deliver?"

"You'll be looking for a life raft in chest-high chop." He shot to his feet. "Mrs. Rudall, this is Bridget Deel to see Mrs. Powers."

Once Bridget and Lexie Wright arrived and pleasantries were exchanged, the four women retired to the dining hall, a long room with a barrel vault ceiling and huge mullioned windows. They watched twenty teen-agers walk in and seat themselves at three round tables, a teacher and assistant at each to keep order. The students chatted and joked but there was no horseplay or screaming.

"So you run a summer session," Bridget said.

"We do for the high school students only," Sheila said. "We like to accommodate their personal goals and keep some of our teachers employed year-round. It makes the parents happy too."

Bridget watched women in uniforms wheel in carts laden with food platters, which were passed family style. "The students don't go through a cafeteria line?"

"No," Sheila said. "They don't choose who they sit with, and from the uniforms you can see they don't choose what they wear either. The students don't have to eat from every dish passed to them, but we grant very few special requests, so they either eat or go hungry. The chef is so good, however, that we have very few complaints."

"Did I smell bread baking when I came in?"

"You did. Fresh bread every day. By example, the adults at each table lead the students in conversation and teach some manners while keeping track of any student whose behavior or appetite requires a discussion with the parents."

"Wow. That's so old-fashioned, it's . . . ."

Sheila waited for Bridget to finish the thought. When she didn't, she said with a smile, "It's so old-fashioned it's shockingly new. I know."

Lexie spoke up. "Everything we do here is meant to impress upon the kids that learning is serious. Not to say that it isn't fun too. It is. Teachers develop their own lesson plans and personal style, and if effective, we support them. But when parents are paying tuition equal to the per capita GDP of Spain, the students better be safe and happy and learn a lot in the process."

"I'm in love with this place already. And this salmon salad is magnificent."

"Good," Sheila and Lexie said in chorus.

"Now tell me," Lexie said, "did you ever misjudge a person, and if you did, what happened?"

Bridget's jaw dropped. "I didn't expect that question."

"I hope not," Lexie said, smiling.

After nudging Bridget's knee, Kate stepped in to give her a moment to think. "Lexie asked me almost that same question when I interviewed with her. In my case it was Josh Rosen. At first he was just a friend. I thought he'd never be more than that because he was so satisfied with himself, so intent on changing a world he didn't understand. But even though I'd only known him a few months by the time I interviewed with Lexie, I was already beginning to see the real Josh. Now he's my fiancé."

Bridget shot her a look only a sister could interpret. *Then why didn't you warn me about what I might be asked?* "It's a great question when you think about it," Kate continued, pretending not to see her sister's panic.

"Let me think," Bridget said, distracted by her desire to strangle her sister. She felt herself growing warm with anxiety. "Well, yes," she said, taking a deep breath and plunging into her story. "I did misjudge someone. Actually, my story is a little like Kate's only with a different ending. Blake was a very good friend and I really liked him. But I found out who he was at the core in a psychology course, of all places. The instructor formed us into study groups, five students apiece, to write a ten-page paper about whether alcoholism is a disease, an addiction, a genetic flaw, a symptom of depression, or a moral failure. Our group divided up the research and the writing, but Blake never produced his analysis on addiction. I'd never seen that side of him before, so I was shocked."

"What happened?" Sheila asked.

"I pulled an all-nighter to do the research so we could finish the paper on time."

"Did you talk to Blake about it first? Urge him to pull his weight? Remind him of his obligation?"

"We all reminded him about his duty but he just laughed it off."

"Why did you step in to do his work?"

"It had to get done and we were short of time. I was the only one who volunteered."

"So what happened?"

"We got the paper done but it only earned a B." Bridget sighed. "Blake wasn't the only member of the group who skimped on the work."

"What did you learn, Bridget?"

"You know that saying -- a camel is a horse designed by a committee. That's how I felt about the paper we produced. It was a very ugly camel."

She was relieved to hear the women's appreciative laughter.

"I prefer to do my own project all by myself," Bridget continued. "But I can be part of a team -- the right team. Kate and I have three brothers and we grew up on a farm, so we learned early that teamwork makes chores easier. So maybe this is what I learned. Either choose your team members yourself or make sure there's someone in charge who can enforce the rules even-handedly. Our parents were very good at that."

Sheila glanced at Lexie, who said, "Smart girl. What happened to your friendship with Blake?"

Bridget glanced at her sister, who nodded encouragingly. "We broke up because after that I couldn't trust him to be a good partner."

"Ah," Sheila said. "Blake was your boyfriend."

"He was. Just for a few months, though."

"Do you think you did the right thing?"

Bridget frowned. "Which? Doing Blake's work for him or breaking up with him?"

"Both," Sheila said.

Bridget wondered what these women saw in the story that she didn't see. Did they think it weak of her to do Blake's work? Or vindictive to break up with him? "I've had a year to think about it, and I believe I did the right thing. I wanted the work to get done and I just didn't feel the same about Blake after that." She looked around the table. "Did I just blow my chance to work for you? I guess the story doesn't make me look very good."

"It doesn't make you look bad," Lexie said. "I like your initiative, your determination to see a project through to the end come hell or high water."

"And you learn from experience," Sheila added. "Now let's have some fruit cobbler and talk about *Hunger Games II*."

"Oh, *Catching Fire*. I love that movie," Bridget said, relieved at the change of subject.

"I was sure you would. Tell me what you like about it."

When the interview was over, Bridget realized she'd revealed a lot about herself without ever being asked a single stock question, like what's your greatest weakness or where do you want to be in five years. And she realized too how much she wanted to work for Sheila Powers and Lexie Wright.

Kate said she'd done pretty well -- high praise from an older sister.

2

Not for Public Consumption
Monday, July 29, 2013

On the Friday after the interview, Sheila called to say Bridget had a job with Summit Academy, but exactly what her job would be hadn't been nailed down. It would probably involve teaching American history, at least part-time, plus some administrative duties yet to be defined. Yes, Sheila said in answer to Bridget's question. Whatever the duties, the job would be full-time with benefits, but if Bridget could remain flexible, her duties would become clear in time, though not, perhaps, by the day her job officially started.

Meanwhile, Sheila asked, would Bridget like to accompany her to Congressman Bristoll's office for a meeting about a proposed law affecting Summit Academy? She could pick up a copy of the proposed law from Justin.

Though Sheila didn't explain and Bridget didn't inquire why she was being asked to perform this unpaid favor, Kate was pretty sure she knew. "Sheila needs an assistant to help her with government affairs, the founders board, parent relations, fundraising, putting together a structure for a future alumni association, and the like. So you're being tested."

"Tested? But I already have the job, Kate!"

"Your job duties won't be defined until you either pass or fail this test."

"What do you mean?"

"She wants to see how well you relate to the Congressman, how well you know the proposed law on short notice."

"What do I do to pass?"

"Read the proposed law, know it backward and forward. Ingratiate yourself with the Congressman. And don't speak unless asked."

On Monday Bridget arrived early at Summit Academy to prepare for the meeting with Congressman Bristoll. She'd not only read the bill but Googled everything she could find on the subject.

As her sister advised, she listened hard to her future boss expound on the law which would change teacher certification requirements for private schools. "I've hired two men, one a mathematician and one a chemist, to teach high school science courses. They're retired from academic teaching positions. Because teaching at Summit is simply a second career they don't need financially, they have no interest in undergoing the two-year process for certification, but they're superb teachers. If opponents of private schools get their way, they'll be disqualified because they lack state certification."

"Do you know the Congressman?" Bridget asked.

"Oh, yes, through my father. Furthermore, Bristoll's wife, Cordelia, is a member of the Summit Founders Club. She's going to sit in on our meeting with her husband. Her youngest child, Porter, who'll be a junior this year, is enrolled at Summit. And she's endowed a four-year full-ride scholarship for a lucky student. She cares a lot about the school."

"The Bristolls must be rich to afford all that."

"Well, *she* is. Family money. She's from out East but she's made herself a pillar of the Fort Wayne community, even though she only spends half the year here. Just between you and me, I think she much prefers Washington, D.C. That's where she grew up."

"So did Hoosiers get a two-for-one when they elected Bristoll?"

Sheila laughed softly. "You're thinking of the Clintons. Not a bit of it. Cordelia is not the power behind the throne and she has no political ambitions of her own. In fact, she hates politics -- the cut-and-thrust of the power game, the broken promises, the talking points. But if she cares about an issue, she lobbies her husband."

"Why does she have to lobby him if they're married?"

"As two individuals with their own views, they don't agree on everything."

"And does he always do what she wants?"

"No. But her weight behind an issue sometimes tips the balance. I'm hoping that will happen here." Sheila briefly glanced at her new hire. "What do you think of Justin?"

For Bridget, the question came out of left field. "He's very polite."

"Handsome too, wouldn't you say?"

Bridget blushed. "I noticed that."

"I thought you would. Formerly a Navy SEAL, he's physically fit and very smart. And he's single."

"Are you playing matchmaker?"

Sheila sighed. "I guess I am, though for the life of me I don't know why."

"I never imagined myself dating a security guard."

"Oh, Bridget, he's a lot more than that. His character is superb. As for being a security guard, he's had special training in executive protection. What he doesn't know about security isn't worth knowing. Mark my words, one day he's going to head his own international security business."

"Well, finding a boyfriend isn't high on my list. I have a job I'm excited about, and I need to find an apartment plus a roommate if I'm going to afford anything decent."

"Then I'll drop the subject for now. All I suggest is you envision the potential."

"Isn't that courting delusion?"

"Sometimes, I suppose. Maybe you're thinking of Blake. But take me. I was just a middle-school teacher, quite happy at the prospect of retiring in forty years. But Lexie saw something else in me -- something even I didn't see. So focus on the man Justin is becoming, not the man he is at thirty-one."

"You're a romantic!" Bridget exclaimed.

Sheila put her finger to her lips. "Shh. Don't tell anyone."

"Well, I'll keep your advice in mind. But something else you said has definitely lodged in my brain. Why . . . why do you need the level of protection a Navy SEAL with special training can provide?"

"I told Lexie I didn't, but she thinks otherwise. She may be right. After all, both of us have gotten death threats from people who think we're unAmerican, destroying the public schools. Our detractors are furious because we don't take a dime from the taxpayers and our staff isn't unionized, so we can do things the public schools can't. And, of course, if you look at the other side of the question -- which I always do -- we siphon off some of the best students and thus the public schools perform less well than they otherwise would."

"So is Justin your bodyguard?"

"Not outside the school. I put my foot down about that, but Lexie wants the school as safe as possible and I do too. So Justin's job is to protect all of us."

"Why do we need Congressman Bristoll's help? What we're talking about is an amendment to state law, not federal."

"The union proposing the amendment is testing their power in Indiana. If they can force private schools here to hire only accredited teachers, then they hope to get a federal law to supersede all contrary state efforts. Bristoll's behind-the-scenes support would help even at the state level, and as a member of the House committee on education he might even take a firm line in our favor at that level."

"So this meeting today is serious."

"Very serious."

"What's my role?"

"Listen and learn. And, not for public consumption, but Tad Bristoll likes attractive young women. You never know, he may be swayed by your pretty face."

Bridget took in Sheila's youthful hairdo and glowing skin, her sparkling eyes. "Oh, Sheila, yours should do it."

"Thank you, but I'm not twenty-one."

"Is the Congressman's penchant for pretty women okay with his wife?"

"No." Sheila got to her feet, signaling it was time to leave. "Don't take this the wrong way, Bridget. I'm not throwing you at that man, believe me. Nothing like that. And I certainly don't want Cordelia hurt. But flirting is a woman's trade."

"Did you just make that up?" Bridget asked, rising too.

Sheila laughed. "I heard it or read it somewhere, perhaps in a Jane Austen novel. But if not, then I must have just made it up. And I congratulate myself. We women must use all the formidable advantages we were born with."

3

The New Amorous Problem
Monday, July 29, 2013

Chase Sumner was reading a stack of newspapers and gulping coffee, his normal morning routine, when he looked up to see two women walking toward Tad's office. He checked the daily schedule on his computer monitor. Sheila Powers, President of Summit Academy, had arrived. He remembered her, having shaken hands with her shortly after Summit Academy opened. The party to celebrate the academy's opening was attended by PWM -- People Who Matter -- including Tad and Cordelia. He was fortunate to tag along.

But who was that young woman with Mrs. Powers? She was a pretty girl with mischievous eyes and dark wavy hair clutching a leather portfolio against her chest. Was she pretty enough to become the next AP -- Amorous Problem? He'd have to ask Mimi, Tad's secretary.

It made him uneasy that he'd been told his presence at this morning's meetings wasn't necessary. As the Congressman's press aide, Chase felt he could not stay on top of his job unless he monitored every meeting, every public appearance, even every chance encounter with a potential donor, volunteer, supporter -- or enemy. When pretty women were involved, Tad's radar for political survival went haywire.

Chase's radar never went haywire. He was a man on the make.

Having grown up in a family of entrepreneurs who kept choosing the wrong partner or investing in a losing franchise or taking to drink when things went bad, he was determined not to make the mistakes of his forebears. And politics was his game. It was the only way to form the world in his own image. The image he had in mind was complicated. Taking a risk was good, so he believed in free markets and private capital. Losing, however, was bad, so he also believed in generous safety nets and plenty of government control as well.

As a freshman at college, an undistinguished state school that he could afford because it gave him a scholarship for golf, Chase attended a lecture by Tad Bristoll on farm subsidies. He was smitten. The politician sounded confident. He looked it too. Tall, lean, tanned, with a big shock of salt-and-pepper hair, Tad was well-spoken, funny, and dressed in a suit Chase instinctively knew had cost the earth. He wanted to be Theodore Bristoll.

So he interned with Tad, at no salary, every summer after that. The experience was exhausting for his mother, who agreed to take a second job to support him when he pleaded that the internship was an ISS -- important stepping stone -- to a big-time career in Washington, D.C. Three summers of working for the Congressman taught Chase how to be indispensable without being a sycophant. Though writing had never interested him before, he learned to write press releases that caught the media's attention without actually taking a binding position on any subject. He ingratiated himself with Cordelia Bristoll and made a friend of Porter, his mother's asthmatic darling.

The hardest part of his job was keeping Tad's affairs under wraps. Without ever being told what to do, he became the Congressman's "beard," pretending to be the AP's real boyfriend. Fortunately, though Tad's women were always attractive, none had ever appealed to him, so playing the role of suitor *manqué* became second nature -- so second nature he wasn't sure he could ever have a genuine relationship with a woman he chose for himself.

Shortly after Sheila Powers and the mysterious girl walked out of Tad's office, accompanied by Cordelia, he saw Mimi show a young blonde in. She was all pink dewy skin and charming smiles, a voluptuous figure set off by a knockout dress in royal blue. The Congressman's calendar read "Kayla Jesperson, interviewing for Special Assistant."

Chase sighed. He knew what Special Assistant meant. He knew the qualifications for the job: a college degree, beauty, and a willing spirit.

If he were a betting man, he'd stake his life on it: This girl was the new AP.

4

Kayla's Diary
Monday, July 29, 2013

What a wonderful time I had today!!! So nervous at first, but it was more like meeting a hot guy at a bar than interviewing with a BIG SHOT. Congressman Bristoll -- with two L's -- is SO handsome. Tall, slender, lots of hair. Great teeth for his age. He says he works out. He didn't say, but I just know he buys his clothes at some posh place like Saks. He says he vacations a lot in Florida but how does he keep that tan going when he's up north?

Totally awesome.

He's older, as he'd have to be for all that power and prestige, but I've always liked older men. So much more sophisticated than guys my age. Anyway, he told me to call him Tad. SO NICE. He doesn't smile a lot but that LOOK in his eyes -- very FLIRTY.

I flubbed a few questions but he just laughed it off. I know what the Ways and Means Committee does, but my mind simply went blank for a minute because the name sounds so dumb. It's all about taxes and appropriations and is VERY important. I told him the classes I had in poly sci weren't that great, so some things didn't sink in the way they should, but I'm a quick study, so not to worry. I'll work my butt off and I know how to use Wikipedia, I said. "Wikipedia!" he repeated with a laugh.

Anyway, I've got the job. With a CLOTHING allowance, no less, because I'm expected to go to fundraisers and speeches and conventions and such, and I'll even get to go to Washington for hearings and committee meetings, so I'm pretty chuffed, even if the salary is a lot less than I deserve. A LOT less.

Right in the middle of the meeting Asher texted again but I didn't reply. He's working in a warehouse in Elkhart, for God's sake. Just because we dated in Bloomington doesn't mean we're going to keep dating. I'm SO done with him. LOSER!

LUCK was with me all day. In the restroom I met another IU graduate, Bridget Deel. A little straight-laced, I suspect, may not be tons of fun, and she grew up on a farm, but I can tell she's smart. And she's pretty -- a lot prettier than she knows -- but not as pretty as I am, I think, so that works. She'll make a great wing man at bars.

WHAT LUCK, she wants a roommate too, so we're having a drink tonight at Club Soda to talk about it. Just to be sure we're singing from the same hymn book, she said, although I didn't tell her I don't sing hymns. If things go right, we're going to hook up Thursday to look for an apartment. I told her I HATE apartments. Too much like dorm rooms. And I don't like elevators either. I want something charming, big enough for parties, with a place for a grill.

Only problem with the new job is I won't get my first paycheck until September 16, and Tad's secretary Mimi warned me there'll be lots of deductions for things like FICA, which I've heard of before but again I can't remember what it is, so I've got to call Daddy.

He'll huff and puff and then give in like he always does and put a few hundred dollars in my bank account. I'm his little princess, after all. And I intend to stay that way until he dies. Which I hope is EONS away.

5

Bridget's Journal
Wednesday, July 31, 2013

I really like Kayla Jesperson, despite the fact that she's about ten times prettier than I am and her clothes are smashing.

She's got the cutest laugh and says funny things she doesn't even know are funny. We talked a lot about clothes -- probably her favorite subject. She says she likes clothes because naked people never amount to anything -- you never see them at the Oscars or the Olympics or a State Dinner at the White House. She didn't know why I was laughing so hard.

Kayla's a daddy's girl, that's obvious. My dad is very nice but he never spoiled me. She may be spoiled, but she seems very generous and kind and rooming with her should be a treat.

She agreed to look at a couple of apartments, but I can tell she's dead set on finding a house. No more dorm rooms, she said,

If we do find a house we can afford, we agreed we'd get a dog. Gracie, Mom's Golden Retriever, just had another litter in June. Mom's keeping one and selling three, but she told me I could have the runt, a shy little boy that's the cutest thing I've ever seen. I have his picture on my phone.

Kayla's so excited about the puppy she even agreed with me on a name for him.

6

Mac
Thursday, August 1, 2013

From behind a lilac, Mac Bevan watched two women get out of a little green Bug and approach the house next door. He smiled at how young and pretty they were. Exactly the tenants he wanted.

The house he had advertised for rent was a little Craftsman bungalow. A decade earlier, he had inherited it, free of all liens and mortgages, from his crazy Aunt Gladys, whom he had cared for as she lay dying. Her out-of-town children challenged the will, accusing Mac of fraud, forgery, undue influence, and other heinous crimes committed on an old woman who was not of sound mind, but, being of crafty mind himself, he had prevailed. After that, he quit his job at Jiffy Lube, successfully applied for disability due to back pain and stress, and lived rather well as a landlord who sometimes hired out as a handyman skilled in plumbing, electrical, and carpentry. Hating tax collectors of every stripe, he accepted rent payments and handyman fees in cash only.

All his life, Mac had avoided marriage as scrupulously as paying taxes. He'd come close a couple of times, but it was no go. He wasn't about to quit smoking in the house for anyone, and he didn't like being nagged to get a real job. Nevertheless, he liked women so long as they didn't demand anything, did as he said, and lived in their own place.

Mac dropped the hose and whistled at the women, not

flirtatiously but as a signal that they should quit knocking on the door of the empty house.

"Hi, girls. I'm Mac. I'm the landlord."

"Oh," the pretty blonde said, holding out the newspaper. "Is this the right house?"

"It is. And what's your name?"

"Kayla."

"And I'm Bridget," the brunette said.

"Are you two sisters?" Mac asked, though he was sure they weren't.

"No. We're friends," Kayla said. "We just met Monday but since then we've talked and we think we can manage as roommates. We're looking for an apartment -- or a house if the rent is right."

"Well, a house is always better. I'll make sure the rent is right for two such lovely ladies." He unlocked the door. "This is an old house but it's all updated. I did it myself. Two bedrooms, a bathroom for each. New kitchen, eating alcove, freshly painted. Working fireplace." He led them through the house, carefully watching their faces for reaction to the work he'd done. The blonde exclaimed approvingly at everything -- the taupe paint on the walls, the gas stove in the kitchen, the little telephone niche in the dining alcove, the fireplace mantel. The brunette said nothing.

"So what do you think, girls?"

"I love it," the blonde said. "It's charming. Isn't it, Bridget?"

"Oh, yes, I like it too. So much nicer than a sterile apartment. But we need to know if we can afford the rent and whether we'd be expected to take care of anything that breaks down."

"Like what?" Mac asked.

"I don't know. Maybe the furnace or the air conditioning."

"I take it you're the practical one."

Kayla laughed. "Oh, Bridget is for sure. I saw that right away. Me, I'm a romantic and this place fills the bill for me. I leave the practical stuff to her."

"I'm practical too," Mac said. "I live right next door so I'm here 24/7 to take care of any little thing you need," Mac said. "I'm very proud of this house and as you can see I take care of it.

I rewired and replumbed the whole thing a couple of years ago and there's nothing about a house I can't fix. I mow the lawn and shovel the sidewalks and trim the trees. The furnace is old but it's good, and the sump pump is new. Believe me, you'll be very well taken care of."

"Perfect," Kayla said.

"But first we have a couple of other places to check out," Bridget said, putting a restraining hand on Kayla. "We just started looking this morning."

"Tell you what," Mac said. "You go look. Then come back and tell me the rent the other places want and I'll make sure this is a better deal. But first tell me -- I don't want to be nosy here but I want some assurance you can pay the rent whatever it is -- do both of you have jobs?"

"I'm the new special assistant to Congressman Bristoll," Kayla said. "I start in September."

"And I'll be teaching at Summit Academy starting then too," Bridget said.

"So you're going to have some money in the future, but what do you do until then?" Mac asked.

"Well," Kayla answered, "we were hoping to move in September 1 or even a few days earlier if that's possible, so we don't want the rent to start until then."

"You'll be lucky to find a deal like that, girls."

"We have to try," Bridget said, turning toward the front door.

"Hold on. Hold on. You come back to me after you've looked at whatever you're going to look at. I'll not only beat any price quoted to you for a two-bedroom place, but I'll let you move in August 19, rent to start September 1. That's two whole weeks free; no security deposit. But the rent is payable only in cash."

"How nice of you!" Kayla said.

"Why in cash?" Bridget asked.

Mac smiled. "Cash means I can charge you less."

"Less is good," Kayla said, clapping her hands. "This is so exciting."

"You'd really let us move in before we start paying?" Bridget asked.

"For tenants like you? Of course," Mac said. "You look like you'll take good care of the house. But the offer's only good until tomorrow at 5 pm."

The two girls exchanged excited looks. "We'll get back to you before that," Kayla said.

* * * * *

After leaving Mac, Bridget and Kayla chattered about the bungalow they'd just toured while cruising the area in Bridget's old Volkswagen.

"I'd rather be on Forest Park Boulevard," Bridget said wistfully.

"Well, so would I, but that's not going to happen. Besides, Anthony Boulevard isn't bad at all and it's only a block away. If we get a dog, we can take walks all around the places you like best and look at all the pretty mansions."

After debating whether they should conclude the search instead of visiting a couple of apartment buildings, Bridget finally said, "I like the house as much as you do, but I don't like the looks of that man."

"You mean Mac?"

"Who else?"

"He looks very nice for a guy in his forties. Almost handsome, in fact, neat and clean for a guy who works outside with his hands. I'm surprised he isn't married."

"Still."

"Still what?"

Bridget glanced at her new friend. "Something about the look in his eyes."

"What look in his eyes? He's just friendly."

"Friendly? Are you kidding? He leered at you. There's no other word for it. He leered." Bridget turned her head to smile teasingly at her friend. "He looked like a starving man glimpsing a fat roast turkey."

"Are you calling me fat?" Kayla asked in mock indignation.

"No. And obviously not a turkey either. But he'd like to eat you up."

"Oh, that," Kayla said, laughing. "I don't mind. Everyone wants to eat me up."

7

Party Planning
Saturday, August 24, 2013

A week after moving into the bungalow next door to Mac the landlord, before any rent had been paid, Kayla began planning a house-warming party.

"You haven't even completely unpacked yet," Bridget protested. "And we hardly have any furniture. Where would people sit?"

"I just have a couple more boxes to empty, so no worry there. And what do you mean about sitting down? Nobody has to sit. In fact, it's better if people can't plant themselves somewhere. That way, they'll have to move around and mingle. But the Labor Day weekend is perfect. If we do it Saturday, we'll have two days to recover before we start work on Tuesday."

"You don't think Mac will be mad if we start partying before we've paid rent?"

"I hadn't thought about that. . . . . I know. We'll invite him too."

"You're kidding, Kayla! He won't fit in."

"Well, then, he can be the grill man or the bartender -- or both!"

"Why would he want to do that?"

Kayla giggled. "Just to be over here. I'll tell him what to wear and make him feel so special he won't notice he isn't really a guest."

"Are we going to offer food? Baked beans is about all I know how to make."

"Food isn't the point, so we'll just serve hamburgers and hot dogs, nothing expensive. And we'll ask everybody to bring their own booze. All we'll have to do is set up some tubs of ice."

Bridget looked around the long living room. Except for mismatched armchairs on either side of the fireplace -- the chairs in which they were sitting while drinking their morning coffee -- and an old wicker lounge near the front window, the room was bare. "I don't know, Kayla. This room looks pretty rough."

"So let's go look at sofas and end tables. We need some lamps too."

"Like we can afford a sofa. My credit card is maxed out and even if it wasn't, I have a big school loan to start paying."

"So do I, but we can't let little things like debt take the fun out of life." Kayla leapt to her feet. "Come on, Bridget. Macy's might have just what we want. You can always say no to whatever I pick out."

"And you'll have a tantrum in the aisle if I do."

"It'll be a very charming tantrum, I promise."

Bridget laughed. "I'm sure of that. But why not start at Sofa Mart?"

"Because I like Glenbrook and I haven't been there in months. If we don't find furniture we like, at least we can buy a lipstick or something."

8

Advice from a Warrior
Saturday, August 24, 2013

Fortunately, Kayla found no sofa at Macy's that suited her idea of glamor or Bridget's idea of economy. Neither was unhappy. What they really wanted all along was to cruise Macy's for cosmetics, perfume, and costume jewelry -- Kayla to buy something, Bridget to scope out what was new.

After Kayla had a new face applied by an eager cosmetics clerk, she said she needed a caffeine lift. Starbucks was crowded, every table taken, when a handsome young man beckoned at Kayla as she and Bridget picked up their caramel lattes and looked for a seat. "Didn't I see you at Tad's office?" he asked, getting to his feet. "Sorry, I don't remember your name."

"Tad? You mean the Congressman?" Kayla asked uncertainly.

"I'm his press aide, Chase Sumner. If you know his nickname is Tad, then you must be an insider. I remember seeing you a month or so ago in the office but we didn't get a chance to meet."

"Kayla Jesperson," she said, accepting his proffered hand. "You must have seen me when I went in for an interview."

"Are you the new special assistant?"

"I am. I can't wait to get started."

"I saw you walk by my office, but I was all tied up with something, so I couldn't introduce myself then. I noticed you too," he said, nodding at Bridget.

"Oh, let me introduce you," Kayla said. "This is my roommate, Bridget Deel. She's starting at Summit Academy the day after Labor Day."

"Please join me," he said, smiling and pointing at two empty chairs. "This place is packed. Doing a little shopping?"

"Looking for a sofa we can't afford," Bridget said drily. "How about you?" She wanted to hear more about him. Apparently in his late twenties or early thirties with no wedding ring, he had a pleasantly square face, regular features, short brown hair, and good manners.

"Just taking a little time off." He turned his attention to Kayla. "So you're Tad's new special assistant. You're going to love the job. You've got the face for it."

"What do you mean?"

"There's a social aspect to the place, you know, so most of the people in the office are not just smart but good-looking too. PWM relate to handsome men and beautiful women."

"PWM?" Bridget asked.

"People who matter. Television and social media make politics as much a game of beauty as brains.... Speaking of beauty," he said to Kayla, "you know who you remind me of?"

"No idea."

"Jennifer Lawrence."

"As Katniss Everdeen?"

"That's it, only you're blonde. And not sweaty or dirty. She's my heart throb."

"I'm flattered. But I'm not an actress. Just a political junkie. And I do like to socialize, of course. I'm even getting a clothing allowance, if you can believe that."

Apparently Chase could believe that. Bridget listened to their banter, a bit envious of the attention paid to Kayla.

Finally, he turned to Bridget. "Kayla said you're roommates. How did that happen?"

"Not the way you'd think," Bridget said. "We both just graduated from IU. Kayla's degree is in political science. Mine is in education. As luck would have it, our paths never crossed in

Bloomington."

"By chance," Kayla said, picking up the story, "we met at the Congressman's office. Bridget was there with her boss, Sheila Powers, to talk to the Congressman about ... about ...."

"About a law affecting teacher certification," Bridget said. "The two of us got talking in the restroom about looking for a place to live."

Chase chuckled. "I once saw a play that took place, all three acts, in a women's very fancy restroom. Apparently, that's where the best conversations happen."

"Oh, it is," Kayla said. "Is it the same with men?"

"Not in my experience. So have you found a place to live?"

"We have. You'll never believe our luck," Kayla exclaimed. "The first place we looked at was a little bungalow on Anthony, completely redone. Very charming. And the landlord, who lives right next door, takes care of everything. He even let us move in two weeks before the rent starts."

"I envy you. I'm in a studio on the river. All by my lonesome."

"But you must have a lot of friends in your position."

"Sure. Not really good friends, though. I don't have a lot of time for socializing that isn't work-related. Working for Tad, as you'll discover, is a full-time job -- and I do mean full time."

"Well then," Kayla said brightly, glancing again at her roommate for permission to continue but not waiting for a signal, "you'll have to come to our house-warming party and meet some new people. It'll be fun. Bring your girlfriend."

"I would if I had one. After college, I spent a few years in the Army, so I know a bunch of fraternity brothers and military guys like me, but not a lot of women."

"Even better. Bring all your single men friends. It'll balance out the numbers."

"What do you two do for fun -- besides give parties?"

Kayla and Bridget looked at each other and laughed. "You'll never guess what we just did," Bridget said.

"Don't tell me. Let me guess. You strolled the beaches in Cabo and partied hard at night, doing jello shots and dancing on tables. I've been there, so I know what it's like," Chase said. "I'm sure you made your boyfriends jealous and left a herd of heartbroken men behind."

"Not even close, especially about beaches, jello shots, or boyfriends," Bridget said. "We drove to Virginia to take a wilderness survival course -- four days, three nights. It was a chance to get to know each other and do something different."

"So, Kayla, you really *are* Katniss, aren't you?" he chuckled.

"You're so far off. We didn't have any bows and arrows and weren't running for our lives."

"Then what could you possibly have learned in four days?" Chase asked with a faint smile.

Is that question condescending? Bridget wondered. *Or am I paranoid?* Despite feeling a little intimidated, she spoke up. "We learned a lot: how to read a compass, construct a shelter, climb a tree, make a fire, find water, evade predators, that kind of thing."

"Not how to catch rabbits and squirrels for food?"

"No," Bridget said with a little shiver. "The heat and relentless physical activity were exhausting, but we came back feeling like -- speaking of Katniss -- survivors of the hunger games."

"I doubt that four days in Virginia really prepared you for surviving the worst nature has to offer, but I'll give you this. It was smart job preparation," he said, tipping his empty coffee cup in their direction. "I'm an ex-Army Ranger myself, so I know what I'm talking about. You'll find politics is rougher than the wilderness."

"Oh, dear," Kayla said. "You're scaring me. What's that mean?"

"Stay alert, keep your weapon loaded, watch your back at all times."

"You make politics sound like war," Bridget said.

"It is."

"But I hear Representative Bristoll is a good guy and easy to work for," Kayla protested.

"Very principled, on the right side of the issues," Bridget added.

"Oh, don't misunderstand me. He is all that. You're both right.

But Tad has to play a rough game, so there's plenty of collateral damage, as they say in war."

Kayla looked worried. "What's that mean for me when I start work?"

He patted her hand reassuringly. "Silent treatment from the losers who think they deserve your job, but not from me. Nor from Tad. If the past is prologue, he's going to love you."

Suddenly Bridget nudged Kayla. "Don't look now, but isn't that Mac standing over by a kiosk, pretending to be shopping for sunglasses?"

Kayla turned discreetly. "He's not pretending. He actually is trying them on."

"But looking our way," Bridget protested.

"Who's Mac?" Chase asked.

"Our very attentive landlord. Kayla says he's kind and just cares about us. But I think he cares a little too much."

"What makes you think that, Bridget?"

"Well, for one thing, letting us move in two weeks early, rent free, no security deposit."

"Maybe you were the best tenants he saw."

"Maybe. But he also hangs around a lot, trimming bushes, mowing the lawn, asking to come into the house to inspect things for the hundredth time. Yesterday he checked to see that all the windows open and close easily and lock properly from the inside."

"That doesn't sound bad."

"Wait. I haven't finished. After Mac left, I checked all the window locks. And guess what?"

Chase tipped his head inquiringly.

"The windows in Kayla's bedroom weren't locked. So I locked them."

"You didn't tell me that!" Kayla exclaimed.

"I didn't want to worry you, but now you know. I think he's in love with you."

"Why doesn't that surprise me?" Chase said, giving Kayla yet another look that left Bridget wishing it had been directed to her. He was so solid, so confident, the kind of man she'd like to know better.

"He's not in love with me. He's just a harmless flirt," Kayla said with a giggle.

"Maybe," Chase said, shooting another look in Mac's direction. "He looks ordinary enough. Flirt or not, though, he may also be a stalker, and stalkers always look harmless. That's how they get away with what they do."

"Thank you," Bridget said, feeling vindicated.

"A word of advice from a warrior," Chase said, looking at Kayla while collecting the three empty coffee cups and getting to his feet. "For your own safety, assume Bridget's suspicions are correct. You may turn out to be right that Mac is just a very good landlord and a harmless flirt, but that thing about the window locks is a red flag. So don't let him into your house unless you're both there."

9

Anything You Want
Saturday, August 31, 2013

The day of the party was perfect, 82°, partly sunny, a light breeze, no rain.

Kayla was excited, popping in and out of Bridget's bedroom, sometimes to ask an opinion on her own outfit, which she kept changing, sometimes telling Bridget, "Not that top. You've got to have something sexier than that. Here, wear this number. And for heaven's sake, put on those black shorts I like; you have great legs, so show them off. Here, let me fix your hair. I've got just the barrette to match that eyeshadow. That's the wrong color lip gloss, you know. Why didn't you go to the tanning bed with me? Next time, you're going. I mean it."

"What are you doing to my hair?" Bridget asked. "I never do anything except comb it."

"That's the problem, girlfriend," Kayla said. "I'm putting a long braid on the side so it stays out of your face. See? You look like you just got back from the islands."

Bridget turned her head this way and that as she inspected herself in the mirror.

"Say you like it," Kayla giggled.

"I do. I think I'm actually cute."

By the time she stepped out the back door to see how Mac was doing with the grill he'd dragged over, Bridget knew she looked the best she ever had. Not trashy but a lot sexier than she would have if left to herself.

Mac glanced at the puppy in her arms. "He'll be safe without a leash since I fixed the fence, but if you want him to stay in one place, I pounded a stake in the ground over by the lilacs, so you can tie him up in the shade."

"Thanks," Bridget said, carrying the squirming puppy over to the lilacs and attaching a 30-foot leash to his collar. "It's nice of you to fix the fence."

"No problem. Better put out a dish of water," Mac added, walking over. "What's his name again?"

"Doug."

"Doug," Mac repeated in a disapproving tone. "Not a good name for a dog." He put his hands to his mouth and called "Here, Doug. Here, Doug." He looked at Bridget reprovingly. "Half of the guys in the neighborhood will come running. You want that?"

Bridget couldn't help laughing. It did sound weird.

"Me, I'd name him Norman."

Bridget laughed louder. "Norman! That's as bad as Doug."

"Nobody's named Norman any more, so nobody'll come running. Doug reminds me of my days at Jiffy Lube," Mac continued. "One of my mechanics was named Doug." He crouched to rub Doug's belly. "Jiffy Lube Doug was a runt too but not as cute as this little guy." He stood up. "Tell me again, how many people are you expecting?"

"Oh, gosh, Mac, I don't know. Twenty? Twenty-five? I can't keep track of who Kayla's invited, and she can't remember."

"She's a live wire, ain't she? If she wasn't homecoming queen wherever she went to high school, then somebody should be shot."

Bridget giggled. "Lucky for somebody, Mac, she really was homecoming queen. But let's think about this party. We've got a big pan of baked beans in the oven, and last night Kayla made a tub of potato salad, but I'm worried it's not enough. I've put a couple of six packs of Bud in the ice tub in case people forget to bring beer, but who knows what'll happen?"

Mac walked back to the grill. "No need to be such a worrier, girl. I've got a dozen hamburger patties and hot dogs in the freezer and at least one case of beer in the basement, so nothing's going to go wrong. I guarantee it."

Just then Kayla bounced out of the back door, carrying a portable stereo. She looked smashing, her blond hair caught up in a messy bun with rogue tendrils framing her heart-shaped face. Her eye makeup and blush looked completely natural, though they had taken an hour to apply. Her shorts were very short indeed and her tank top left little to the imagination. Still, she somehow looked all-American, the wholesome girl next door. Kayla had a gift.

"Is there a way to hook this up, Mac?" she asked, holding out the stereo. "We're going to need some music."

"Doesn't it run on batteries?"

"No."

"Well, then, bring me a long electric cord."

"We don't have anything like that."

"I do. I'll go get one. But first let's set up the corn hole boards on that flat ground over there. Now, we need twenty-seven feet between them, so let's walk that off. Unless you have a measuring tape."

"A measuring tape?" Kayla asked.

"Never mind. Let me run to the garage."

"By chance," Kayla asked, flirtatiously touching her hair, "do you have a folding table we can put the food on? And maybe some lawn chairs."

Mac smiled and gave her the eyebrow flash. "I got anything you want. And more."

10

Prince Harry
Saturday, August 31, 2013

"Is that Prince Harry walking across our lawn?" Kayla asked, shielding her eyes as she looked toward the street.

It was four-thirty in the afternoon and the party was in full swing. At one point Bridget counted forty-one people, but the number kept shifting as some left and others arrived. Surprisingly, men outnumbered women almost two to one. Unfortunately, her own sister Kate was at the Gretna Green Golf and Tennis Club with the Wrights and their guests, but Peter, one of her brothers, had shown up with a six-pack of beer. Another guest had brought a second corn hole game; both Mac's and the new one were in raucous use. Most of the lawn chairs were empty, guests preferring to circulate. At all times, Doug, the rambunctious puppy, was being petted and rubbed by an ever-shifting group of dog lovers.

Bridget, the worried hostess, had just surveyed the scene. A 55-gallon drum was a third full of beer cans. All the beans and potato salad were gone. Having run out of hamburgers, Mac was still grilling hot dogs by the dozen. She had just returned from checking on a girl she didn't know who had gotten sick -- from too much sun, she claimed, though she reeked of beer -- and was now lying on the wicker lounge in the living room.

Bridget turned to look in the same direction as Kayla. "Oh, that's Justin. He's in charge of security at the academy. I didn't think he'd come." She waved. "Justin. What a nice surprise. Meet Kayla, my roommate."

Kayla's eyes sparkled at the sight of him.

"Hi, Bridget. Thanks for inviting me. Where do you want me to put this six-pack?"

"Over there," Kayla said, pointing to a folding table. "I'm Kayla. You look exactly like Prince Harry, the hottest gingy in the whole wide world. You're tall too, just like him."

"I don't think gingy is a word anybody but a redhead is allowed to use," Justin said with a smile, "but I'll let it go. By coincidence, I'm exactly, to the day, two years older than Harry."

Kayla frowned. "So how old does that make you?"

"Thirty-one on the 15th of September."

"Are you having a birthday party? Oh, I hope you do. We'll come. Bridget says you work security. You're certainly built for it," Kayla said, squeezing his bicep. "Are you single?"

"Yes, ma'am."

"Well, come along. Put the beer down and meet some people. You don't mind, do you Bridget? A couple of my sorority sisters are here. You've got to meet them. I think there's some beer left. Do you like the corn hole game?"

With an apologetic smile, Justin let himself be dragged off to meet Kayla's friends.

With a start, Bridget realized Mac was signaling her. "What's up?" she asked. "Oh, my, your face is so flushed. You've been working like a trooper, Mac. We certainly owe you one." He'd looked pretty good in his chinos and t-shirt that morning, but now he was rumpled, smoke-stained, and shiny with perspiration. Lanks of hair that normally covered his balding scalp hung damply on one side of his head.

"Don't mind at all, but I'm running out of hot dogs. We ran out of hamburgers an hour ago and my freezer's empty. What do you want me to do?"

Bridget sighed. "Shut it down. I can't leave in the middle of the party to go get anything."

"You could order some pizzas to be delivered."

"I could," she said hesitantly, wondering what to use for money. All she had in the house was cash in the amount of the rent due to Mac the very next day. She shook her head. "I'll go find Peter. Maybe he can go to Kroger's for more hamburgers and buns, so on second thought, keep the grill going."

She found Peter talking with Justin and Chase. All three men smiled warmly.

Justin was holding the puppy, massaging its neck while trying to avoid sloppy kisses. "You've got quite a buddy here. What's his name?"

"Doug."

Justin laughed. "I've known one or two Dougs but none this hairy And fortunately they never tried to lick my face."

Chase backed away, frowning as he swiped his pant legs. "He's too friendly, if you ask me. He used my trousers like a towel and now I've got dog hair all over them."

"Wait till he gets big enough to go for the crotch," Justin replied, laughing. "Judging from the nibbling he's doing on my hand, I'd say he's hungry."

"Well, that's exactly the problem," Bridget said with shame in her voice. "We're out of food and it looks like the party's going to go on for hours. God knows how many more people are going to show up because I don't and Kayla doesn't either. So, I was wondering, Peter, if you could run to the store for hamburgers and chips.... I'll have to pay you later."

Peter nodded conspiratorially. "Got you. I'm off."

"And I'm going with you," Justin said before glancing at Chase. "You coming too?"

"Wish I could, but there's no time. My boss is at another party up north with PWM. I think I better check on the action there, see if Tad needs anything." Chase turned to Bridget. "Tell Kayla I'll be back to help clean up."

As Chase strode away, Justin smiled at Bridget. "PWM?"

"People who matter."

"A guy who doesn't waste words is one serious dude, don't you think?"

"Maybe that's his military training," Bridget said. "He's an ex-Army Ranger."

"A Ranger who goes nuts over a little dog hair on his pants. That's a new one. . . . By the way," Justin said, tugging lightly on her braid, "I like this. Pick up a sword, put a falcon feather in your hair and you'll look like the goddess Freya."

"Who?"

"The old Norse goddess of love and war. She's not usually pictured with brown hair, but that's just a detail."

She gave him a rueful smile. "Who are you? A Viking warrior?"

"Just a guy who likes strong women."

11

Surprise Surprise
Saturday, August 31, 2013

Bridget was just telling Mac that soon there would be more hamburgers to grill when she heard Kayla's joyous squeals over the noise of the crowd. "What -- ?"

And then, surprise surprise, she saw Congressman Bristoll striding across the lawn like a model stepping out of a Polo ad: rich and well-bred but pretending to be just one of the boys. His glorious hair was rakishly mussed. A two-day stubble took twenty years off his chiseled face.

Good heavens, he was handsome. And out of place in every way imaginable.

Before heading to greet their distinguished guest, Bridget glanced back at the party scene: the carelessly dressed crowd buzzed on beer, youth, and bad jokes, the 55-gallon drum of empty beer cans, the messy array of cheap lawn chairs, the stained paper covers on the folding tables, the corn hole boards, the smoking grill with nothing cooking -- and wanted to disappear.

But Kayla was unfazed. "Oh, Mr. Bristoll, what a pleasure! How did you know about the party? You remember my roommate Bridget. Can I get you a beer?"

"Hi, girls," he said, flashing a big smile and briefly putting his arm around Kayla's waist before shaking hands with Bridget. "Aren't you two a sight for sore eyes?" He explained that he and his wife were partying at Gretna Green with the Wrights but he thought he'd sneak away for an hour or so to meet the "real" people -- the nation's treasure, the hope of the future. He'd have to get back, of course, but it was too fine a day to spend only with people he already knew. No, he wasn't hungry but he'd accept a beer. Yes, he liked the corn hole game and would play if the stakes were tempting enough.

Bridget watched with curiosity as the Congressman maneuvered to make Kayla his partner in the game and then selected another pretty young woman to act as stakeholder for modest bets that escalated, along with the cheers and groans of onlookers, as the hour wore on.

"Who is that?" Mac asked with a frown. "Why's Kayla all over the guy?"

Bridget explained that it was the Congressman who on Tuesday would be Kayla's new boss.

"She acts like she's known him for years."

"Well, she hasn't. I think she only met him once. But you know Kayla," Bridget said with a laugh. "She never met a stranger. You want me to introduce him to you?"

"Not right now. Is he married?"

Bridget patted Mac's back. "He's married. To a very rich woman."

"Well, that's all right then. So when is the food coming?"

"You're in luck because I see my brother just getting out of his car."

"This guy," Peter said, setting down two big sacks of food and nodding at Justin, who was also laden with sacks, "wouldn't let me pay me for a thing. So, Bridget, you owe him."

"Nobody owes me anything," Justin said, tipping his head at Bridget. "You want some help, Mac? Go get yourself a beer. Peter and I'll take over for awhile."

An hour later, Mac was back at the grill, and Peter and Justin were playing against Tad and Kayla, when hell emitted a little puff of sulfur and smoke.

Cordelia Bristoll, accompanied by Chase, suddenly appeared

on the lawn, elbowing her way through the crowd to where Bridget was sitting with Doug under the lilacs. "Hello, dear. Bridget, isn't it? I remember you from my husband's office."

"Oh," Bridget said, scrambling to her feet. "Hi, Mrs. Bristoll." Having no idea what to make of this formidable woman's unexpected appearance, she was at a loss for words. "You're back, Chase," she said inanely. *Why are you glowering like that?*

"I'm back."

"Is my husband here?" Cordelia asked abruptly.

"He is." Bridget turned and pointed. "He's over there. So nice of him to come. We didn't expect him, you know. He's really got the crowd excited." *Stop babbling,* she thought. *This can't be good. Something's going to happen.*

Bridget picked up Doug and held him against her like a protective pillow as she scrambled in Cordelia's wake.

It took a few minutes for Tad to notice his wife. When he did, a fleeting look of horror passed over his face. But he recovered quickly. "Friends, this is my wonderful wife, Cordelia. What are you doing here, love? Is it time to return to our other party?"

Cordelia smiled graciously at the crowd. "Hi, folks. Good to see you all having so much fun. Beautiful day, isn't it? But I'm afraid Tad is being very naughty. I hope you'll forgive me for taking him away. My wandering Odysseus must return to his Penelope and his kingly duties in Ithaca."

With amusement, she took in the puzzled faces of the clueless guests, who were not sure whether to laugh or applaud or slink away. Poor benighted souls, they knew nothing of Greek mythology. She enjoyed their painfully obvious ignorance, which could only remind Tad of her unique qualifications as his wife.

On the other hand, Cordelia had no desire to humiliate Tad. Like a royal wife, she let him walk a few steps ahead of her to the sleek black car waiting at the curb. As if nothing awkward was happening, she progressed regally, shaking a few hands and uttering a few meaningless greetings, all the while smiling charmingly.

Watching them walk away, Bridget giggled nervously.

"What's that giggle about?" Justin asked, suddenly appearing at her side and reaching over to scratch Doug behind the ears.

"I don't know. Because what just happened isn't really funny," she said weakly.

"I don't know what happened. That was like a one-act play with no point."

"Oh, it had a point, I think," she said.

"Explain it to me."

"When I'm sure of what I saw, I will."

12

Kayla's Diary
Saturday, August 31, 2013

I'm SO tired, but I've got to write about the day.

I almost jumped out of my Kate Spade sandals when I saw Tad coming across the lawn like a god deigning to visit us poor earthlings. But he didn't act like a god at all. NOT AT ALL.

He was wearing the most gorgeous sport shirt I've ever seen. And that stubble is PERFECT. Pity, but he can't keep "the facial adornment," he said. Actually, he whispered it into my ear like we're really good friends. He smells so good I asked what he was wearing. He said some foreign name I can't remember.

He's really good at corn hole, like he's played every day of his life, which anybody with a brain knows he hasn't. Way too busy for that. He drank two cans of Bud, joked with everybody, acted just like one of the boys. And even though he won over fifty dollars, he didn't keep a dime. Instead, he gave it ALL to me to help pay for the beer.

Bridget says I should give the money to Justin, the gingy, because he paid for some extra hamburgers when we ran out. Bridget's a little mad at me for not planning better. I could see a fight coming, so I just joked around, saying better to let life happen than do too much planning. She said, "No chance of that happening."

Should I give the money Tad won to Justin? I had expenses too, so I don't really see how that's FAIR.

If I give it to anybody, it should probably be Mac. He worked his butt off. But we're already paying him rent, so really, that ought to be enough.

But Bridget admitted the party was FUN except for two things.

First: She hardly got to see Chase, she said. I think she's got a little crush on him. I could see that when we met him at Glenbrook.

Two: She was upset about Mrs. Bristoll coming to take Tad away. She thought it was awkward and asked why he came in the first place. Did I invite him? I told her NO. It was a big surprise that he showed up, but NOT awkward when he had to leave. Of course, he had other places to go.

Then Bridget tried to get into a DEEP girl talk about not having relationships at work. I think I see where that's going. She's doesn't want me to fall for Chase because she wants him for herself. Well, she can have him.

Usually, I like our cozy little girl talks when we trade secrets and dreams, but I told her I was too tired for it tonight. So I came in here to write a little before going to sleep.

I'm going to sleep like a BABY.

13

Icarus

Friday, September 6, 2013

At the end of her first week at Summit Academy, Bridget was exhausted but flying high. She liked everything about her job.

She was teaching three courses in the morning, one on American history, another on the country's founding documents, and the third on civics. Each class had fewer than twenty students. Mornings were good because the students' minds were as fresh as they were ever going to be.

For the American history course, Sheila Powers had said yes to her proposal to compare the American Revolution to the French. "That way," Bridget explained, "the kids will see from the blood spilled why a democratic republic is better than a tyranny. Why America is unique."

"I grant you that," Sheila said, amused. "But beware, they'll be far more fascinated with the guillotine and the Bastille and Marie Antoinette's necklace than with the crossing of the Delaware in winter. Have you thought about that?"

"No," Bridget said, chagrined. "But I will."

"Perhaps you could liven things up with that HBO miniseries on John Adams. We could arrange for your class to watch an episode once a week in the auditorium while eating box lunches. Follow it up with a discussion of key points."

"I never thought of that."

"And what's your idea for the civics course?" Sheila continued.

"Well, the textbook you recommended. Plus, once a week, I'd like to bring in real people involved in all three branches of government to come in and talk to us. Congressman Bristoll, for example. His press aide, Chase Sumner. And your father, Judge Johnson."

"Don't stop there. How about a taxpayer, an administrator, a journalist covering politics? Make a list. Let's involve as many parents as we can."

"Good idea. I thought maybe the speaker could have the floor for fifteen minutes, then lots of Q&A."

"You might also want to pick a political topic for the Debating Society and stage the debate. Find some media people to be the judges. We'll get exposure that way, a mention on the local news."

"Oh, I'd love that," Bridget said, scribbling notes.

"Just so the students aren't stuck in the classroom every day, let's arrange a few outings. I'll bet most of our scholars have never been in the County Building or the courthouse. Maybe they should see the Congressman's office and my dad's courtroom. And I've got another idea. The senior trip to D.C. could involve a day in the visitors' gallery in the House of Representatives to listen to a debate, a private meeting with one of our Representatives, and a tour of the National Archives to see the original Declaration of Independence."

"Who goes with them?"

"You'll be one of the adults."

"Really?"

"Really. There's a catch, though. You have to arrange the day's activities, so there's a challenge. Congressman Bristoll might be a big help. And let me warn you, chaperoning teenagers is no picnic."

"I'm up for it. I've never been to Washington before."

Bridget happily settled into a routine that was comfortably predictable overall but full of the little surprises that kept her guessing. She arrived an hour before school started, chatted with Justin a few minutes, then joined the other teachers in the faculty lounge. After that came three morning classes for seniors, followed by lunch, and then an afternoon of home room, grading papers and preparing for the next day's classes. Some of the young single teachers then adjourned to a popular bar to decompress before heading home.

The wild card was her new administrative duty to promote the academy. The goal was to swell admissions to five hundred students within a year without lowering academic standards or endangering financial stability. She had no training in marketing or finance and thus no idea where to start.

Like many successful people -- Valedictorian of her high school class, Dean's list in college, a great job right out of the box -- Bridget was bedeviled by feelings of being a fraud. Surely, some day she'd be exposed as an impostor. She felt like Icarus, flying high -- but maybe too high. Thus her unexpected assignment from Sheila triggered every misgiving she'd ever had about her abilities.

Still, she was determined to sprout wings and soar.

14

Jabberwocky
Friday, September 6, 2013

By seven Friday evening, Chop's Wine Bar was packed, but Bridget, thinking ahead, had made a reservation for four. She and Kayla were the first to arrive.

"Let's both sit against the wall," Kayla said. "The guys can sit in chairs with their backs to the room."

"Fine with me."

"You sit opposite Chase so it looks like he's your date," Kayla said with an uncharacteristic frown as she unzipped her bright red moto jacket and slipped into her place on the banquette.

"Why?" Bridget asked.

"I want to look at Justin."

"Again, why?"

"I like looking at him. It's like looking at the Prince. And I don't want to be close to Chase."

"But you work with him!"

"That's the point, Bridget. I see way too much of him. He says it's his job to know everything, but really! Does he have to be up in my grill all day long?"

"You don't think he's just doing his job?"

"For Pete's sake, he isn't the chief of staff. Yet."

"Shh. That's him coming in."

"Hi, Chase," Bridget said, pointing at the chair opposite her. "I like that sport jacket you're wearing."

"Brooks Brothers. My dad never wore Brooks Brothers, so that's all I wear."

"Oh, oh," Bridget said, "there's a story there."

"Not a good one. I think Justin's right behind me."

Which he was.

"Oh, Justin, it's so good to see you," Kayla exclaimed, getting to her feet and giving him a hug. "Umm, you smell good. Are you packing?"

"What?" he asked with a puzzled smile.

"You work security so maybe you're packing. I like a man with a gun."

"Oh, that" he said, looking relieved. "Sorry to disappoint. Chase, how are you doing. Bridget, we've got to stop meeting like this."

She smiled at the joke. They'd seen each other in the morning and then again briefly when she left work.

From there, the conversation meandered through a wide range of subjects -- work, movies, books, restaurants, survival training, and clothes. But two themes stood out for Bridget.

One was Kayla's account of her new job. She wasn't as happy about it as she expected to be. The hard part, she said, was that she'd been asked to write an idea paper on how the federal government could increase regulation of small businesses while extracting more revenue without bankrupting them or causing a political firefight. It was such a boring topic! She knew nothing about small business or government regulation. Nor had she found anything useful on the subject in Wikipedia.

And even worse than that, Congressman Bristoll was hardly ever in the office. She'd expected to see him a lot. That was the whole point of the job, wasn't it?

"If I have to sit at that stupid little desk all day outside Tad's office, I'll lose my mind," she said in conclusion. "The desk isn't even real wood."

After the laughter died down, Chase spoke up. "Why didn't you tell me this before, Kayla? Of course Wikipedia doesn't have the answers, but I know how to find them, so if you just tell me about the snags you run into, I can help."

"That's very nice of you," Bridget said to Chase. "See, Kayla? You're lucky to have somebody like this guy in your corner."

Kayla rolled her eyes and, after draining her glass of wine, held it up like a panhandler. "I'm going to need a lot more of this stuff. Somebody, order me another one."

Then Kayla asked Justin what thing he'd done that week that was the most fun.

"I started a new book by Bernard Cornwell."

"Never heard of him," she said. "What's it about?"

"It's called *The Last Kingdom* about the ninth century Danish incursions into England. Cornwell writes historical novels about a lot of different subjects -- the Saxon conquest of Britain, the Napoleonic wars, even the American Civil War. All his books involve sailing. When he describes a Viking ship, I can see it."

"But if it's fiction," Bridget asked, "how can you be sure it's historically accurate?"

"You don't read historical novels?" Justin asked. "I'd have thought you would."

"Oh, I do, but they make me feel guilty for not going to the primary sources."

"Well, I don't feel any guilt. And in answer to your question, I can't check the historical accuracy. But Cornwell's credentials are impressive. He brings the stuff to life in a way that seems pretty credible."

"I don't think that's the best way to dig into history," Bridget persisted. She didn't know why she was challenging the guy.

"For a history teacher like you, it probably isn't. But I need adventure and good writing and Cornwell is where I find it." Justin played with his wine glass. "You don't even watch programs like *The Vikings?*"

"Not so far." For no reason at all, Bridget heard herself recite in a singsong voice, "'The time has come,' the Walrus said, 'to talk of many things: Of shoes -- and ships -- and sealing-wax --.'"

"'Of cabbages -- and kings -- and why the sea is boiling hot

— and whether pigs have wings,'" Justin concluded with a smile.

"What are you two talking about?" Kayla asked.

"Sailing ships," Bridget said, "made me think of that Lewis Carroll poem. For the life of me, I don't know why."

"What poem?"

"*The Walrus and the Carpenter,*" Justin said. "Hasn't every kid read it?"

"Not this kid," Kayla groaned, shaking her head. "I don't see how reading a book is the most fun thing you did this week. And the only poetry I like is on greeting cards. But you mentioned sailing. Now that's fun. Are you a sailor, Justin? Oh, I hope you are. My daddy has a sailboat and I love it when he takes us all out for the day."

"I have a little sailboat on Lake Wawasee. Nothing elaborate, but during my time in the Navy, I learned to sail. I love the water."

"I'm scared to death of the water," Bridget said, feeling contrary for no good reason. "How about you, Chase?"

"I have to like it because Tad has a boat too. Also on Lake Wawasee but not a sailboat. So in the summer when he can't find anybody else to crew with him, I'm pressed into service. It's not hard work and most of the time it's fun. You ever sail on Lake Michigan, Justin?"

"I've been on Lake Michigan but not in a sailboat. Last year I had a scary day on Lake Erie with a friend who owns an ocean-going sailboat. We hit a storm and almost didn't make it, but that's another story. Erie's not a lake to mess with."

"Isn't that where the *Edmund Fitzgerald* sank?" Bridget asked.

Justin shook his head. "No. You're thinking of Lake Superior. Which is also a scary lake."

Unfortunately, I wasn't thinking of Lake Superior, Bridget thought. *I was trying to show off, but now I just look stupid.*

"Oh," Kayla cried, reaching across the table to grasp Justin's hand, "you've got to tell us all about your escape from death. I know. You told us at our party that your birthday's September 15, so why not give yourself a birthday bash? Take us to Lake Wawasee for a day of sailing on your boat and tell us the whole story." She looked at Bridget. "What do you say? Wouldn't that be a great outing?"

"If I live through it."

"Oh, ye of little faith," Justin said with a wry smile. "I won't put you through more adventure than you can handle."

Kayla got out her phone to check the calendar. "The fifteenth is next Sunday, so it's perfect. Anybody see a weather forecast?"

"I'll check when I get home," Justin said. "What are you doing now, Bridget?"

"I'm taking a picture of you and Chase. Then you can take one of Kayla and me. And when the waitress comes by again, I'll have her take one of all four of us."

"What are you going to do with the pictures?" Justin asked. "My mom throws them in a box and never looks at them again."

"Put them in my journal."

"Of course. I should have known that," Justin said.

"Why?" Kayla asked.

"Why? Because Bridget's so organized."

Bridget pretended to pout. "You make that sound like a fault."

Justin shook his head but before he could deny that organization constituted a fault, Kayla jumped in. "I want copies of the pictures for my diary."

Back home, Bridget printed the pictures in her bedroom and then pasted them in her journal.

The picture of the four friends lined up on the banquette was strangely disturbing. Justin had his left arm stretched around Kayla so that his hand reached all the way to Bridget's right shoulder. Chase, who was to Bridget's left, stretched his right arm across the top of the banquette so it touched no one. How odd. How cold.

She looked again at the picture of Chase and Justin with their backs to the room. They were both handsome, the most attractive men in the bar. And then she saw something in the background of the picture that jolted her. Across the room at the long bar behind Justin and Chase, one of the nondescript guys had turned just enough that Bridget could make out his face.

It was Mac.

15

Bridget's Journal
Friday, September 6, 2013

What a strange evening.

I was mean as rat poison to Justin, who's actually nice to me, but a simpering schoolgirl around Chase, who ignored me.

It's not that Chase dislikes me -- at least I don't think so. He just doesn't see me. All his attention is directed to Kayla, but not like a lover. More like a warden. Is he asexual or what? I can't tell. For a guy as good-looking and well-dressed as Chase is, he's strangely without affect, as my psychology professor used to say about certain depressed people. Chase gives very few clues to what he's thinking.

So why do I want him to notice me?

Justin, on the other hand, always looks a little amused by something the rest of us haven't figured out yet. He's polite but not stiff. He's mature without condescension. He's really kind to me -- though I don't think that's anything special because he's kind to everybody. Sheila thinks he's husband material and I should try to date him.

So why don't I see what she sees?

And then there's Mac. Kayla thinks he looks fine, but his close-set eyes and long face set my teeth on edge. I keep checking his feet to see whether he's grown cloven hooves.

How creepy that he was right there in the bar, maybe the whole time we were. Was it just a coincidence? Should I tell Kayla?

Or -- horrible thought -- should I ask him?

16

Asher

Friday, September 13, 2013

Kayla was at her desk -- the ugly one not made of real wood -- doing her best to sort out the arguments for ethanol mandates, when she heard a commotion around the corner near the entrance to the office. She looked over at the Congressman's secretary. "What's going on?"

"No idea," Mimi said, frowning as she thumbed through a stack of correspondence. "If there's anything I hate, it's all these complaints from constituents. They want this, they want that. Whatever bill Tad sponsors, it's not quite good enough or it's even dead wrong. Every vote he makes is nit-picked to death. If he compromises with the other party, he's a traitor. If he doesn't compromise, he's an obstructionist." With a shrug, she looked up at the ceiling. "They think they could do a better job? Then try running for office. That's what I'd like to tell them."

"But you won't," Kayla said gently.

"No indeed. The angriest letters get farmed out to a free-lance journalist who used to work on the Hill. She writes a response."

"How does she know what to write back?"

Mimi laughed. "It's not that hard. She writes that the Congressman hears their concerns but for the good of the country did this or that, whatever it was. Yada, yada, yada. In closing, the journalist thanks the writers for their interest and assures them that the Congressman remains focused on representing his constituents in keeping with his Constitutional duties. I could write those letters in my sleep."

"Isn't that kind of bland?"

Mimi gave her a strange look. "Of course. That's the point."

And then the mystery of the commotion was abruptly solved. Asher Stroheim was right in front of Kayla's desk, glowering. Two women with worried looks stood in the background, stunned by the intrusion in an otherwise quiet day. Neither the Congressman nor Chase happened to be in the office just then. The guy who manned the printer and sorted the mail in a nook the size of a closet was too old and deaf to be any help.

Kayla looked up at the man she once thought she loved. Asher was just this side of handsome, his long nose overpowering the thin mouth and weak chin. Now Asher's face was flushed bright red and his big brown eyes, normally his best feature, were bulging out of their sockets.

"Why don't you answer my texts, Kayla? Why don't you take my calls? Huh, Miss Nose in the Air? You're too good for me now?" He swept the office with angry eyes. "Just because you got this stuffy white-collar job, sitting all day, dressed up like you're going to a club, pretending to work, now you think you're special."

Vituperation continued to spew all over Kayla like lava from a volcano. Wisely, she said nothing -- which only infuriated Asher further. He leaned over, his sweaty face inches from hers, and knocked the coffee mug off her desk. "How do you like that?" he growled.

"Oh!" she yelped. "Look at my blouse. It's ruined."

"Good, you little piece of white trash. What's the matter now? You going to cry and whine about your precious clothes? I'm not done." Without warning, he jerked the silver chain from her neck. He tossed the chain up and down in his hand, then examined the pendant as if he hadn't seen it before. "Scorpio. You told me that's your zodiac sign and believe me it fits because I found out it means a scorpion, a predator with poison in its tail. And that's exactly what you are. If you're going to treat me like this, the least you can do is return all the stuff I gave you. I know where you live and I'm coming over tonight to collect, so you better have everything packed up or all hell will break loose."

Kayla remained mute, though she scooted her desk chair back to the wall, as far from Asher as she could get.

Suddenly, the Congressman rounded the corner, Chase close behind.

"What's going on here?" Tad asked the stranger. "I could hear you yelling all the way from the elevator. Who are you?"

"This is Asher. He used to be my boyfriend."

Tad took in Kayla's ruined blouse and pale face before noticing the mark on her neck. "What's happened?"

"He knocked my coffee mug to the floor, then pulled my necklace off," Kayla said, rubbing the wound. "It was my birthday gift last year but he wants it back."

Asher threw the necklace on the floor. "I don't want it back! I want my girlfriend back."

When Chase started to say something, Tad waved him away without taking his eyes off the intruder. "What an asswipe you are! Trespass in a government office, assault and battery, robbery, harassment, intimidation. You know how long you could go to jail for all that? You're going to leave now, the easy way or the hard way, take your pick. What's it going to be?"

Asher was having none of it. Caught up in his own drama, unable to halt the yelling and thrashing about, he failed to notice Chase punching a button on his phone or the bulky man who entered the office a minute later. It was Tad's driver, Tarik, a short, burly immigrant with a round face and slits for eyes. Without saying a word, Tarik strong-armed the enraged suitor, still yelling and thrashing, out of the door, into the elevator, and back to the street. To Asher's incoherent threats, Tarik responded with a laugh eerily conveying both mirth and menace. Then he opened his suit jacket just far enough that Asher could see the holstered gun. "You try anything, *cetnik*, and you get big storm, big taste of hell."

Asher had no idea what the strange epithet *cetnik* meant but he suspected it wasn't anything good. He swaggered to his banged-up Chevy, doing his best to look like a gunslinger bored with his cowardly opponent. As he pulled away from the curb, he rolled down his window and, in a last gesture of rage, pointed his index finger at Tarik.

Tarik didn't see the finger, but if he had, he'd have laughed.

17

Mugged
Friday, September 13, 2013

Shaken, Kayla allowed Tad to guide her to his office, where he placed her in a guest chair, closed the door and took the chair next to her. She spent the next ten minutes tearfully explaining who Asher was and what he had done before Tad arrived.

The Congressman was all sympathy and soothing words. He handed her a clean handkerchief to dry her tears before pulling her to her feet in a fatherly embrace. "Let me soothe that boo-boo," he said, kissing her neck where it was red and scratched from the violence with the necklace.

Eyes fixed on the floor, Kayla tried to pull back. "I'm so ashamed, Tad. I thought Asher had gotten the message that we're over, but I guess he thinks he owns me. I never wanted anything like this to happen, believe me. I just want to fit in, to be the best special assistant you ever had."

Tad assured her that she fit like a glove and was invaluable. But after such a harrowing experience, he said, she deserved the rest of the day off. Tarik would drive her home. And if Asher carried through on his threat to go to her house, then she was to call him immediately.

Then came another embrace, this one not at all fatherly. Kayla could feel the heat of his body and the beating of his heart; she could see the passion in his eyes. She wanted to linger, to melt into him, to be protected like this forever, but something told her to cool things down.

She broke the spell with a glance at her ruined blouse. "Thank you, Tad, but I'm going to ruin your shirt this way. I'll go home to put something else on and then come right back."

"No you won't. I mean it when I say, take the rest of the day off."

"There must be a dumb blonde joke for this situation," Kayla said shakily.

"Never," he whispered.

She forced a smile. "How do you tell that a blonde has been mugged?"

"How?"

"When she's got coffee all over her. . . . Mugg-ed. Get it?"

Tad tipped his head in amusement. "I get it. If you just made that up, there's nothing dumb about you. You're a good sport. But let me ask you something. What exactly have you done to end things with that lunatic who was just in the office?"

"I don't text him back. I don't take his calls. I just ignore him."

"That'll never work, my darling girl."

Darling girl? For a moment, she was flustered by the tone of his voice, his words. "So what should I do?"

"Have someone else tell him how bad it could get if he keeps harassing you."

"Like who?"

"How about your father? Or your brother?"

She shook her head. "They wouldn't. Daddy loves me -- a lot because I'm his princess -- but he's not a guy who's going to scare anybody. And my brother's only fifteen."

Tad rubbed his chin. "I know a couple of people who could scare him, but I think in this case I might suggest Tarik."

"What would he do to Asher?" she asked nervously.

"Nothing that won't heal."

"Oh!" Kayla exclaimed. "Are you hinting at . . . ?"

"I'm not hinting at anything. I'm *saying* that once Tarik is done with the asswipe, you won't hear from him again but not because he'll be dead. He'll be alive and a lot wiser."

"I hate violence. I can't even kill a spider."

"Then let me take care of it," Tad said, adjusting his tie and smoothing his hair.

"You'd do that for me?"

"And a lot more," he said, stroking her cheek. "Now go home, rest, have a glass of wine. But first, let me buzz Chase so he can take you downstairs to the car. Tarik will make sure you get home safe and sound."

18

SEAL Breeze
Sunday, September 15, 2013

From the dock Bridget watched Justin and her brother Peter as they readied the *SEAL Breeze* for an afternoon of sailing. Having been raised on a farm where he did hard work from the age of ten, Peter was muscular and strong but he was not built like Justin, who stood four inches taller. Seeing Justin for the first time in a t-shirt and khaki shorts, Bridget could not help but admire his physique -- wide shoulders, bulging biceps, a true six-pack, narrow hips, muscular legs. His movements were smooth and unhurried, efficient, no wasted effort. Without making a production of it, Justin was clearly in charge.

After the gear was stowed and ropes and pulleys adjusted, Justin held out his arms and told Bridget where to step so she could board without fear of falling. Even so, she lost her balance when she hit the gently rolling deck and fell against his chest. It was like hitting a rock. He smelled like sun and soap.

"Steady on. Do you know where Chase and Kayla are?" he asked, glancing at his marine watch. The fine red hairs on his arm glowed in the sun.

Bridget swiveled in the direction of The Channel Marker. "Kayla dashed into the restaurant for something, so she should be here in a minute. I don't know about Chase . . . . Oh, that's him coming out now, isn't it? Not sure, though. I've never seen him in shorts before, or with sunglasses and visor. Whoever it is, Kayla's not with him."

It *was* Chase, and he had surprising news about Kayla. "Sorry to tell you this, but we're going to be one person short. We ran into Tad in the restaurant. Kayla's left with him, saying to have a good time. Tad wants us all to meet up at the yacht club at six. Dinner's on him."

"What . . . how did . . . ?" Bridget sputtered. "She didn't tell me she had plans with anybody else."

Chase stepped on board before answering. "She probably didn't. Tad's wife and son are out of town. He's taking out a few friends for the day, so he asked her to join them." He smiled at Bridget. "You want to put on a life vest now? You might feel a little more relaxed. I brought dramamine for anybody who needs it. And visors."

Bridget accepted a visor but declined the life vest and dramamine. She was one woman among three men, any one of whom looked ready to sail alone across the Atlantic. She couldn't bear to fall into the stereotypical role of the weaker sex. She would be brave and comradely. She would watch and learn what she could about sailing.

She was very nervous for the first half hour after the sheets were released, but gradually her mind emptied of fear, filling instead with pleasantly unfamiliar sensations -- the sound of sails snapping in the wind, the warmth of sun on her face, the shock of cold spray on her bare arms, the feel of the boat as it heeled and tacked.

At one point, Justin invited her to join him at the tiller so she could find out what it felt like to steer the boat. Peter and Chase were up at the bow. Encircled in Justin's arms, ostensibly because she needed help with the tiller, she suddenly felt his mouth near her ear.

"Remember what you said at your party?" he asked.

"What did I say?"

"Someday you'd tell me what was going on when the Congressman's wife showed up."

"But someday hasn't arrived because I don't know yet," she

said. "Not for sure."

"You want to trade guesses?"

She turned to look into his eyes, aware of how close their faces were. Why had her heart skipped a beat? "You first."

"A triangle is forming. The Congressman, his wife, and your roommate. The wife doesn't like it."

"I'm thinking the same thing," she murmured.

"Do you really think the Congressman is going to have a lot of other passengers on his boat today?"

Bridget's head jerked. "Yes, I do."

"What do you want to bet?"

She laughed. "I watch *The Vikings* if you win. You watch some ponderous six-hour PBS program about the history of Rome if I win."

"You're on."

Suddenly he gently pushed her hands away from the tiller. "The wind has changed and we're going to have to come about. Watch out for the boom. Once this maneuver is done, let's eat."

The ham and cheese sandwiches Justin had packed tasted more delicious than any gourmet meal, and though she didn't like the smell of beer, she found that the frosty bottle of Blue Moon, with a little slice of orange, tasted like the nectar of the gods.

When the wind died down, Peter asked Justin about his training to be a Navy SEAL. She listened in wonder to graphic tales of surf torture and drown-proofing. How did anyone survive such things? A man who did deserved respect.

But the man who surprised her most was Chase. He didn't ignore her, as he had at Chop's Wine Bar. Instead, he acted almost like a boyfriend. Did she want him to spray some more sunblock on her legs and arms? How about a dramamine? He had plenty. Here, he'd take her empty bottle so she wouldn't have to get up. What did she think of the water now?

She thought the water was still a little frightening but quite liked the sensation of skimming across it in a bit of molded fiberglass propelled by canvas sails snapping in the wind.

She also quite liked the attentions of two very attractive

men.

19

Nerves of Steel
Sunday, September 15, 2013

"You look flushed, Kayla."

She and Bridget were combing their hair and applying lipstick in the ladies' room of the yacht club.

"Just a little sunburn except for around my eyes. I had to wear my Jackie-O sunglasses, but now I look like a raccoon," she giggled.

"What happened?" Bridget asked, leaning into the mirror to check her mascara.

"What do you mean, what happened? I went for a great boat ride."

"Why didn't you stick with our plan? I thought you wanted to hear all about Justin's brush with death on Lake Erie. After all, you're the one who goaded him into doing this on his birthday. Instead of getting to take it easy, he worked like a Trojan all day."

"Oh, I know, Bridget. I'm really sorry. I wanted to be with you. But when Tad unexpectedly showed up and invited me to join him on his power boat, what could I say? He's my boss, after all."

"How did he know where to find you?"

"He called me Friday night to be sure Asher hadn't shown up and somehow we just got to talking about the weekend."

"Chase said Tad's family is out of town."

"His wife and son flew to D.C. because on Friday Cordelia's

mother went into the hospital for surgery. She's supposed to be discharged today. Tad said the procedure was a carotid endarterectomy."

"How in the world did you memorize those words?"

"Daddy's an anesthesiologist, so I've heard lots of medical terms my whole life."

"So," Bridget said, zipping up her cosmetic purse, "I understand you met some of Tad's friends today."

"I did?" Kayla asked with a frown. "What are you talking about?"

"Chase said Tad was taking out a bunch of friends."

"Tad never said anything about that. We were alone. His boat's fantastic, a new Tiara, with lots of seating in the back. You know that smell of new leather? I love it. At full throttle, the whole prow rises like the Lock Ness monster rearing its head out of the water. The deep growl of the engines, the power -- so thrilling. I want to do it again. He said if the weather holds he'll take me out again before he has to put it in dry dock for the winter."

"What else happened?"

"He let me drive for awhile. I never did that before, but he said I was a natural. And I helped him by walking along the hull to tie up at the dock where he gassed up the boat. I have great balance from all those years of ballet classes, so I'm good at that too. He said I have nerves of steel."

"You do have nerves of steel if you're spending the day alone with a married man -- your boss, no less -- on his new boat while his wife is away tending to a sick mother. If the papers find out, if there were any photographers around, who knows what will happen?"

Kayla held the door open. "Are you scolding me?"

"Just being a friend, Kayla. He didn't do anything you can't tell your mother about, did he?"

"Of course not!"

"You're blushing. So something happened. What was it?"

"Oh," Kayla said with a giggle, "he's a touchy-feely kind of guy, but nothing like what you're thinking. Maybe an accidental touch here and there, a few compliments I didn't expect, something flirty in the eyes, a lot of smiling, edgy jokes. You know the way men are."

"Probably not the way you do," Bridget said under her breath.

"How about you and Chase?" Kayla asked with a knowing look.

"Why ask about him? Why not Justin?"

"Come on, Bridget. I know how you feel about Chase. Me, I'd go for Justin if . . . well, if things were different."

"Meaning what?"

Kayla looked away. "Lots of things. I just mean, you're a little mean to Justin, who I think really likes you. But you're not mean to Chase. I see how you look at him."

"I'm not mean to Justin. We're friends. We talk every day at work. But I'm more attracted to Chase. At least I thought I was."

"You've changed your mind?"

Bridget shook her head. "I may have lost it altogether."

"Love is funny, isn't it?"

"We're not talking about love here. Whatever it is -- chemistry, sexual attraction, pheromones -- it's about as funny as going to sleep in a grizzly bear den."

"Oh, Bridget. That's ridiculous. Love is the most fun there is. So quit stalling. I told you about my day. Now it's your turn."

"Chase is definitely not a touchy-feely guy like you say Tad is, but he was nice to me."

"He didn't find an excuse to put his arm around you or anything?"

"No. But Justin did."

"Did you like it?"

Bridget nodded.

"Well, don't look ashamed."

"I'm not, Kayla. I'm just confused."

20

Bridget's Journal
Sunday, September 15, 2013

Justin liked my gift, a folding yachtsman tool with a spike and shackle key, whatever those are. The salesman at Dick's Sporting Goods said he'd love it, and he did. At least I got that right.

Actually, the day was pretty good, considering that Kayla deserted me. Now I'm wondering if she hadn't arranged to meet her boss all along. Justin hinted at that. The idea makes me mad because she could have warned me when we drove to the Lake.

After what she told me in the restroom, I watched her and Tad at the dinner table. They didn't sit next to each other or really even look at each other. Their pretense that nothing's going on between them was so elaborate I know something is.

Tad mostly paid attention to the men, especially to Chase and Justin, asking questions about their military experience, all in the guise of deciding how to vote on certain appropriations for the Defense Department.

Justin shocked me. I'm not sure, but I think he was challenging Chase about Ranger school. He asked Chase questions about his training that went right over my head. But the questions hit Chase squarely between the eyes. At first, he looked flustered, as if he'd been caught in a lie. But then Chase challenged Justin about his Navy SEAL training. Justin wasn't fazed in the slightest.

My eyes swiveled between the two as if watching a tennis match. I like both men but I don't think they like each other. I've never seen Chase uncomfortable before. Nor have I ever seen such mockery in Justin's eyes; usually, he just looks pleasantly amused, the coolest guy in the room.

Fortunately, Kayla piped up to tell about our survival course in Virginia. She made everybody laugh when she said what she learned about evading a predator was not to outrun it but to outrun me.

21

All Gone
September 15, 2013

Late Sunday Asher sat across the street from the little bungalow on Anthony, munching on beef jerky and swigging Red Bulls in between tokes on a hand-rolled cigarette. Every few minutes he glanced at the loaded handgun on the passenger seat, just to be sure it was there. He hadn't decided whether to use it.

He wished it was dark and cool instead of sunny and hot. He wished he hadn't drunk so much beer an hour earlier because now he needed a wizz but didn't want to drive to a gas station.

The little bungalow had shown no signs of life since he parked. The curtains were pulled. The door never opened. And Kayla did not respond to his texts.

He was furious at the way Kayla had dumped him. The day after graduation in June, he helped pack her car so she could return to her home in Fort Wayne. She said she'd call to let him know she arrived safely, but she didn't. Then he got on her Facebook and found out she had switched her status to single. The selfie showing the two of them at an IU football game had been taken down. The picture of him playing tennis was gone.

He'd evaporated from her life like the smoke from his cigarette.

His spirited performance in her office, his threat to reclaim all the stuff he'd given her, didn't seem to have persuaded her to take him back. Kayla was still ignoring him.

He put his head back with a groan.

He should have known how this would end. She was out of his league from the get-go and he knew it.

Even his best friend said Kayla was at least fifteen points more attractive on a hundred-point scale than he was; couples more than ten points different never made it. A year ago Asher thought his best friend's drunken observation was crazy; now he wondered. Kayla was like a young movie star on her way up. He was like a character actor reduced to the role of dimwitted muscle man.

There were differences other than looks. Kayla's father was a doctor. His stepfather worked in an RV factory in Elkhart. Her vacations were spent at Caribbean resorts. His were at Six Flags. Kayla read magazines and the occasional book for fun. He was addicted to Candy Crush. She always wanted to "do" something on the weekends. He just wanted to watch action movies and crush beer cans.

At the sound of a dog barking, Asher turned. A slender man with a long face and stringy hair had just emerged from the house next door to the bungalow. He had a bouncy puppy on a leash. Asher tensed when he realized they were crossing the street in his direction.

"What's up?" he asked the guy with the dog.

"You been out here a long time. Just wondered if you need help with something."

"Who are you?" Asher snapped. The stranger's eyes were *so* weird and he smelled like kerosene.

"Mac. This here pup is Doug. And you are?"

"Asher."

"Well, Asher, you been staring at the house next to mine for an hour. What's that about?"

"My girlfriend lives there. She was 'spose to meet me an hour ago."

"Which one?" Mac asked. "The blonde or the brunette?"

"The blonde. Name's Kayla. You know her?"

"I'm her landlord. But you must of made a mistake about meeting her today. She's up at the Lake with friends, not going to be back until real late. This here's her dog I'm taking care of." Mac leaned in to look at the passenger seat. "You planning to use that gun?"

"What's it to you?"

"Might be nothing, pal. Might be something, specially if you're mad at Kayla. You tell me."

"None of your business. I'd take a long walk, if I were you," Asher said, rolling up the window. He watched the pair walk to the end of the block and turn the corner.

He was growing drowsy in the heat. Maybe some more weed and a shot of vodka in the Red Bull would wake him up. He rolled the window back down for fresh air. He started another game of Candy Crush. Still, his eyes grew heavy and his breathing slowed.

When he woke, it was dark. Where the hell was he? He blinked and squinted and tried to make sense of things. Ah, his head was under a bush and ... oh, God, his ear was bloody and he'd pissed himself. When had he gotten out of the car? How had he done it? Why?

He eased himself to a sitting position and looked around. He was near the curb only a yard from where his car was still parked. He crawled to the car and leaned against it before finding the strength to stand up. Keeping one hand on the hood, he slowly made his way to the driver's side.

But nothing was where it should be. The keys weren't in the ignition. He leaned over to check his back pocket. His wallet was gone too. Where was his phone? He checked the glove compartment. No weed.

And then he looked at the passenger seat. Where was his gun? Why couldn't he see it? He frantically patted the place it had been, leaned down with a groan to feel around under the seat, shook the floor mat. Nothing.

He sat up and stared out the window. Still no lights in the bungalow. Nothing seemed to have changed on the block other than streetlights had come on and he could see the flickering of television sets in a few houses. Yet the dashboard clock said almost three hours had passed since he took that last toke.

He clicked on the overhead light and leaned forward to check himself in the mirror. One eye looked dark, and when he touched it, he winced. There was dried blood on his upper lip and his left ear. He ran his finger inside his mouth. He still had all the teeth he'd started with.

Asher couldn't wrap his mind around what had happened. Not a scrap of memory surfaced. He thought about the weed he'd smoked. He'd been warned it was some heavy shit, but it had never knocked him out before.

Obviously, he'd passed out. Then he'd been hauled out of the car and beaten up. He was bloody, bruised, and pissed -- literally pissed. He'd been robbed of everything. A terrible crime had been committed against him.

Should he report it?

It took no more than a millisecond to answer that one. No. Even if he still had his phone, the answer was not in a thousand years would he report what happened. He had no good explanation for why he'd been sitting for hours in front of Kayla's bungalow with a loaded gun on the seat, especially after the threats he'd made on Friday. Who would believe he'd intended to use it on himself if Kayla hadn't agreed to come back to him. He wanted her to watch him die so she'd understand what a bitch she was.

He glanced again at the house where the guy with the dog lived. He seemed a little too familiar with Kayla and saw the gun. Maybe he'd watched and waited until dark to disarm a guy he thought meant harm to Kayla.

Asher rubbed his head. Nah. That dipstick was much too scrawny for the job of hauling a guy weighing two hundred pounds out of a car and beating him up.

He pounded the steering wheel in a sudden burst of insight. Whoever did this must be from that stupid government office. Somebody was getting revenge -- or giving him a warning.

So who was it? The bowling ball driver who threatened "big storm?" The tall smooth dude with the phone? Or the Hollywood-actor type with the deep voice, Congressman Whatshisname, who threatened him with jail and called him an asswipe?

Was an asswipe the same as a *cetnik*?

And then his rage conjured up ever more lurid pictures. Kayla half-dressed, Kayla dancing obscenely, Kayla blowing a man whose face he couldn't make out. She was banging one of the men in that office, he'd bet on it. But which one? If he could figure that out, he'd know how to bring big storm down on Kayla and the unlucky asswipe who thought he could steal Asher Stroheim's girlfriend.

22

Ending the Game
Monday, September 16, 2013

Cordelia was the last of the bridge club members to arrive. "Sorry I'm late," she said to the seven women already standing around two card tables in Maria Steinmacher's family room. She handed her hostess two bottles of her favorite sherry. "This doesn't make up for my tardiness, but maybe after everybody's tasted it, I'll be forgiven."

She looked around at the homely room. She despised wood-paneled walls, built-in bookcases stuffed with bric-à-brac, and chintz drapes. The ceiling was too low and the carpet stained by Mugsy, Maria's insane Chihuahua. Folding card tables were the lowest form of furniture.

For the hundredth time, Cordelia wanted to tell Maria to hire a good decorator. As the wife of Sheldon Steinmacher, who became rich when he founded the biggest alternative fuel business in the State, Maria could afford it. In fact, the Steinmachers could afford a country estate with a mansion and staff if they wanted. But neither seemed to care about their image.

Cordelia could hardly broach the subject of image, however, when she had committed the unpardonable sin of arriving late. So she did what her pride required: elicit sympathy for herself. "I got in late last night, drove Porter to school this morning, ran a few errands, then stopped at Tad's office, where I took a call from my mother that I thought would never end. She just had dangerous surgery, so I couldn't tell her I was too busy to talk."

"How is she?" Maria asked.

"Very well for what she went through. A little hoarse from the intubation but not in pain. She had ninety percent blockage in her carotid, if you can believe it. She could have had a stroke like that," Cordelia said, snapping her fingers. "But you know us old pilgrim stock. We're a hardy bunch. It takes a lot to kill us."

"How old is she?" another woman asked.

"She'll be ninety in October. I was a late baby."

Maria handed round tiny glasses of sherry. Cordelia grimaced. The glass was not a traditional sherry glass but one designed for liqueurs, and the rim was smudged. "Oh, well," she murmured, closing her eyes before draining the sherry.

"Oh, well, what?" Maria asked.

"Did I say that aloud?" Cordelia asked, scrambling for a credible lie. "I was just thinking life is a lottery, isn't it? We think we're in control but we're not."

"You missed a great day at the Lake yesterday," Maria said. "Perfect weather, lots of boats taking their last cruise before winter."

"How do you like my husband's new Tiara?"

Looking puzzled, Maria waited for the women to be seated before answering. "I didn't see it. What's it like?"

"Didn't Tad invite you to join him?"

"He called Sheldon Saturday morning to cancel, saying he wasn't sure he was going to get to the Lake."

"Oh, dear, where's my head?" Cordelia said. "He told me that, but I was in the hospital when he called, waiting for the surgeon to come out to tell us how Mama had done, so I forgot."

Cordelia was a master bridge player and she hated losing, but that day she couldn't focus. To her partner's dismay, she played too quickly and overcalled two hands.

Her mind was elsewhere. Last night Tad claimed he'd spent the day alone on the boat but met Chase and some of his friends for dinner. But had her husband really been alone on the boat? It wasn't like him to pass up a chance to show off his new toy.

And who were the friends with Chase? Did they include the new special assistant, the bouncy blonde she'd seen at that beer party on Anthony?

When she was young, she accepted her husband's infidelity as the price of being married to a rising political star propelled aloft by his charm and ruthlessness and her illustrious heritage and money. But given the shifting political winds, she no longer saw any hope that Tad would ever be elected to the Senate or appointed Treasury Secretary or, even better, assume the exalted post of Ambassador to the United Kingdom. Either Tad would end his stupid games or she would end them for him.

She sighed deeply, not because she'd lost the hand by neglecting to count the hearts and her partner's face was now tight with fury, but because of what lay ahead of her.

First, check the obvious. She'd rifle through her husband's dressing room to see if he'd bought new underwear. She'd scrutinize credit card statements for charges from fitness clubs. If roses were delivered for no good reason, she'd be sure there really was a reason -- one she wasn't supposed to know about.

If she found nothing, then she'd arrange separate lunches with both Mimi and Chase. Mimi always dished without quite realizing what her gossip revealed. Chase, however, was a harder nut to crack, loyal to Tad and no one else.

She laughed silently at the idea of Chase being a hard nut to crack. Even he couldn't escape the force of Cordelia Tilley Bristoll, nutcracker *par excellence*.

23

Much to Fear
Wednesday, September 18, 2013

"Oh, Mrs. Bristoll, what a lovely home you have," Kayla said. "But I just knew you would. Mimi says you're the most elegant woman she's ever met. She says what you don't know about lifestyle wouldn't fill a teaspoon. Do you want me to take my shoes off?"

Cordelia looked at the girl's feet. She recognized the stilettos as Kate Spade. "Not at all. Here, let me take your jacket. I'm so glad you could join me for a little *tête-à-tête*."

"A what?"

"A private conversation, just between the two of us." Cordelia noted the dress, a graphic black and white sheath. Kayla Jesperson wasn't dressed in the ill-fitting pantsuit she'd come to expect on Tad's special assistants. Her face wasn't tight with ambition. She wasn't carrying an iPhone. This girl definitely wasn't in the mode of Madison Alley or the four special assistants who preceded her.

"*Tête-à-tête*," Kayla giggled. "If you don't know what it means, which I don't, it sounds kind of . . . you know . . . kind of weird, almost suggestive. But tasteful. I'll have to remember that word. *Tête-à-tête*. It sounds elegant."

Cordelia smiled in spite of herself. "It sounds elegant because it's French."

"I suppose so," Kayla said doubtfully. "I've never been to

France, but I've been to St. Martin, which was dirty and full of hairy armpits, so not everything French is elegant."

"You've been to St. Martin?"

"Only once. Last year Daddy took us there for Mommy's birthday. Wasn't she lucky to be born in the summer? My birthday's in November and it's always dreary then. How about you?"

"I was born in February."

"Oh, well," Kayla said in a pitying tone, "what can you do? Who else is coming?"

"Just you."

"Really? Just me? How sweet of you."

Cordelia winced. She wasn't used to being called sweet. She didn't like it. She led the girl to the back of the house overlooking a manicured lawn surrounded by oak trees and a high fence. "I like to get to know my husband's employees, make sure they're happy."

"I am happy," Kayla exclaimed. "I love politics, don't you?"

"No, I don't."

Kayla looked shocked. "But you're married to a Congressman. Mimi says your family has been in politics for generations and generations."

"My ancestors started as politicians but rose to be statesmen and ambassadors. Tad might never get to that status."

"But people treat him like a rock star. He gets special treatment everywhere he goes. That's pretty special, isn't it?"

Cordelia recoiled at the idea that Tad was a rock star but said nothing.

Kayla stopped short upon entering the glass-enclosed room filled with plants. Next to a softly gurgling fountain sat a charming little bistro table holding two luncheon place settings. "What a pretty room. Is this where we're eating? What is this room called?"

"I call it my conservatory. I grow orchids. When I'm on the East Coast, I have a man who comes in to take care of them so they don't die in my absence." Pointing at a fat glazed container, she said, "I collect these *pots de jardin* for my biggest and best plants."

"Po what?"

"*Pots de jardin,* French for garden pots. Do you like flowers?"

"Adore them. What do orchids smell like?" Kayla leaned down to sniff one, then looked up with a little frown. "It doesn't smell. Why not?"

"Why? I don't know. They just don't. They're very hard to grow."

"Is that a good thing or a bad thing?" Kayla asked, the V between her eyebrows deepening.

"Both. I like a challenge. When I succeed, I know I've done something worthwhile."

"Gosh, I should be more like you. I don't like hard things because . . . well, because they're hard. I prefer easy."

Cordelia laughed. "Is your job hard?"

"Harder than I expected. So much research. I was never good at that. Chase is trying to teach me, though. He calls research an ISS."

"Meaning what?"

"An important stepping stone to a better job. He has acronyms for everything."

"What do you think of Chase?"

"Other than all those acronyms?" Kayla asked with a laugh. "He's nice, very composed, never flustered. I can see why Mr. Bristoll likes him so much because Chase tries to do everything for him. Every time I turn around, there's Chase, checking schedules, asking how I'm doing with my assignment, reminding Mimi of something. One time, Tad -- oh, I apologize, I don't mean to sound impertinent, but that's what everybody calls him in the office -- spilled something on his tie, so Chase just took his right off and gave it to . . . to your husband."

"Is Chase nice to you?"

"Very nice, but then he's nice to everybody. We go out sometimes -- always with friends, though. No romance is allowed in the office, you know. Your husband's orders. But if we weren't working in the same place, well, maybe . . . ."

"Maybe what?"

"Oh, you know. But I'm too interested in learning my job right now to get involved with anybody. And I broke up a couple months ago with my college boyfriend. He made a terrible scene in the office last week. Maybe you heard about that. I'm still embarrassed it happened."

"Mimi said something about that yesterday. You have my sympathy. Breakups are hard. As is avoiding office romances. I don't know why office romances are taboo. Where else can young people meet each other when they work so hard at their careers? Especially when they're thrown together in social situations, as you and Chase were at the Lake last Sunday."

"The Lake?"

"I heard you two were at the Lake and had dinner with my husband. Or maybe you were even on his boat."

"Chase and I were at the Lake but we weren't together, not like a date or anything. A whole bunch of us went up to celebrate a friend's birthday on his sailboat. Let's see," Kayla said, ticking names on her fingers, "my roommate Bridget, her brother Peter, Justin who works with Bridget, Chase and me. It was Justin's birthday and his sailboat. We met your husband for dinner. It was a wonderful day."

"I wish I could have been there."

"Oh," Kayla exclaimed, "where are my manners, talking about the fun we had when you were probably worrying yourself sick. Your mother was in the hospital that day, wasn't she? How's she doing? Mr. Bristoll said she had an endarterectomy."

"You know the word?" Cordelia asked in surprise.

"Daddy's an anesthesiologist, so I've got a headful of useless medical terms. He wanted me to go into nursing, but I can't even say 'vomit' or 'pus' without gagging."

Cordelia smiled. "I'm with you on that one. My mother's very well, thank you for asking. So I had no choice but to miss a beautiful day on the water."

Cordelia had not gotten the answer she wanted about the Sunday boat trip. Mimi had known nothing; Chase was avoiding her. And now Kayla chattered without really saying anything.

Somehow the girl had deflected the suggestion that she might have been on Tad's boat. But she couldn't probe further about who exactly was with her husband without sounding like a suspicious wife -- thus giving away the entire reason for this *tête-à-tête*.

And that was the problem. Kayla was charming and artless. She was smarter than she appeared, but modest about what she didn't know. She was prettier and more feminine than any of the other women in Tad's life, all of whom had resembled her in significant ways.

But this woman, except for the color of her beautiful blond hair (which in Kayla's case was natural), didn't resemble her physically or in any other way. If Kayla was Tad's new infatuation, then he had changed in ways she never even suspected.

Throughout lunch, Cordelia kept glancing at the girl's purse sitting on the floor beside her. It wasn't the prim structured bag she favored, the kind that firmly snapped closed and signaled its owner was a lady. Instead, it was a vintage Coach bucket bag, a jaunty wink to the Seventies. It wasn't uninspired like the bags the other APs carried. Her high-fashion daughter in London, who openly mocked her style, also carried a bucket bag, a tasseled one from H&M.

Though she was Lady Astor living in a Miley Cyrus world, Cordelia felt queasy in the presence of Kayla's bucket bag. Kayla was young and fresh. She was old and fusty.

"How old are you going to be in November, Kayla?"

"Twenty-two," she chirped. "The second year I've been legal to drink. You said your birthday's in February. How old will you be?"

Cordelia blanched. It was impolite to ask a woman her age. Yet she'd just done it to Kayla. "How about dessert?" she asked. "Or don't you eat dessert?"

Kayla winked. "Don't tell anyone, but I eat everything, especially dessert."

A terrible thought struck Cordelia. If she had secretly given up on Tad's political career, why couldn't he have secretly done the same thing? And maybe given up on their marriage as well?

She watched Kayla throughout the rest of the lunch without uncovering anything she could well and truly mock or finding any way to intimidate her. Instead, she found much to fear.

24

Kayla's Diary
Wednesday, September 18, 2013

It was SWEET of Mrs. Bristoll to invite me to her beautiful house for a private lunch. When I told Bridget about it, she frowned and said maybe I better rethink that. Sweet might be the wrong word.

Bridget asked flat out if there's something going on between Tad and me. So I told her about what REALLY happened after Asher was thrown out of the office -- Tad kissing the boo-boo away, holding me in his arms, his pupils dilating the way they do when men are aroused. Then I told her about what really happened on the boat. We didn't go all the way; not quite.

Then Bridget did that thing where she sounds like a tough lawyer, making me tell her every single thing about the lunch with Mrs. Bristoll.

I don't think I gave anything away about how I was ALONE on the boat with Tad. I wasn't exactly trying to be deceitful but something told me to be careful -- well, actually Tad warned me not to give anything away. So when Mrs. Bristoll asked about Chase and me being on Tad's boat, I blathered about how Chase and I aren't exactly a couple without saying where either of us was and I mentioned her mother to distract her. I also made a point about how her own husband put the kibosh on office romances. Nobody told me to say that. It just came to me and it was pretty clever, right? So here's a pat on MY back.

Tad told me I'm to pretend to like Chase so people won't know what's going on. I told him I don't really like Chase but my roommate does. Tad said don't even breathe a word to Bridget about the game I have to play with Chase. I told him that would be hard, but he pointed out that since I really wasn't going after Chase, there would be no reason that he couldn't hook up with Bridget if he wanted to.

I really mean it when I say I don't want to hurt Tad's wife's feelings. She's NICE. I know I shouldn't fall for Tad the way I'm doing. So fast too.

When I told Bridget that for me and Tad it's love at first sight, she pooh-poohed me. She said it's just lust and lust is dangerous, especially when it's all mixed up with big-stake politics and women like Cordelia.

Well, maybe it is lust. But it's LOVE too. Lust and love aren't mutually exclusive. And love doesn't kill political careers, right? I don't want to hurt Tad's career. He said I won't so long as we keep everything quiet until the time is right. Right for what? I asked. He mentioned the Cayman Islands and how he might have enough to get out of the political racket if it came to that. But he wants to stay in office as long as he can, so we have to keep things under wraps.

Tad told me his marriage has been over for ever and ever but until he met me, he just stuffed all the pain down into a DEEP DARK HOLE where there was no time -- no past, no present, no future.

He said something clever about time that I remember word for word because it was so strange. "Time is how fast the atoms are dancing," he said. "In black holes, the atoms aren't dancing at all." Then with a big laugh he grabbed me and danced me around the deck.

I don't know what that stuff about atoms and black holes means. But he made me feel like dancing until the time is right, which I hope is SOON.

25

ISS

Friday, October 18, 2013

"You're packing all that stuff and you're only going to be in D.C. for a week?" Bridget asked from the doorway of her roommate's bedroom. Clothes were heaped on the bed and an armchair in the corner, and shoes were scattered all over the floor. Scarves and belts hung from the arm of a pharmacist's lamp; colorful lingerie spilled out of a dresser drawer; and jewelry was heaped on the night table.

Kayla turned with a smile. "Come on in and keep me company. I need a lot of clothes for six days. I'll be in Tad's office almost every day, so there's that. He said I'll also be attending a hearing and a couple of committee meetings, one cocktail party, one lunch with a colleague, two dinners with lobbyists, and an afternoon on another Congressman's yacht. I need a different outfit for each activity -- as I found out to my embarrassment the first time I went out there with Tad."

Bridget picked up a sleeveless cocktail dress in red. "This is beautiful. I haven't seen it on you before, have I?"

Kayla took it from her and held it up to herself. "Isn't it pretty? I'm christening it at one of the dinners in Washington. I found it at Susan's on sale, half price. Here," she said, taking a little black dress off a hanger and picking up a pair of pumps with black and white feathers on the back. "How about this combination? Simple dress, fabulous shoes. They're from Jophiel's. Tad says my taste is exquisite."

"I'll bet he's thinking about you rather than the clothes."

"Oh, no, Bridget. He's a very unusual man. He really notices the clothes women wear. He likes simple with some touch of the unexpected. 'A little flash with the cash,' he says. Isn't that original? I wrote that in my diary the minute he said it. He says so many things I don't want to forget."

"And whose cash is buying all this flash?"

After pushing a suit away to make room, Kayla sat down on the bed beside Bridget. "My clothing allowance, of course. My salary isn't much, but there are perks. Plus when Daddy heard how much time I'm spending in D.C., he secretly deposited some money in my account."

"Secretly?" Bridget asked.

"Mommy wouldn't like it. She thinks it's time for me to live on what I make. But Daddy understands this job is an ISS."

"Not you too!" Bridget exclaimed. "I thought you hated Chase's way of talking. Why can't he -- why can't *you* -- just say important stepping stone?"

Kayla giggled. "Oh, I make fun of Chase right to his face. But it's kind of infectious, talking the way he does. It's so cool."

"So is he going to D.C. with you and Tad?"

Kayla pretended to pout. "Of course. He's Tad's shadow. Besides, if Chase is with us, people think Chase and I are an item."

"So that's the game."

"Oh," Kayla said, putting a hand to her mouth and then to Bridget's. "I wasn't supposed to let anyone know that."

"Even me?"

"Even you. But I'm glad I slipped. I want you to know Chase is available if you want him. He's no more interested in me than I am in him."

"Does Mrs. Bristoll know about this game?"

Kayla bolted to her feet and began sorting through her lingerie. "Don't mention her. I feel guilty enough without that."

"Is she going to Washington with you?"

"Yes, but only for a day. Then she's going to Boston to see her mother."

"Where are you going to stay?"

"Tad has a little apartment near Dupont Circle. He calls it a *pied-à-terre*. So as soon as Cordelia leaves, he'll join me there."

"And where does Chase stay?"

"With an old buddy who lives in a row house near the Capitol." Kayla erupted in hysterical giggles. "*Tête-à-tête. Pied-à-terre. Pots de jardin.* If I'm going to live with Tad, I'm going to have to learn French, I think. He has fancy words for a lot of things. We're not having a love affair, you know. Oh, no. It's a *liaison amoureuse*."

"Suddenly I'm beginning to understand why you feel guilty about Cordelia. The life she's constructed is crumbling."

Without answering, Kayla disappeared into her bathroom to pack a toiletry bag.

"Kayla," Bridget said, walking to the bathroom door. "Talk to me. Talk to me about the guilt."

"I don't like hurting anyone, but what Tad and I have isn't just a fling. It's the real thing."

"Oh, for Pete's sake, that's the title of a corny country and western song. 'This isn't just a fling, girl. It's the real real thing.'"

Kayla flushed to her hairline. "Corny or not, we love each other. Yes, there's guilt, but it's not the main thing."

"It *is* the main thing, at least as to Tad's wife. You should leave your job and break off the relationship before it goes any further and the guilt swallows you whole. Otherwise, you're going to ruin Tad's career and Cordelia's life -- not to mention your reputation. Have you thought about that?"

"Too late." Kayla brushed by her roommate and began folding clothes and putting them in her suitcase. "We're going to have big news soon."

"What big news?"

Kayla straightened and turned with a startling face: furrowed forehead, flushed cheeks, troubled eyes, a defiant smile. "So big we won't be able to hide it, so there'll be no choice but to tell the world."

26

Pig at a Trough
Monday, October 21, 2013

Chase Sumner glanced at his iPhone as the Congressman conducted a long telephone conversation with the Majority Whip. Then, when the conversation veered to personal subjects, he pretended not to be listening by turning his attention to the walls of this much-coveted office suite in the Capitol Building. There they were: photos of Tad with Bush 41 in the last year of his presidency, Tad with Bill Clinton in the first year of his, Tad with several different Indiana governors, Tad wearing a flak jacket and helmet with soldiers in Iraq, Tad with world leaders at the 2013 Economic Forum in Davos. A photo of Tad hitting a baseball at the annual Congressional Baseball charity event was blown up to newspaper size, as was a closeup of Tad as coxswain of the Harvard rowing team. Various plaques in wood and bronze and framed awards and diplomas rested on a floating shelf hung at eye level.

Not everything glorified Tad. A landscape painted by Bush 43 held pride of place above an antique sideboard dating back to the Revolution, a Tilley family heirloom. Uncirculated silver coins from the year of Tad's father's birth mounted on black velvet in plexiglass broke up a wall of photographs. A model of the P-61 Black Widow night fighter his grandfather flew in World War II was suspended above the black walnut partners' desk that Tad claimed had belonged to an even earlier ancestor of his. A seriously out-of-date giant globe on a teak stand stood within reach of Tad's chair.

Chase once heard a visitor from Indiana ask her husband, "Are these walls about three decades of fame or shame?" The husband shushed her but not before she managed to ask in a stage whisper, "Why no picture of a pig at a trough?"

Chase didn't think Tad's self-promotion was shameful at all, nor did he equate public service with pigs at a trough. His ambition was one day to sit in this same office, not as a press spokesman, but as The Honorable Chase Sumner, U.S. Representative, Speaker of the House, third in line to the presidency. He too would have wonder walls plastered with accolades and celebrity handshakes, but the special face and name would be his, not his mentor's.

When Tad hung up, Chase asked, "So what's the deal on defense?"

"More cuts."

"And the budget?"

"No squeezing of the President. The consensus is, the House gives him what he wants so we can fight another day. If we don't win next year's mid-terms, we won't have anything to fight with."

"And the IRS investigation?"

"No special counsel."

"How about Benghazi or the Obamacare individual mandate?"

"We just keep plugging away. Same with the NSA and Fast and Furious. When your opponent is losing, don't get in his way. . . . Why are you shaking your head, Chase?"

"It's all just so damn frustrating trying to change the world. One step forward, two steps back. That's the way it feels."

"But you love politics."

"Most days."

Tad settled back in his chair, his hands locked behind his head. "Think of politics as baseball, slow and elegant, gentlemen's rules, a fly ball here, a two-base hit there. Nothing spectacular. Then comes the crack of the bat, the ball winging its way over the fence, a home run that thrills the crowd. Home runs are thrilling precisely because they're rare and come out of nowhere, and they happen just as you bite into a hot dog or spill your beer and you almost miss the whole thing. Our home runs will come, but not when we expect them. If we go to the stadium just for the home runs, we'll die of boredom or go ape-shit crazy."

"You don't think we're going to have some 'splainin' to do with our backers? Businessmen don't sit and watch home plate or spill their beer. They hustle. They build a whole brewery in the time it takes to play one leisurely game of baseball and then get on with building a pub to serve the beer and then something else. They don't contribute thousands of after-tax dollars to a campaign for the hell of it. They want that home run. From where our supporters are sitting, we look like pigs at a trough."

He sucked in his breath, surprised he'd said that. He hadn't meant to. "Not that we are pigs, of course," he added lamely. "But you know what I mean."

Tad got to his feet. "I do know what you mean. Fortunately, we're the only game in town, aren't we? Businessmen who want tax reform or protection from unions or help with OSHA or a lucrative government contract, they come to me. Where else are they going to go?"

Suddenly Tad's eyes shifted over Chase's shoulder and his face brightened. Chase turned around to see Kayla in the doorway. She was holding a leather portfolio against her chest and wearing a pink suit that somehow managed to look about as businesslike as a ball gown. "Ready, Mr. Bristoll?" she asked with an infectious smile. "I'll fill you in on the NFT's view of Common Core on the way to the restaurant."

"Common Core?" Chase interjected. "What about it?"

"Indiana's probably going to be the first state to reject it," Tad said. "The NFT is on the other side, of course. I suspect it's worried that the Education Committee might go soft at the federal level. Am I right?" he asked with an eyebrow flash to Kayla.

She nodded in the affirmative.

"In any case, it's a great lunch at Marcel's, so I'll listen."

"Common Core doesn't have anything to do with private school teacher accreditation, does it? I hope we're still with Cordelia on the school issues." In a strange way, Chase liked

Cordelia even better than Tad. She'd always been good to him. He did his best to be good in return. He knew from their last private conversation that she was on to Kayla as the new amorous problem -- or AP, as she called it with a little laugh about sharing his secret language. If only he had a woman like Cordelia in his life, he'd already be running for public office.

Kayla reddened. "I don't know about Cordelia's position. What the Congressman chooses to do is up to him, isn't it?"

Ignoring Kayla, Chase stood up so his eyes were once again level with his boss's. "Of course it's up to you, Tad. But don't let me be the last to know."

"Oh, you won't be." Tad flipped the gold Cross pen he'd been twirling back on the desk, then quipped, "We may be awhile, so don't wait up."

Chase watched Tad and Kayla hurry through the door into the short hallway before turning right. He wondered what had happened to Tad's political principles. He seemed so gutless. The man he'd once admired as rock solid now resembled a scampering little chameleon flashing a rainbow of color as it mindlessly hunted crickets and meal worms.

Chase shuddered at the unworthy thought. What had gotten into him? Theodore Bristoll was a good man. He had freely chosen a life of public service, only to find himself in a pit of vipers. Of course it was natural that he would become a little serpentine and spit a little venom now and then. Tad had also freely chosen a magnificent woman to marry, albeit at a very young age, only to find himself the object of many other pretty women's ambitions. Given the unending temptations, it was thus natural that he would fleetingly succumb to this or that feminine charm.

But Tad always returned to the path of the unselfish statesman and good husband.

Stepping out to the hallway, Chase caught a last glimpse of Tad and his new AP. He wanted to warn the lovebirds that Kayla's newly adopted formality in addressing her boss was a joke. Nobody was fooled.

27

Grave Robber
Saturday, October 26, 2013

Hitching a ride on Sheldon Steinmacher's corporate jet, Representative Theodore Bristoll, his press aide Chase, and his special assistant Kayla arrived back in Fort Wayne early Saturday morning after a busy week in Washington. Cordelia Bristoll arrived late that afternoon, having started in Boston and missed her connecting flight in Detroit. She was grumpy and made sure her husband and his press aide shared her mood.

Kayla, however, was not grumpy at all. She was elated. She had met dozens of new people -- PWM, in Chase's special lexicon -- and dined at the best restaurants, always wearing the right thing. At a party at the French Embassy, a powerful Department Secretary had flirted with her and even promised she could come work for him any time she grew tired of Tad Bristoll. At lunch, a lobbyist for the NFT had taken her aside to offer her a job as a meeting coordinator. Chase had graciously taken over the duty of preparing an elaborate paper on educational issues, a paper she had dreaded writing. And she'd spent several very cozy nights with Tad.

After unpacking and taking a nap, Kayla emerged from the bathroom, wearing a fluffy robe and a towel around her wet head, in search of strong coffee and company. When she settled in a chair by the fireplace, Doug jumped up on her lap for a snuggle.

Bridget, who'd spent six nights alone with Doug in the little house, was glad to see her. "So, Kayla, what do you want to do tonight? I've got Season Four of *Downton Abbey*. Or we could go to Piere's with some of my friends from the Academy. Grave Robber is performing live."

Kayla shuddered. "What in the world is Grave Robber?"

"A local metal band that plays something called shock rock or horror punk. I've never heard of them, but one of the teachers at the Academy raves about the music, especially *Fear No Evil*, claiming it sounds like Alice Cooper."

"The name Grave Robber bums me out. They're probably depressing."

"Maybe, maybe not, but what do we care? We've always said, let the event either be really terrible or really terrific. Either way, it'll be an experience we won't forget."

"Oh, I wish I could go, but a couple dozen of Tad's supporters are honoring him tonight at the Marriott, and I'm invited. He's expecting to raise a hundred thousand dollars, so it's a big deal. I've got to look my best."

"Is Cordelia going to be there?"

"Yes, of course. But not at Tad's table. I always sit next to him."

"Isn't that awkward?"

"Not really. Tad tells her she's his greatest asset, such a good hostess -- which she is. That's why they have to separate at these events so they can impress as many people as possible. And Chase hosts another table. So everything works out perfectly, at least for me."

Bridget walked to the living room window and looked out. "You do know a big storm with powerful winds and lashes of rain is predicted for tonight, right? Mac warned me about it at least half a dozen times, telling me to have candles and flashlights handy in case the electricity goes off. He's out on the lawn right now, sawing off a huge limb from the oak tree so it won't fall on the roof." She turned to look at her roommate. "It's not going to be a good night for man or beast, so are you sure you don't want to stay home with me? We can make the Irish coffees you like and sneer at Shirley MacLaine's attempt to hold her own with Maggie Smith and all those other accomplished British actors."

Kayla giggled. "My favorite kind of girls' night, but I just can't. I'll make it up to you tomorrow, I promise. How about driving down to Indy and spending the day at the Fashion Mall? I need more shoes."

"Right, Imelda. There's no such thing as too many shoes," Bridget said. "So what are you wearing tonight?"

Kayla jumped up, disappeared into her bedroom, and returned with a yellow cocktail dress. "I found this in a Georgetown boutique. It's pure silk. Notice the criss-cross ruching at the waist. Isn't it fabulous?"

"Fabulous. You're going to need a raincoat, you know."

Kayla closed her eyes with a big sigh. "Somehow I never get around to the practical stuff, so I'll have to borrow yours again. Okay?"

"Okay."

Hours later, Kayla was still applying lip gloss in the front hall mirror when Tad's sleek black car pulled up at the curb. Bridget had been deputed to watch for its arrival. "Your chariot is here, Cinderella," she announced. "Don't wear the coat open. Button it all the way to your throat and put the hood up because the rain's already coming down in buckets and the wind is fierce."

"I'll be late, so don't wait up," Kayla said.

"How late?"

"Probably not before midnight."

"You have your key?"

Kayla opened her little clutch. "I do, Mom. I have my phone and a credit card and a lipstick too."

Bridget made a screw face. "I'm not your mom."

"Oh, really?" Kayla asked, blowing a kiss as she opened the door to the howling storm.

From the living room window, Bridget watched her roommate, wearing six-inch heels, pick her way over the wet stepping stones leading from their bungalow to the car. The hood of the coat flew off Kayla's head instantly and the skirt billowed like a parachute, exposing the precious yellow dress to the elements. Poor Kayla. She'd look like a drowned rat before she arrived at the hotel.

An hour later, despite the storm, Bridget left for Piere's for an evening with the Grave Robber. She wasn't sure she was ready for horror punk but she didn't want to spend the night alone in a storm.

Part Two

"If you don't read the newspaper, you're uninformed.
If you read the newspaper, you're mis-informed."

Mark Twain

"I'm a simple man, a man of the people."

Congressman Theodore M. Bristoll

28

Outrunning a Demon
Saturday, October 26, 2013

Bridget had been at Piere's almost an hour when the crowd momentarily parted and across the packed room she glimpsed something that bothered her far more than she expected. Justin was standing with his arm around a slim young woman, probably Hispanic. The pockets of the woman's blinged out jeans emphasized a nicely rounded rear, made even more rounded by knee-high suede boots sporting very high heels. When the woman turned, Bridget noticed that the pleated chiffon top was stretched to the maximum over ample breasts but narrowed to skim a tiny waist. A jaunty black beret set off a mop of blue-black curls. The woman's gestures were dramatic and her high-pitched laugh so loud that little snatches of it could be heard soaring above the crowd's atonal chorus.

Bridget had no idea that Justin had a girlfriend and even less idea that she would be so flashy, so sexy and exotic. He told her once he liked women who were strong like Freya, not hot like a Cosmo model. She'd resisted viewing him as boyfriend material, but now she realized he didn't see her as girlfriend material either. Her stomach flipped at the humiliating knowledge that what she thought she was rejecting wasn't hers to possess anyway.

"What?" she asked with a hand behind her ear and leaning halfway across the bistro table when she realized that Suze had just said something to her. The noise was deafening.

"Isn't that Justin over there with the *chica*?"

"I think so."

"Who is she?"

Bridget shrugged and mouthed, "No idea."

"Who would have guessed?" Suze said, wiggling her eyebrows. "You like the music?"

Bridget shrugged again. "Not bad."

After that, Bridget couldn't concentrate on anything but Justin and the *chica*. They were a little too animated to be a real couple. Their movements weren't coordinated. Maybe they weren't romantically involved after all, she rationalized. The more she watched, the more they looked like a blind date or a fix up that was more exciting for the woman than for Justin. If Justin had chosen to spend the evening with the *chica*, he had to be temporarily insane.

A headache that had started behind Bridget's eyes bloomed into a red fog. Her scalp felt hot and her fingers cold. The second strawberry Margarita just delivered to her looked poisonous. She glanced at her watch. Eleven o'clock. Tired and troubled, and starting to feel nauseous from the noise and funk of the room, she said her goodbyes, donned the yellow rubber slicker she'd been forced to wear (Kayla having commandeered her good raincoat), and muscled her way to the entrance to the club.

There, to her dismay, she saw Justin and his date standing near the door, watching the storm, apparently deciding whether to brave the onslaught or wait it out. The woman, who was even more stunning close up, flashed Bridget a big smile.

The scene outside was dreadful, rain blowing horizontally, loud cracks of thunder punctuating lightning flashes that ripped holes in the sky. Why had she ever left home?

She would have to pass within inches of Justin to get outside. The last thing she wanted was for him to notice her. Her thin frame was no match for the *chica's* voluptuous figure. Her rubber slicker looked pathetic beside the *chica's* balloon-skirted raincoat. Justin Creed had a stunning date clinging to him; Bridget Deel was alone on a Saturday night.

So, thinking she could make herself invisible, she tucked her hair into the hood of the slicker and hunched her shoulders as if she were already battling the storm. Head down, she scuttled to the door and tried to open it.

But she couldn't. The wind had the force of a battering ram. After her second try, Justin leaned in to help. "Bridget," he said, peeking under her hood. "Is that you?"

She smiled weakly. "Oh, hi, Justin. Didn't see you. Got to run. See you Monday." Then she gestured at the storm as if it prevented all further conversation.

Heart racing and face burning with embarrassment, she ran to her car, spun out of the parking lot, and sped through one yellow light after another as if outrunning a demon.

29

Oak Tree
Saturday, October 26, 2013

As Bridget pulled into the driveway alongside the bungalow, she looked for lights in Kayla's bedroom window. There were none. Bridget's stomach sank. She didn't want to be alone, not tonight of all nights. She wanted to talk about the strange reaction she had to Justin and his exotic date at Piere's. She wanted Kayla to prepare an Irish coffee to soothe her headache and then distract her with stories of her brilliant night at the fundraiser. If she had company, the storm would feel cozy instead of wild and threatening.

Doug was curled in Bridget's chair by the fireplace. He must not have heard her come through the back door, but when he saw her round the corner from the kitchen, he leapt down and with wild gyrations of his tail and little squeals of delight threw himself against her legs.

"Oh, my darling little man, at least I have you. Let me get my jacket off and I'll find you a treat. Do you need to go out to potty?" She opened the living room door. Doug stood on the threshold, head down, blinking away raindrops. He sniffed the air. Upon hearing a crack of thunder, he shook himself violently and snorted twice. No, he didn't want to go out in *that*.

"Well, then, Doug, let's watch a happy movie. Something funny."

Halfway through *Groundhog Day,* when Bill Murray threw the

alarm clock on the floor for the second time, Bridget glanced at her watch. It was almost one in the morning. Where the hell was Kayla? She texted her and walked to the front window just in case the sleek black car suddenly appeared.

Nothing. No reply. No car.

She sat down on the wicker lounge to watch the street. And then it happened. A wicked bolt of lightning hit the old oak tree, which split down the middle, one half falling toward the street. All the lights went out. Doug whined.

"Damn it!" Bridget cried. The whole day had been crap from one end to the other and now this. Civilization died when the lights went out. It felt like a bad omen.

Momentarily blind, she waited on the lounge for her eyes to adjust before feeling her way to the kitchen for a candle and matches. But before she could do that, a flashlight suddenly bobbed toward the house.

"Who is that?" she asked aloud. Doug barked.

And then someone was pounding on the door.

Bridget put her eye to the peephole. Mac! He had thoughtfully pointed the flashlight up at his own face. The strands of hair that had been covering his scalp hung limply to one side, dripping rain. His eyes seemed to have migrated into the bridge of his nose.

She attached the chain and opened the door a few inches. "What do you want, Mac?" she yelled over the noise of the storm.

"Open up. Let me in."

"Now?"

"Yes, now. I've got to check the sump pump. I don't want the basement to flood."

Ever since that day at Glenbrook when Chase warned them not to let Mac in if either was alone, she and Kayla had meticulously followed that instruction. "I'll check it myself."

"I'm drowning out here and you don't know what to look for, so open up."

"I'm alone."

"That's okay."

Wavering about what to do, Bridget looked down at Doug

and whispered, "Are you big enough and mean enough to protect me here? Or will you show Mac where the cash is and invite him to take the jewelry too?"

Before she had to decide whether to be stupid by detaching the chain or rude by slamming the door, a car pulled up at the curb and in seconds Chase, also holding a flashlight, was standing beside Mac.

Bridget detached the chain and opened the door wider.

"What's going on here?" Chase asked.

"This is Mac, our landlord. He wants to check the sump pump but I'm here alone and the lights are out, so . . . ."

Chase patted Mac on the back. "Man, don't be insulted by her hesitation. Women don't let strange men into their house at night."

"I'm not a stranger," Mac barked. "Who are you?"

"You don't remember me from the Labor Day party? I'm Chase, a friend of the girls. So come on in with me and go check the basement."

After Mac disappeared down the basement stairs, Chase said, "I won't be a minute. You said you're alone, so I take it that Kayla hasn't returned."

"I've been waiting up. Isn't she in the car?"

"No. Tarik drove Tad's wife home when the fundraiser was over. After the donors cleared out, Tad took Kayla to the hotel lounge, telling me to return in an hour to pick her up. But she wasn't there. The doorman said she left. He offered to call a cab, but she said no, and he didn't see her get into a car."

"She just walked outside? In this storm?"

"That's what the doorman said."

"Why would she do that?"

Chase looked away briefly. "I hate to tell you this, but she had an argument with Cordelia in the lobby. It got ugly."

"How ugly?"

"Words. I didn't hear what Cordelia said, but her tone was angry and made Kayla cry. Nothing physical, no slaps or anything like that, but words hurt, of course. So maybe Kayla got mad and went outside to cool off."

"That doesn't sound like Kayla."

"Well, whether it does or doesn't, the doorman told me she left on foot and he didn't see her come back in. So I drove around downtown, trying to guess where she might go. I drove all over hell, but I never found her."

"Where's your boss?"

"He snagged a ride home with a friend, so he's fine."

"Did you check her cellphone?"

"I don't have her number with me. . . . Oh," he exclaimed, "there we are. The lights are back on. You mind if I sit down a minute?"

"Have a seat. Here's Kayla's number."

After a few seconds, he gave her a worried look. "Goes to voice mail. Where would she go this time of night?" Chase reared back when Doug suddenly put his paws on his knees and nosed his crotch. "Oh, here, boy, down. Thank God I changed clothes, but still . . . ."

"Sorry," Bridget said, pulling Doug away. "I was wondering about those jeans. Kayla left here in a fancy cocktail dress, so I assumed you'd be wearing a tux."

"Not a tux, but we men were in good dark suits and the women -- well, they were pretty fancy but not as colorful as Kayla. Speaking of whom -- ."

"I don't know where she'd go this late. She's never not come home when she said she would. Should we call the police?"

Chase looked surprised. "Why would we? She's not missing, not in the police sense. She's just late. But I feel responsible for her welfare. Tad told me to take her home and that's what I intend to do come hell or high water." He looked out at the street. "Or come the storm of the century. I'll go out again and drive back downtown. Maybe this time I'll find her."

"Find who?" Mac asked, suddenly appearing in the hall.

"Kayla," Bridget said. "She wasn't at the hotel when Chase went to pick her up."

"You talking about the Marriott?"

Bridget blinked. "How do you know that?"

"I heard something about a fundraiser there for Bristoll tonight. I happened to be driving by when the Congressman arrived in that fancy car of his. I saw Kayla get out. I wanted to jump out and hold an umbrella over her head. How come nobody did that?"

"Well, that's not the issue now," Bridget said. "She left the hotel without getting into a car and hasn't come home. Maybe she hailed a taxi but we don't know that. Chase has been trying to find her."

"You want me to go looking? Where do you think she walked? If she's to be found, I'll find her, let me tell you."

"No need for that. How's the sump pump?" Chase asked pointedly.

"Fine," Mac said, shuffling his feet. "But I want to know where Kayla is. I want to find her."

"So do we. But let's not panic. No need to talk like she's missing or something bad has happened. We don't want to start any rumors that might embarrass her. Right, Mac?"

"Right you are. She got any friends living near the Marriott?"

"Not that I know of," Bridget said. "And everything's closed this time of night, so no stores to duck into."

"Well, I'm going to go looking for her. She could get hurt by downed power lines or catch her death of cold, so don't try to stop me."

Neither Bridget nor Chase tried anything of the sort.

After Mac left, Chase said. "For sure that man's a little strange. Now, I'm going to retrace my steps in case I missed something. Put my number in your phone, call me the minute you hear anything."

At the door, he hugged Bridget reassuringly, saying everything would be all right and Kayla would be back soon. It was the first physical contact she'd ever had with him.

Bridget wanted to believe that Kayla would be back soon. And she wanted Chase to hug her again.

30

Bridget's Journal
Saturday, October 26, 2013

It's really Sunday already, but it doesn't feel like it. Saturday will never end, though the storm has finally passed on east.

When I get up tomorrow, I'll write all about the strange day I had: the savage storm, Justin and the chica at Piere's, the ruined oak tree, lights out, Mac at the door, and Chase hugging me.

But it got stranger ten minutes after Chase left.

I knew I couldn't sleep until I heard from Kayla so I made myself some hot chocolate with a splash of bourbon. That always puts me to sleep. And of course I gave Doug a little treat because he couldn't sleep either.

I had just turned on the TV to find something mindless to watch when my phone buzzed. It was a text from Kayla. I was so relieved, I almost fainted.

Back TMR. : -)

I hate emoticons. I thought she did too. She's never used them before. But at least I know what they are. So she means she'll be back tomorrow -- smiley face.

I immediately texted back, "Where are you? What

are you doing?"

She texted back, Nosy. X-P

Another emoticon. She's sticking her tongue out at me.

Then I tried calling her, but her phone went to voice mail.

So I forwarded her texts to Chase with a note that I tried to call her. He texted back that he was glad she was okay and was calling off the hunt.

I called Mac too. He started asking questions but I was in no mood for that, so I just hung up.

31

Sunday Breakfast
Sunday, October 27, 2013

Tad Bristoll looked up from *The New York Times* to take another bite of scrambled eggs. Then he glanced out the window of the breakfast room. "Did you notice that one of the oak trees came down last night?"

Cordelia sipped her coffee, then turned to look out at the yard. "Yes. I noticed it when I got up. The fence is broken too. And the birches in the front are toast."

He returned his attention to an article about Syria. From behind the paper, he asked, "Who takes care of that kind of stuff?"

Cordelia shut her eyes in frustration. "The tree service we've always used. The company that put up the fence."

"Does the insurer need to be notified?"

"Yes, of course."

"So you'll take care of that tomorrow."

"Naturally."

"Don't sound so burdened," he said, glancing at her as he turned the page. "I've got a big meeting tomorrow with my campaign staff, so the last thing I need is to worry about a few trees damaged in a storm."

Cordelia glanced at her son, who had inhaled his breakfast and was now occupied with his iPad. "You may be excused, Porter. Did you finish your homework yesterday?"

"Uh-huh."

"Have you taken your antihistamine?"

He nodded.

"Well, then, off you go. Don't forget your appointment this afternoon with your math tutor. Come down at a quarter to two. I'll drive you."

"Ah, jeez, Mom. I can drive myself."

"Great. I'll fumigate your room while you're gone. And don't say jeez."

After Porter left the room, Cordelia waited a few minutes before speaking. "Tad. Look at me."

He snapped the paper down on the table. "What now?"

"That girl, Kayla. She's getting on my nerves."

"You're getting on hers too, calling her a bitch in the hotel lobby. She cried for an hour."

"I kept my voice down. Nobody but us heard. And hanging on you the way she did, right in front of our friends, it was like a slap in the face."

"Hanging on me? She never touched me."

He was right. Cordelia looked away, momentarily confused. What was it that had been so offensive? "Something about the way you two act together, that's what I meant." She straightened her shoulders. "Whatever it is you're doing, it's offensive. So in my view, she deserved everything she got from me. And it's unseemly of you to be serving as her defense attorney."

"She works for me, Cordelia, so who else is going to defend her? What you don't realize is that she's good for morale. She's nice. She does her job. Everybody at the office loves her."

"Including you."

Tad glared at his wife. "Including me."

Cordelia sneered. "It's time for you to grow up and see the difference between lust and love."

"I've always known the difference, believe me."

"What time did you get home?"

"Late." He poured himself another cup of coffee.

"Why?"

He sipped his coffee, taking his time to snarl his answer. "I had things to do."

Cordelia studied his face, normally handsome, now ugly with fury. The two of them had never had an argument like this before, not over his infatuations. She'd casually murmur something about how it was time for this or that special assistant to move on. He wouldn't object, implying by his acquiescence that the assistant hadn't been special anyway and thus it was of no moment whether she moved on or not.

So her instincts were right: this affair was different. It had meaning. She was therefore entirely justified in what she'd done to Kayla.

"Just so there are no surprises," she said, "I'm catching an early morning flight to Boston tomorrow. Mama needs me. You don't."

"How long are you going to be out there?"

"What do you care?"

"I'm your husband. We're in the public eye. I'm expected to know where my wife is."

"I'll be out there until things blow over."

"I think they blew over last night," he said, pointing at the window and laughing at his own joke.

"And while I'm gone don't send me flowers."

Tad snorted his contempt. "What happens to Porter?"

She once again closed her eyes in frustration. "Do you notice nothing that happens around here?"

Tad made a production of picking up his newspaper and pretending his wife was invisible.

"Mrs. Brighton, of course," Cordelia said before she left the room. Then, *sotto voce*, she added, "In the last sixteen years, who else has come in to take care of your son when I'm gone?"

32

Sunday Cleanup
Sunday, October 27, 2013

When Bridget heard Mac light up his chainsaw, she went to the window. That kind of noise on a Sunday would ordinarily cause her distress, but not today. She needed the distraction.

She finished her toast and coffee and looked out again. Given the size of the tree that had been struck by lightning, Mac was going to be there all day. So she went out.

He looked up from his work when he caught sight of her. He shut down the saw and laid it aside. Two short chunks of the fallen half of the oak tree had already been rolled to one side. "Sorry to see this old tree go," he said, pulling his ear muffs down and pushing his goggles up, "but we'll have plenty of firewood for the winter."

"I don't know what I can do, but can I help?"

"See those leaf bags over there? And the rake? You can gather up the twigs and leaves and put them in the bags."

"Let me bring Doug out and tie him to the stake so he can get some exercise without running into your chainsaw."

"Any more word from Kayla?"

"No," Bridget said. "But she said she'd be back today."

"When?"

She shrugged. "No idea."

Mac shot to his feet. "I know that car."

Bridget looked across the street. An old blue Chevy, one fender painted black, had just shuddered to a stop. A young guy rolled down his window and stared at them.

"You know the guy who's driving?" she asked.

"Name is As- . . . Asser . . . Asphalt. Something like that. He was here that day you and Kayla went up to the Lake. Waited out there for hours in the heat. Finally, real late, a tow truck come along and took the car away."

"Could his name be Asher?"

"Asher. Yeah, that sounds right."

"Asher Stroheim. He was Kayla's boyfriend at college but she broke it off the day she graduated. I never saw him before. But one day, not long after she started work, he made a big scene in Kayla's office. I don't think she's talked to him since."

"Well, he wanted to talk to her, sat out there for hours, smoking weed. Not a lucky guy, I'd say." Mac barked a laugh.

"What's that laugh about?" Bridget asked.

"You don't want to know." Mac swaggered to the curb and called out, "You need something, boy?"

Asher got out of the car and walked across the street. Bridget decided to join the men.

"Who are you?" he asked Bridget.

She tilted her head at the rudeness.

"I mean," Asher said, "are you the brunette your friend here mentioned who lives with Kayla?"

Bridget nodded.

"What's your name?"

She hesitated. "Bridget."

"I need to talk to Kayla. Bring her out here, would you? You can stay right beside her if you want. I'm not going to hurt her. I just want to get my stuff back."

"What stuff?" Bridget asked. He was a big guy with a big nose and long untidy hair; his windbreaker was open over a plaid flannel shirt and jeans ripped at the knees. His steel-toed boots were oddly immaculate. Asher Stroheim was attractive in a lumberjack kind of way.

"Stuff I gave her. Silver necklace, teddy bear, a portable stereo, a couple of DVDs, a wristwatch. Oh, and a tennis racket, a Wilson. Kayla was never good at the game, though, so I might as well have it back."

"She's not here."

Asher looked at the bungalow. "She's gotta be here."

"Well, she isn't."

"You mean, she went out already? Not like her. She always liked to sleep in on Sunday."

"She's not sleeping in and hasn't gone out," Bridget said. "The fact is, she never came home last night."

"You shittin' me?"

"No," Bridget said, blinking at the vulgarity.

Asher removed half a hand-rolled cigarette from his jacket pocket and lit it with a lighter shaped like a shotgun shell. He took a puff, then offered it to them. "Want some? It's good shit."

Mac looked longingly at the cigarette, but when Bridget shook her head, he did too.

"I tried to give her a ride last night. Saw her downtown on a deserted street, pretty late, thought she might be in danger, maybe her car wouldn't start or something, but she told me to get lost. I pulled over and opened the door, talked real nice and everything -- raining like a son of a bitch, you know; her coat was blowing up and her hair was a mess -- but she just kept walking in those silly shoes. Wouldn't even look at me. Wouldn't you know, a cop was right on my tail, so I had to move on. I rounded the block -- well, a couple a blocks on all four sides, damn one-way streets, you know -- but by the time I got back she was gone. Vanished. Couldn't see her anywhere. I thought she'd probably gotten a ride from someone she knew or maybe found a cab. Either way, she should have been here a long time ago."

"What really happened?" Mac asked suspiciously. "Did you take her somewhere?"

"Not a chance, bro. I told you all I know. So," he said, looking at Bridget, "you mind if I go in and look around, find my stuff?"

She stepped back, appalled at the effrontery. "Of course you can't come in. And if Kayla *was* here, she'd say the same thing."

"Oh, come on. I won't take anything that isn't mine. Won't disturb a thing."

"It's time for you to go."

After taking a last toke, he pinched the cigarette and put the remains back in his pocket. "Did Kayla say nasty things about me? Write crap in her diary? Or are you just the unfriendly type?"

Bridget hadn't noticed Mac slip behind her but suddenly he was beside her again, brandishing the chainsaw, pulling on the starter rope.

"Whoa!" Asher said, hands in the air. "No need for that, little man. You're wired a little too tight, should a toked a little. You too," he said, grinning at Bridget. "You'd both be nicer."

He had reached the middle of the street when he turned back. "You're not bad looking, Bridget. You play tennis?"

Bridget finally found her words. "You're breathtaking, you know that?"

"That's what she said," he answered with a lascivious grin. "So do you play?"

Mac started up the chainsaw. Laughing, Asher pointed his finger at Mac, threw an air kiss at Bridget, and sauntered to his car.

33

emails
Sunday, October 27, 2013

Bridget to Chase:

Still no word from K, tho I texted her 100 times. U?

Chase to Bridget:

Nada.

Bridget to Chase:

Shd I file missing person report?

Chase to Bridget:

No! :-(She's probably licking wounds from last night and will show up in the office tomorrow.

Bridget to Chase:

I don't think so. But let me know ASAP

```
if U see K -- or hear from her before then.
```

Chase to Bridget:

```
    Will do.  Just don't do anything hasty.
Talk to me first.
```

Bridget was just getting into bed when her cellphone buzzed. The text from Kayla read:

```
    Don't worry.  I have a lot to think about,
want to crawl under a rock.:$
```

Bridget immediately texted back:

```
    What's :$ mean?
```

Kayla replied:

```
    Embarrassed. Now I'm really embarrassed.
Do I have to spell out everything?
```

Bridget asked:

```
    Where are you?
```

Kayla's reply was infuriating:

```
    Things are upside down, but just know I'm
well.
```

Bridget's response:

```
    You're making me crazy.
```

Kayla replied:

```
I'm still a tease.:-)
```

Why don't you just say where you are? Bridget thought. Frantic to hear her roommate's voice, she punched in Kayla's number, but there was no answer, only voice mail. She forwarded Kayla's texts to Chase. He replied:

```
Just what I thought. :-))
```

So you're really really happy, Chase. Why not just say so?

34

Whose Call?
Monday, October 28, 2013

"So," Sheila said to Bridget and Justin, "are you two ready for the challenge?"

Both nodded without looking at each other. Bridget squirmed in her chair.

Sheila had just informed them that as tour leaders and chaperones both would be accompanying the Summit Academy seniors on their Washington, D.C., trip in two weeks. Bridget was in charge of arranging a morning at the House of Representatives; Justin was in charge of arranging an afternoon at the Smithsonian's National Air and Space Museum. Both would report to a parent who had volunteered to be the trip director.

Ordinarily, Bridget would be thrilled at the idea of spending five days in the nation's capital. But it would also be five days with Justin, whose taste in women definitely didn't include her.

"You think the government shutdown is really over?" Justin asked.

"It's been eleven days since operations resumed," Sheila said. "Congressman Bristoll assured me last week that everything's back to normal and will stay that way. He'll be happy to have our students visit his office in the Capitol. His assistant -- your roommate, Bridget -- will take them to the Rotunda and Statuary Hall. . . . Do you think she actually knows anything about their history?"

Bridget was uncomfortable.

"What's that look?" Sheila asked.

"I didn't want to bring it up today, but I haven't seen Kayla since Saturday night. And I'm worried about her."

"I saw her at the fundraiser at the Marriott," Sheila said. "She was at Tad's table."

"Well, she supposedly walked out of the hotel -- ."

"In the storm?"

"That's what the hotel doorman told Chase. She wouldn't let him call a cab and no car was waiting for her. Worse, she never came back to the hotel."

"Why would she do that?"

"Chase said Kayla had an argument with Cordelia in the lobby. Maybe she got mad about something and just wanted to cool off."

"But to go out in the dark in a raging storm, even just for a few minutes, is a whole lot of crazy," Justin said.

"She isn't crazy," Bridget said. "But I have to believe she walked around a little. Chase said he was supposed to pick her up but she'd already left the hotel, so he drove around downtown trying to find her, which he never did. Her ex-boyfriend actually saw her on the street but she wouldn't get in his car. Even our landlord went looking once he found out she hadn't come home."

"Hold it right there," Justin said. "What are all these guys doing driving around trying to find her?"

"Chase drove to the hotel because his boss told him to pick Kayla up at a certain hour and take her home. I don't know how Asher happened to see her when he did. Mac didn't go looking for Kayla until Chase showed up at my house and found out she hadn't come home yet. The strange thing is she's texted me a few times without saying where she is or what's she doing. Here, let me read you the texts she sent me."

When she was done, Justin said, "Weird. . . . Did you check Bristoll's office this morning?"

"Not yet. But Chase promised to let me know at once if she showed up or they heard from her."

"Have you spoken to Kayla's parents or informed the police?"

Bridget shook her head. "No, I haven't. Chase told me it's too soon to treat her as a missing person. She's texting me, after all, and she's an adult, so if she wants to disappear for awhile, she can."

"But this isn't like her, is it?" Sheila asked, checking her watch and scooting back her chair.

"No. She and I text a dozen times a day. I always know where she is and what she's doing, even what she's thinking. She's never done anything like this before."

After a short silence, Sheila tapped her pen like a gavel and said, "Call Bristoll's office first. Find out if she's shown up. If she hasn't, then I think you have to call Kayla's parents. Tell them what you know and forward their daughter's texts. See what they want to do. It's their call, not Chase's or yours."

Bridget looked at Justin. "Do you have anything to add?"

"No. It sounds like a plan."

"Time to go to work, folks," Sheila said over her shoulder as she left the conference room.

As Justin and Bridget followed their boss down the hall, he said, "You left so fast at Piere's, I didn't get a chance to introduce you to Julieta."

"That's okay. I saw her, though. She's very pretty. Congratulations."

"Congratulations! For what?" he asked, puzzled. "She's -- ."

But before he could say anything else about Julieta, Bridget quickened her pace and fled to her classroom.

35

The Heir
Monday, October 28, 2013

Lexie Wright was ten minutes early for her appointment with Congressman Bristoll. Mimi, his secretary, ushered her into Chase's office.

"Mrs. Wright," Chase said, straightening his tie before shaking hands, "so nice to see you."

"I'm early."

"That's fine. Let's go into Tad's office -- much more comfortable than mine. What can I do for you?"

"Where's Tad? I need to speak to him."

"He's in Indy this morning, meeting with the Governor about a couple of issues."

Lexie did not hide her irritation. "Nobody called to tell me that. We could have rescheduled."

"I thought about that, and I know how busy you are, but I may be able to help you. At least I can tell you where the Congressman's thinking is right now and promise that I'll do whatever I can."

Lexie glanced out the window, deciding whether to stay or leave. She liked Chase, but she needed to talk to her Representative. *Oh, well, I'm here, so why not make the best of it?* She shrugged and sighed.

"I have every federal agency on my back and I'm sick of it, up to here," she said, gesturing with a swipe across her neck. "First, the

IRS demanded an audit. That cost me a fortune in accountants and lawyers, all to find we owed nothing. Then OSHA. Ten thousand in fines for stupid things like a worker not wearing a seat belt on a Bobcat. EPA did a surprise visit about permit compliance. Again, no violations were found but the inspection took two days of staff time plus a fee to our outside environmental engineer. And -- if you can believe it -- Alcohol, Firearms and Tobacco visited the scrapyard last week." The scrapyard was Summit City Metals and Scrapyard, a fourth-generation family business that Lexie inherited from her father.

"AFT?" Chase asked in shock. "Why?"

"Checking to see that we don't take any guns as scrap. They were there two days. I said people don't typically throw guns away, but if any slipped through, which they never have, we'd notify the authorities at once and turn the gun over."

"Jeez. You must be livid."

"That's not all. The FBI may be next. We've heard through the grapevine that a disgruntled former employee is pretending to be a whistleblower, claiming we take stolen iron and copper. We don't, but the threat of an embarrassing and very costly investigation is hanging over our heads."

"I take it that that much attention from the government is unusual."

"Unusual?" she exclaimed. "It's downright unprecedented. It looks like a coordinated attack on me."

"And why would the government be coordinating an attack on you?"

"That's what I want to talk to Tad about. I haven't founded any Tea Party organizations, but I've given to them. I've donated to Tad, as you well know, and to other politicians that support tax and regulatory reform and fiscal responsibility. I'm sure the IRS knows about those donations. Therefore, I suspect that's the activity that put a mark on me. And I want it to stop."

"What can Tad do?"

"That's for him to tell me. I have the problem; he better have the solution. For starters, unless the House gets a handle on the

IRS, I'm not giving another dime to Tad or any other politician because all it does is bring the government down on me. It doesn't matter which party I support anyway because the result is the same: more heavy-handed government."

"I understand your position, Mrs. Wright. Completely. But Tad just doesn't . . . ."

"Doesn't what?"

"How do I say this?" Chase looked uncomfortable.

Lexie closed her eyes in frustration. "Spit it out, Chase."

"He doesn't seem to be in a mood to fight right now. The Speaker and Majority Whip aren't either, so it's not just Tad. They won't appoint a select committee to investigate the IRS or enforce any contempt proceedings or subpoenas. The prevailing mood in the House is to put off any real fight until after the mid-term elections."

"Do you talk with Tad about this?"

"Every day," Chase answered, rubbing his hands through his hair. "I wouldn't do things the way Tad is, but I'm just his spokesman, so all I can do is give him my best advice."

"What would you do?"

"I'd fight like a hellcat. The House controls the nation's purse, so I'd close the purse. That way the administration would have to cooperate with the House or defund its favorite programs."

"Well, tell Tad this: If he and his buddies keep putting off the fight, they're not going to have any money from business owners like me to fight with. It's just spitting in the wind."

"But you just wrote a big check Saturday night," Chase gently reminded her.

He shrank when she turned her beautiful brown eyes on him. That glare was like a drill into his brain. "And I'm beginning to regret it, Chase. And there's one more thing."

"What's that?"

"Speaking as the founder of Summit Academy, I want to know what he's going to do about accreditation for private schools. Can we continue to hire unlicensed teachers or not? If we can't, he'll never see another dime from me."

"Tad might be a little soft on that one too. As a matter of principle, I'm in Mrs. Bristoll's corner, of course -- which is your corner. But I'm not sure Tad is listening. The NFT has a lot of money for politicians who go their way and, as you know, they want to kill private and charter schools."

Lexie got to her feet. "Maybe you should be my Representative, Chase. I'm beginning to think Tad should find something else to do."

"Oh, Mrs. Wright. I don't know what to say."

"Say nothing for now. Not a word to anybody about what I just said. But just between us there's a whole cadre of people like me ready to find somebody else to run next year and your name has come up. Don't tell me you've never thought about it."

Chase humbly ducked his head. "I'm ready whenever Tad throws in the towel. But I don't expect he'll do it any time soon."

"Has he ever said anything to you about taking his place when he retires?"

"Yes. As a matter of fact, he has. Behind the scenes, he's been grooming me as his successor."

"If he takes money from the NFT to oppose the Indiana bill on teacher accreditation, then maybe somebody should step in to move the succession along. And if he doesn't do something to help me with the *federales*, then I'll have to reconsider my support for him."

"Yes, ma'am."

Chase got up to open the office door for her. Lexie laid a hand on his arm. "And, Chase, be smart about this. Lay low until we see what Tad is going to do. The head of the heir to the throne never rests securely upon its owner's shoulders -- not until the throne is empty."

"I have no wish to see the throne empty yet."

"Whatever you say, Chase. But keep me informed."

"That I will. Let me walk you to your car."

36

Guilt

Monday, October 28, 2013

At six, Bridget parked beside The Oyster Bar on South Calhoun. Once again she checked her phone in case Kayla had texted her again. But there had been no messages since Sunday night. In the visor mirror, she checked her hair, mascara and lipstick. Nothing she could do about the worry lines creasing her forehead or the guilty look in her eyes.

The guilt was irrational, she knew. She felt guilty because it was noon before she could find the time to call Chase and ask if Kayla had shown up. When he said she hadn't, Bridget sighed. "Then my boss says we have to inform Kayla's parents. It's their call, she says, whether to report her as missing."

"I don't think the police will take kindly to such a report when Kayla's texting you of her own free will and she's only been away from home less than forty-eight hours. But your boss is right, let her parents know what's happening and let them decide what to do."

"I dread the call."

"Understandable. So don't make that call to the Jespersons by yourself. Let me help you."

"You'd do that?"

"Of course. Let's wait until after work, though. Who knows, she might still show up today or text you again. Besides, both

Kayla's parents work, so it's better for them if we wait until evening. We'll review the situation and decide what to say over dinner."

"Dinner? The last thing on my mind is food."

"Don't let yourself get run down. We both have to eat, after all, and it'll give us a chance to think of the right thing to say."

As she left the school, Justin got up from his console and signaled her to stop. "Don't run away again, Bridget. We need to talk. You want to catch a drink later?"

She barely paused in her haste to get away. "Can't. I'm meeting Chase downtown and I'm already running behind."

She blushed when recalling Justin's words. "Don't run away again." She must look like a silly schoolgirl to him, running from him at Piere's, then twice running from him at the Academy. Well, what did it matter what he thought of her? If she'd ever had the idea of becoming his close friend -- or even his girlfriend -- that idea died Saturday night. But now, in the worst possible circumstances, solid, handsome Chase cared about her.

He was waiting for her at the bar, talking to the owner. But when he spotted her, he shot to his feet and held out his arms in welcome, then gave her a big hug and took her coat. "You okay, Bridget?"

"Not really. But it's good to see you." And it was. She took a long look at his friendly face, handsome as ever but strangely, given the circumstances, more relaxed than she'd ever seen him before.

"Good to see you too," he said. "What are you drinking tonight? The beer is great here."

"Perhaps a wine spritzer. I want to relax but not lose focus."

"Good girl," he said, signaling the bartender. "I like a girl who's sensible. Remember that night at Chop's Wine Bar when Kayla got drunk?" He shook his head. "The more she drank, the sillier she sounded."

"Oh, Chase, that's a horrid thing to say. She was just tipsy."

"Tomato, tomaato. I say drunk, you say tipsy. If we can't see her the way she really is, it's going to be hard to guess where she's hiding out." He signaled the bartender for dinner menus. "You weren't in Washington with us at the French Embassy party, but she got a little squiffy that night too. She was flirting with a bigwig in the administration, so openly that Tad took her aside and told her to cut it out. So I'm wondering, did she get drunk Saturday night and maybe get in the wrong stranger's car? Just to get out of the storm, if nothing else."

"That doesn't sound like her at all," Bridget said stoutly. "Besides, wouldn't you know whether she was drunk when you saw her at the hotel?"

"Actually, now that you make me think back, she seemed okay. But after the party broke up, she spent an hour alone in the bar with Tad before I returned to take her home, so who knows what she drank then?"

"What did your boss say when she didn't show up for work today?" Bridget asked.

Chase sipped his beer. "He's down in Indianapolis, meeting with the Governor. He won't be back until tomorrow. I don't want to tell him anything until I see him in person."

"Maybe Kayla's in touch with him. Maybe he knows where she is."

Chase waggled his head. "That's possible, I suppose."

"So maybe before we call her parents, you should find out what the Congressman knows."

He smiled. "That's a little delicate under the circumstances. We all know Kayla's the new AP, but -- ."

"AP?"

"Amorous problem. But in Tad's presence, we pretend she's just his assistant."

Bridget raised her eyebrows. "So talking to the Congressman is delicate because you'd be acknowledging what you know but pretend not to know about your boss's relationship with Kayla?"

Chase nodded. "Exactly. In effect I'd be revealing that I know they're having an affair because an employee who's hiding out for some unknown reason wouldn't ordinarily keep her boss posted on what she's doing."

"But . . . but the Congressman has to know that you know about the affair. You're with him practically day and night."

"That doesn't mean we ever actually talk about it. We're men. We don't talk about our love lives."

"Do you think," Bridget mused, "there's any possibility that Kayla's home with her parents and there's nothing to worry about after all?"

"Let me see her texts again."

Bridget handed him her phone.

"While I'm looking at Kayla's messages," he said, pointing at the menu in front of her, "take a look at the appetizers. I want you to eat something. How about the steamed mussels? We can share. And the oysters sound good. Let's see if we agree on how to eat them: raw or cooked, spicy or mild."

A few minutes later, he shook his head. "I don't think Kayla's at home. If that's all she did -- ran home to pout -- she'd say so. Don't you agree?"

Bridget agreed. She also enthusiastically seconded the mussels and raw oysters with horseradish sauce. She was much hungrier than she thought.

As she and Chase shared appetizers, they also shared stories about Kayla. Chase wanted to know everything about her so that they could figure out where she might be and what she was doing.

"If I could figure out the motive for this strange behavior, that might get us somewhere," Bridget said.

"Motive is always mysterious," Chase said. "Too subjective."

The guilt that oppressed Bridget for not taking action sooner gradually shrank from the size and weight of a bowling ball pressing on her chest to a whiffle ball floating somewhere in her midsection.

Finally, by the time they left to return to the Congressman's office to make the call, they had decided on the right message for Kayla's parents.

37

Bridget's Journal
Monday, October 28, 2013

What a day! Until a few minutes ago I felt almost happy.

Chase is so articulate, but then I suppose a press aide should be. After we shared appetizers at the Oyster Bar, we drove back to the Congressman's office to call the Jespersons. Chase didn't turn on the overhead lights, so we sat in his office, the darkness relieved only by the green accountant's lamp on his desk. Spooky. But cozy too.

He was factual and comprehensive in his account of the events but warm and hopeful in his conclusion. "We have every reason to think she'll be in the office tomorrow morning," he said to Kayla's parents.

Dr. Jesperson then asked me if there was anything else I could add to what Chase had said. I said I couldn't think of anything but I would forward Kayla's texts to him, which I did. He also asked if he could come over to the house tomorrow night and of course I said yes.

When Chase hung up, I asked him why he was so hopeful that Kayla would turn up tomorrow. Did he know something he wasn't telling me?

"No," he said. "Not exactly. But those texts from Kayla read like a puzzle, and I'm good at puzzles. I don't tell many people this, but I'm a member of Mensa."

The society for geniuses? I asked.

He said something about how he didn't view himself as a genius, he just tests well. But he admitted he has a good brain and likes to use it.

I asked him why he thought Kayla's messages were a puzzle. She never liked puzzles -- crossword, jigsaw, riddles, nothing.

"But she likes to tease you," he said. "She even says so in her last text. A tease is sort of like a puzzle."

I must not have looked convinced because he said, "Just wait. I'll bet you hear from her again."

I told him that even if Kayla contacts me again, that doesn't mean she'll show up tomorrow.

"I know," he said. "But I don't want her parents to give up hope. You either. Because I am going to find her."

And then, guess what? Another text from Kayla a few minutes after I turned out the lights.

With what fruit do you poison a princess? :'(

That's all. The emoticon means she's crying I think. Crying about what?

Again my call went to voice mail.

What is Kayla talking about? Has she been poisoned? She can't have been. Otherwise she couldn't have texted me, could she?

I'll forward her new message to Chase and the Jespersons in the morning. No use in them being as crazy scared as I now am.

When I looked at the text again, I realize Chase is

right. Kayla's teasing me. When did that start?

    I wonder: is Chase the kind of guy to spike the football? If he is, I'll never hear the end of it.

38

Weird Game
Tuesday, October 29, 2013

"Where's Kayla?" Congressman Bristoll asked his secretary as he strode into the office Tuesday morning.

"I don't know," Mimi answered, mouth pursed when she saw that he wasn't wearing a tie but was wearing tasseled loafers, which she despised as Eurotrash. "She didn't show up yesterday either and didn't call in. Are you ready to go over your schedule? You have -- ."

"Is she sick?"

Mimi got to her feet, adjusted her belt, and picked up a folder. "If she is, she hasn't deigned to inform me."

"Get her on the phone before we go over the schedule. Where's Chase?"

"He stepped out to get some coffee. He hates what we brew here."

Tad unlocked the door to his office. "What the hell am I dealing with? Two spoiled children?"

"You tell me," Mimi answered under her breath as she dialed Kayla's home number.

But Kayla wasn't at the bungalow she shared with Bridget and her cellphone went to voice mail. "No answer, sir. Chase is back. Should I send him in?"

"At once."

"Where the hell is Kayla?" Tad snapped.

"That's just it," Chase said, placing a steaming latte in front of his boss, then taking a guest chair. "Saturday night when I went to pick her up, she wasn't at the hotel. The doorman said she walked out. So I drove around downtown, trying to find her, but she'd vanished into thin air. Since then she's texted her roommate several times but hasn't communicated with anybody else. I thought you might have heard from her."

"No, I haven't. You have any idea where she is?"

Chase shook his head. "No idea. I talked to her parents last night. They haven't heard from her either."

"What's she telling her roommate?"

"Not much. First, she said she'd be back Sunday. After that, just strange little phrases, like 'Just know I'm well. Want to crawl under a rock.' Stuff like that. But the text Bridget forwarded this morning is a little more alarming." Chase scrolled to the latest text. "'With what fruit do you poison a princess?'"

Tad leaned forward, obviously alarmed. "What's that about poison?"

"No idea."

"Have you reported this to the police?"

"No. I wanted to talk to you first. Kayla's not exactly a missing person since she's texting her roommate. She's twenty-one -- ."

"Twenty-one, yes," Tad barked. "Twenty-two on November 20. I'm taking her to Paris to celebrate."

"I didn't know that," Chase said, taken aback at his boss's vehemence over such a small point. "Yesterday she'd been gone less than forty-eight hours, and as an adult she has every right to disappear for awhile if she wants to. I didn't think the police would do much at that point."

"Well, now it's more than forty-eight hours, so they might. What are her parents going to do?"

"They didn't say, but Kayla's father is going to visit her roommate tonight at that little house where Kayla was living."

Tad turned to stare out the window, his face dark with emotion. Finally, he said, "On second thought, let's not call the police."

"I thought that might be best. Do you want to talk to Kayla's parents?"

"No. But I don't want them calling the authorities either."

"There's no way we can prevent that, Tad."

"But you could talk to them."

"What would I say?"

"I don't know, Chase, but you're the wordsmith. Come up with something. The publicity is going to be terrible. Every dirty bull terrier of a reporter is going to start nosing around, digging dirt, exhuming graves -- oh, my God, what did I just say?" Tad shut his eyes in horror. "No graves, nobody dead, not Kayla. We can't go there. Kayla's just playing a weird game of some kind. She's probably still mad at me for what Cordelia said to her at the hotel. She's punishing me. When she comes back I'll strangle her -- oh, my God, there I go again."

"I understand, Tad. A slip of the tongue. That kind of thing happens when emotions are running high. And that's why you let me do the talking to the press, to her family, to the cops if it comes to that, to everybody."

"I don't want the cops involved." He raked his hands through his carefully coiffed hair and spoke to the ceiling. "Oh, Kayla, what are you thinking? Why do this to me now, seven months before the primaries? The publicity will be terrible."

"Speaking of publicity, I had a thought last night. You could hire your own investigator so we keep some control. That might be enough to mollify the Jespersons so they don't go to the cops. It might even persuade the cops if they hear about it to put the case on the back burner. At this point, it's an adult woman who for reasons unknown is hiding somewhere but still in contact with her roommate. Not a big deal when you see it from that angle."

"Kayla isn't a case and she is a big deal," Tad growled. "Let me think about it."

"We could use that guy who found nothing in Congressman Doyle's background to support a charge of tax fraud. Can't remember his name, but he knows what's what. Just in case."

"Just in case of what?" Tad barked.

"Nothing. Nothing at all."

Tad glared at him. "You're thinking of Sly Poolow. Not a name you forget when you have something to hide. Which I don't."

"Sorry." Chase nodded, then got to his feet. "What do I tell the staff?"

Tad mussed his hair again. "Kayla's taken some time off because of family issues."

"Okay. But if I'm to get anywhere with the Jespersons, what do I tell them? I'd better know your intentions about a private investigator before this evening."

"You will." Tad impatiently waved him out of the office.

39

Dr. Jesperson
Tuesday, October 29, 2013

Dr. Jesperson took Bridget by surprise. He was short and slight with gray eyes, short gray hair, and pockmarked cheeks. His manner was reserved. She assumed that as the father of the beautiful, effervescent Kayla, Ed Jesperson would be big and handsome with a colorful personality to match. And given the circumstances, she also expected him to be agitated. But he wasn't. Though a man of few words, he radiated serenity and kindness.

The moment Ed was seated, Doug gave him the sniff test, accepted a neck massage, then lay down at the man's feet, unwilling to move.

"So tell me what you think Kayla is up to," Ed said to Bridget.

"Up to?" she asked, startled. "I don't think she's up to anything. Saturday night everything was completely normal. I'm as shocked as you that she's not come home or told me where she is. But it does raise a question in my mind. Has Kayla ever just taken off before?"

Ed rubbed his mouth. "She was eleven or twelve when she ran away the first time. It was a hot summer day. She took a little Hello Kitty bag with her, stuffed with her favorite teddy bear, a package of cookies, and her mother's best perfume. But we found her a few hours later at the house of an old couple down the street who adored her and had no idea she'd run away. When it got dark and she refused to go home, they called us. That happened several more times. Then, after her junior prom, she stayed out all night with her boyfriend. They slept in his car apparently. Her mother was furious for breaking curfew and not calling us, but I just saw it as teenage nonsense that would pass in time.

"So," he continued, "the answer is yes. She's done a bunk before, but the last time was almost six years ago. This is different, if only because of her age."

Just then, there was a knock on the door.

"Expecting someone?" Ed asked. "Am I intruding?"

"No," Bridget said. "Absolutely not."

She was thrilled to find Chase at the door. She hadn't invited him to meet Kayla's father but she was glad he'd come.

"I hope I'm not interrupting anything," Chase said, looking over Bridget's shoulder into the living room. "I'm here on behalf of Tad. Is that okay?"

"Of course. Dr. Jesperson, this is Chase Sumner, Congressman Bristoll's press aide. He works with Kayla."

Ed rose and shook hands. "Call me Ed. I've heard a lot about you from Kayla. Nice of you to come over."

Bridget led the men to the dining alcove where there were enough chairs for all three.

When they were seated, Chase said, "Tad -- my boss, Theodore Bristoll -- wants you to know we're concerned about Kayla. She's missed at the office and we want to do everything we can to find her. Just so we know where things stand, have you filed a missing person's report?"

"No. But we're considering it."

"Let's talk about that before you decide what to do."

"Fair enough. I don't mean to be nosy, Chase, but Kayla said that you two are dating. Is that right?"

Bridget studied Chase's face, curious about how he'd answer that. He studiously avoided her gaze. "We like each other and we spend a lot of time in each other's company -- the nature of the job, you know -- but we're not dating, not in the usual sense of that term. Besides, even if we were inclined that way, there's no dating in the office. The Congressman's rules."

"I see," Ed said in a voice suggesting he didn't see at all. "Tell me, what do you think has happened to Kayla?"

"I wish I knew. All I can think of is that she has some personal reason for needing some time to herself."

"What personal reason?"

Again, Bridget studied Chase's face, wondering if he'd mention Cordelia's attack on Kayla in the hotel lobby.

"Kayla and I are friends, but I don't know her well enough to even make an educated guess."

"Any idea where she is?"

"Again, I have no clue," Chase said.

"What do you think of the strange messages she's sent Bridget?"

Chase glanced at Bridget. "I think she's taunting us."

"Taunting?" Ed was incredulous. "Whatever do you mean?"

"Wrong word," Chase said, shaking his head. "Testing us. Teasing us. Are we smart enough to figure out where she is, what she's doing, and why? If we aren't, she's safe."

"Safe from what?"

There was a long pause. "That's the question, isn't it?" Chase said, glancing at Bridget. "What do you think? You know her as well as anyone."

Bridget looked away. A disturbing thought suddenly rattled her brain. Once -- when was it? -- Kayla had said that she and Tad would have a big announcement soon, a big surprise that couldn't be hidden. Was Kayla hinting that she was pregnant? Had she sneaked off to get an abortion? But that possibility was so unlikely -- yet so awful if true -- she couldn't voice it, not to Kayla's father.

"You look like you've thought of something, Bridget," Chase prodded.

"No. But that last message about poisoned fruit is so dark, so unlike Kayla."

"But it doesn't suggest foul play," Chase insisted. "She's just depressed about something, so the police will not act on a missing person's report. The best thing we can do is to hire a private investigator to find Kayla. My boss has authorized me to hire someone, no expense to you."

"Why would he do that?"

"May I be frank?" Chase asked.

"By all means," Ed said with just the merest hint of asperity.

"As you probably know, Tad's running for reelection. He has two formidable opponents this year, so the primary is going to be expensive and hotly contested. Any little thing that goes wrong is fodder for the opponents' attack ads. As you can imagine, the worst possible spin will be put on a missing employee, so the publicity will be terrible not just for Tad but for your family as well. You'll have reporters camped outside your door, hounding your every step, poking into every aspect of your life, trying to ferret out your secrets."

"We don't have any secrets," Ed said.

A look of skepticism briefly flickered across Chase's face. "If you say so. But even the most innocent parts of a life can be twisted by the tabloids, you know. So as Kayla's employer, Tad feels it's his duty to protect your family while doing everything humanly possible to see that Kayla is safe. Tad thinks the best way to do that is to keep the cops out of this and hire a private investigator."

"Just so you understand that I'm not naïve, Chase, the arrangement is probably better for the Congressman than for me since he's willing to pay for it. But I see its value."

"It's not better for -- ."

Ed held up his open hand. Bridget realized this gentle doctor had a spine of steel when he said, "Don't argue with me. I have one condition."

"What's that?"

"I choose the investigator -- subject, of course, to the Congressman's approval."

"Why?"

Ed hesitated. "Just to be sure I'm comfortable with him."

"You know of somebody?" Chase asked.

"I do. We had a serious problem at the hospital a couple years ago. The guy we hired was superb."

"Remember his name?"

"Walter Richardson. He's an ex-CIA investigator, specializing in industrial espionage. But he's handled a couple of homicide investigations in Fort Wayne."

"Homicide?" Bridget asked, alarmed.

Ed patted her hand. "Kayla's not dead. I'm sure of it. I think I'd know if she were. That's not the point. But this is my only daughter and something is terribly wrong, so I want the smartest, most dogged and honest person on the case. Otherwise, I go to the police. And the press." He looked at Chase. "So what do you say?"

"I think Tad has someone else in mind, someone he knows from a colleague's tax fraud case in Washington."

"And how did that case turn out?"

"No tax fraud. Complete exoneration."

After a pause, Ed said, "I see. Then I must insist on Richardson."

Chase looked like a cartoon light bulb had just gone on over his head. "You think -- ?"

"Never mind what I think," Ed said evenly. "Richardson or the police, take your pick."

"I'll convey your proposal to Tad and let you know."

Ed stood and looked at his watch. "You have one hour to get back to me, Chase. Otherwise, I'm calling the Chief of Police. He's an old friend of mine. In fact, I'm the guy who made sure he kept breathing but felt no pain when his spleen was removed last year, so we're bonded. He'll turn the City upside down to find my darling Kayla."

40

Say a Prayer
Tuesday, October 29, 2013

After Bridget watched Chase pull away from the curb, she returned to the dining alcove, where Ed was standing at the window. "That was interesting. I'm so glad there's going to be an investigation because I don't know what to do." Without warning, she began to cry.

Ed led her back to the living room, helped her to a chair, and handed her his handkerchief. "Poor girl. I know you're worried too."

"I'm sorry," she said. "I didn't want to cry, not in front of you. You're her father, after all. I'm just her roommate. And you're so strong. I should be strong like you."

"That doesn't mean I'm not worried sick. I am. It's okay to cry." Ed took the chair on the other side of the fireplace. "I'd like you to tell me something, Bridget. Why didn't you let me know Sunday morning that Kayla hadn't come home Saturday night? That she'd walked away from the hotel but no one saw her again."

Bridget looked stricken. "I feel guilty about that."

"I'm not scolding you, Bridget. We just need to understand each other."

"Do you remember that text from her, the one that came a few hours after she should have come home? She said she'd be back the next day, so I stopped worrying."

"But she didn't come back. So why not call me Sunday night?"

"Chase told me not to."

"Did he say why?"

"That she wasn't missing, not in a police sense."

"And yesterday?"

"Well, Chase and I did call you yesterday. He wanted to wait until evening though because he still thought she would show up at work."

"He's a patient man, isn't he?"

"I - I guess so. He's very concerned about Kayla. Everybody at the office likes her a lot."

"I take it Chase does too. He said they're not dating, but what's the truth?"

"They aren't dating. Kayla and I have had a few outings with Chase and a friend of mine from the Academy, but we're all just friends. It wasn't like a double date or anything. None of us hooked up."

"Hooked up," he repeated. "How I hate that phrase.... Chase says he went looking for her Saturday night but never found her. Do you believe him?"

Bridget was shocked. "Of course. If he'd found her, she'd be here right now."

"Is Kayla dating someone else?"

Troubled by the slight deception she was about to engage in, Bridget had a hard time meeting his eyes. "No. Since I've known her, she hasn't dated anyone." *Because her relationship with Tad isn't what I'd call dating.*

He got to his feet. "Before I go, if you'd indulge me, I'd like to take a look at Kayla's room. Come with me."

Ed walked around the room, touching this and that, then opened the closet door. "Good heavens. So many dresses. So many shoes. Where does all this stuff come from?"

Bridget laughed shakily. "Her salary isn't much, as I'm sure you know."

Ed nodded.

"But she has a clothing allowance, which is pretty generous."

"Never heard of such a perk. I wonder why she has it."

"Be- because she's expected to attend a lot of social functions as part of her job."

"With Chase?"

"With the Congressman . . . and his wife."

Ed stepped back and looked again at something that had caught his eye on Kayla's dresser. He picked it up, a fine gold chain from which dangled a gold pendant with the initials "K" and "T" intertwined. "Whose initials are these?" he asked.

Bridget thought fast. When a week ago she asked Kayla that very question, the answer was that "K" stood for Kayla and "T" for Tad, but the world was supposed to think the necklace was a leftover from Asher, whose first name was actually Tyler. She didn't want to lie to Dr. Jesperson, but neither was she ready to give Kayla's scandalous secrets away.

"Asher's first name is Tyler. That's what Kayla said the 'T' is for."

"She broke up with Asher months ago," Ed said. "And this is the first I ever heard his first name is Tyler. Did he buy this for her?"

"She never said who bought it, but I suppose that's a logical assumption. I know Asher's gone, but Kayla likes it because the necklace is pretty and it's made of gold -- which costs the earth these days, you know -- and the initials are so ornate, most people can't even identify them."

"Did she really wear this? I never saw it before."

"Oh, yes. The night she was getting ready for the fundraiser, she put it on, but at the last minute took it off because -- because she decided her earrings were enough." In fact, Kayla almost forgot she was wearing the necklace; it was Bridget who warned her to leave it behind lest Cordelia figure out that it was a gift from Tad.

"I think I'll take this home with me." He shoved the necklace into his left trouser pocket and with the other hand reached into his right pocket, took out a roll of bills, peeled off several, and handed them to her.

"What's this for?" she asked, backing up half a step.

"Kayla's share of the rent. And a little extra. If I know my princess, she owes you for something else as well. She told us you're the best friend she's ever had, so she'd want me to do this until she gets back from wherever she is. You just let me know what you need. We're in this together."

"Oh, that's my phone." She ran to the living room, picked up her cellphone, listened a few minutes, then turned to Kayla's father. "It's Chase, for you."

"Yes," Ed said curtly into the phone. Thirty seconds later he hit the off button. "Walter Richardson, it is. Unassuming guy but smarter than the devil, and that's smart. Have you ever met him?"

"Who?" Bridget asked with a shaky laugh. "Richardson or the devil?"

Ed chuckled despite himself. "We've all met a few devils. But I'm talking about Richardson. You'll love him." He turned at the door. "Say a prayer for my princess."

Bridget nodded, tears in her eyes.

41

Suspicions
Wednesday, October 30, 2013

The next day in Boston, Rupert the butler showed Theodore Bristoll into the sunroom of the Tilley family mansion in Beacon Hill. Millicent, his mother-in-law, was lying on a chaise longue under the canopy of a giant avocado tree she had reportedly grown from a pit thirty years earlier. The tea table beside her was littered with tissues, a pitcher of sweet tea, books, reading glasses, and prescription bottles. The atmosphere was thick with humidity and earthy smells.

When she heard footsteps, Millicent pushed her eye mask up.

"Ah, Theodore," she said, her voice as strong as ever despite her very advanced years and recent surgery. "The black sheep. I haven't seen you in months. You didn't even visit me in the hospital."

"My schedule isn't my own. Politics is a cruel mistress," Tad said, bending down to kiss her forehead and grasp her arthritic, perfectly manicured hand.

"All mistresses are ultimately cruel," she said acidly, pushing his hand away.

"Wives are worse," Tad said, just as acidly. "Where is Cordelia?"

"She's upstairs getting ready to meet some friends for lunch at the University Club. Did you want to talk to her?"

"Eventually. But I'm glad we're alone for a few minutes."

"I hardly see her, you know," Millicent complained. "Even as a little girl, she couldn't sit still. Always on the move. In those days it was play dates and sleepovers. Now it's shopping, playing bridge, having lunch, planning a party, calling somebody, organizing something. You know what I tell her?"

Tad shook his head, though he knew the answer. He tugged a bergère near the chaise and sat down.

"You're always moving, Cordelia, because you don't want to think your thoughts. Too scary to confront what's in your head."

"You know your daughter, Millicent. I give you that."

"And why only that? Shouldn't you give me more?" she asked, her dark blue eyes sparkling maliciously. She loved to spar with her son-in-law.

"I'm in no mood for hair-splitting today," Tad said, elbows on knees, head in hands. "Exhilarating as our little tiffs are. Something's come up in the Fort Wayne office that's giving me a headache."

"And what is that?"

"My special assistant is missing. She walked out of the hotel where we had a fundraiser Saturday night and hasn't been seen since."

Millicent eyed him with suspicion. "What makes her a *special* assistant?"

Tad sat up, eyes closed in frustration. "That's her title, that's all. But you know what the tabloids will make of a missing employee if they get wind. Lots of publicity, all of it bad. And I have a tough primary fight coming up."

"Is the girl alive?"

"Apparently. She's texting her roommate but won't say where she is. And now I've been backed into a corner to hire a private investigator whom I don't know but who is said to be very good at his job."

"Grab my shoulders, Theodore. Help me sit up straighter and scoot that chair around so I don't have to crook my neck to look at you. And before you say another word, hand me one of those pills and pour a glass of tea for me. This is interesting. I don't want to miss a word."

When Millicent was settled, Tad resumed. "I have no idea what has happened to the girl or why, but for that very reason, I'm concerned at what the investigator will find. He'll be nosing into every aspect of my life on the theory that if something bad has happened, look first to the people closest to her."

"You haven't done something to her, have you?" Millicent asked.

Again, Tad shut his eyes in frustration. "No. But if I had, would I tell anyone? Does anyone admit to . . . to whatever has happened to make her disappear?"

"You'd tell *me*, Theodore. I know you would. You've always told me everything and you've never had a better advisor than me. Cordelia loves you, so her counsel is a shade off because it's emotional. But I don't love you. . . . As you well know."

"As I well know."

"However, I want you to succeed so the family reputation isn't tarnished. And I'm not emotional. Therefore, you have to admit, my advice, cold as it is, is worth its weight in gold."

"Always cold and often harsh, but yes. Your advice is gold."

"Rupert," she said, gesturing at the door. "What is it?"

"Mrs. Bristoll just left, ma'am. I told her that you" -- nodding at Tad -- "are in here, but she said she was late for her lunch date in the Back Bay."

"Did she say anything else?" Tad asked.

"No, sir."

"Wait just a second, Rupert. Bring Theodore some of that plum cake and -- coffee or tea?" she asked, smiling at her son-in-law.

"Coffee, strong, with cream and sugar. And a sandwich. I'm starving."

"Tell cook to make a sandwich out of that brown sugar ham. And I think there's some French potato salad left over from yesterday. She'll know what to do. And close the door, please."

"So," Millicent resumed once the door was closed, "let's start over. You said the special assistant isn't special except for her title. You're lying. I always knew when my Sebastian lied about things like that."

Tad shook his head. "How . . . how do you know?"

"It's a female thing. Servants have the same ability to sniff out secrets. Rupert could write a scandalous book about the family, but, of course, he won't because he's not suicidal. We women don't have the power you men do, so we have to be sensitive to the nuances. Does this assistant have a name?"

"Kayla. She's personable and pretty. She and I are close."

"I knew it." Her eyes glittered with triumph. "Cordelia told me about the others."

"I never denied it, did I? After the fundraiser, when we were all standing in the lobby, Cordelia called Kayla a whore, said she dressed like a whore and acted like one."

"Is that true?"

"No. Kayla's a lady. She started crying. Tarik drove Cordelia home in my car. I took Kayla to the hotel lounge -- ."

"Just to the lounge?"

"Yes, Millicent. Just to the lounge, where we shared a bottle of champagne. I let her cry and tried to comfort her. Finally, Kayla excused herself to the ladies' room. She said she was fine, she'd wait for Chase to come back and take her home. So I got a ride home with a friend. But Chase never found her, though he drove around downtown looking for her. The doorman said she simply walked out of the hotel without letting him call a cab or coming back. And the hell of it was, we had a huge storm sweeping through, so Kayla walking out in it makes no sense."

"And what is it you fear?"

"Where do I start? Maybe some random stranger saw this lovely woman on the streets, alone, in the dark, and did something to her. That happened a few years ago in Bloomington to a coed. She's never been found."

"Or?"

"Two guys I don't know much about come into the picture. Her college boyfriend claims he saw her on the street but she wouldn't get in his car. And her landlord, who Chase claims is smarmy, went looking for her but never found her. Maybe their claims are bogus."

"Maybe. But that's not what you really fear, Theodore."

"I don't?"

"No. You fear that someone much closer to you did something."

Tad looked away.

"You either are lying to me about doing something to the girl yourself, or you fear Cordelia did -- or even Porter. That's why you're wary of this new private investigator and what he might discover."

"Porter!" Tad exclaimed. "Not him. He knows nothing about any of this. He's sixteen."

"Then Cordelia."

"I didn't see her from the time she left the hotel until the next morning at breakfast."

"Why not?"

"I slept in my den on the sofa."

"Is that where you've been sleeping all along? Have you two reached that dreadful state?"

"No. I love Cordelia. She loves me too. I just didn't want to wake her when I got home. An argument was the last thing I needed because I was exhausted from the fundraiser and all the emotional turmoil afterwards."

"So what about Cordelia makes you suspicious?"

"Nothing in particular, other than the attack she made on the girl. In public, no less. And the fact that she had time to go back downtown in her own car, do whatever she did, and still get home -- I was going to say, get home before I did, but in fact I don't know when she got home. She might have sneaked in after I went to sleep."

"Is your affair with Kayla serious?"

"What do you mean?"

"Why would Cordelia want to kill this girl --."

"She's not dead. Maybe kidnapped."

"Why would Cordelia want to kidnap this girl when she never did anything like that to the others?"

"I don't know," he said, willing himself to give nothing away.

"You wouldn't divorce Cordelia, would you, Theodore?"

"Of course not."

"Good. Because if you have any such intentions, you understand I won't help you."

"I know that, Millicent."

At a knock on the door, she signaled for quiet. "Your lunch is here. We'll talk about how to protect you and Cordelia after you've eaten."

42

Lock the Door
Wednesday, October 30, 2013

"The girl disappeared a week ago and this is the first I'm hearing about it?" Cordelia snapped.

"Four days ago," Tad corrected. Millicent had gone to bed an hour earlier in a wing on the opposite side of the house from the sunroom. Tad closed the door and turned on a couple of table lamps. "It's your own fault because you wouldn't talk to me alone until now. We need to confer before I go back to D.C. in the morning."

"*Confer*! Couples don't confer. They talk. They argue. They settle things. Be real, Tad."

"I am being real," he said impatiently. "The realest I've ever been. According to the doorman, Kayla walked out of the hotel after I left. She wouldn't let him call a cab, even though the storm was in full force. She never came back. Several people went looking for her, including Chase, who was supposed to drive her home. Only one person -- her ex-boyfriend -- saw her but she wouldn't get in his car despite the fact that she must have been cold and soaking wet."

"Stupid girl."

"She's alive somewhere because she's texted her roommate several times, but she won't say where she is."

"Why do you pick up with drama queens, Tad? It's exhausting.

It's embarrassing. Does Mama know?"

"Yes."

"And everybody else in the world?"

"In our world, yes."

"Is it in the papers?"

"Not yet. I've hired a private investigator to find her so this crazy thing doesn't become fodder for the tabloids. And that's why we need to talk."

"I hope the little daffy duck is dead," Cordelia said with a glare.

"No, you don't, Cordelia. Think about it. She's the daughter of a respected doctor, a university graduate, a nice girl with a good job. Nobody's going to dismiss her as a daffy duck. Thus, if something really bad has happened to her, I'll be thrust smack dab into the pitiless spotlight of the tabloids, caricatured as a heartless womanizer."

"Which you are."

"And you'll be caricatured as the self-aggrandizing wife who stays with her faithless man for the fame and fortune."

"What's Mama say?"

"We're going to be interviewed by the investigator at some point, so -- ."

"Sly Poolow?"

"No. I had no choice but to hire someone recommended by Kayla's father. His name is Walter Richardson."

Cordelia got up and walked to the brass drinks cart, where she poured herself another sherry. "You know who he is, don't you?"

"Never heard of him before."

"Well, I have," she said warningly. "If you have anything to hide, let me tell you, it won't be hidden long."

"I have nothing to hide," Tad said emphatically. "Do you?"

From five feet away she threw her sherry in his face. "How dare you ask me that, Tad! Of course, I have nothing to hide."

Trembling with the effort to stay calm, he wiped his face with a monogrammed linen handkerchief. "You asked what your mother said but never gave me a chance to answer."

"Go on," she said, setting down her empty little sherry glass and picking up a cut-glass tumbler, which she poured full of her precious sherry.

"Sit down, Cordelia. I can't talk to you while you're standing. And if you keep drinking like that, you're going to fall over anyway on the slate tiles. I might not want to catch you, you know."

Biting back a retort, she sat down.

Tad resumed. "Millicent says for me to avoid the interview as long as possible. So I'm going to D.C. in the morning. I'm not going to our house -- ."

"But to that little apartment you have on Dupont Circle, I suppose."

He stared at her.

"You thought I didn't know about it, Tad? I know how to check real estate records."

"It's not even in my name," he said weakly.

"But I knew what name you'd use. Sheldon's a very good friend, isn't he? His private airplane, the oceanfront house in Florida, the fishing lodge in Minnesota -- you use them like they're yours."

"He owns those; I don't."

"But the one thing you must own is a love nest. Such a little thing to ask of Sheldon, such a little thing for him to give so long as you continue your support of ethanol mandates. In your book, it's a fair trade, isn't it?"

He sighed. "Could we stay on the subject for a minute or two?"

"Yes, if you stop treating me like I'm blind and stupid," she said acidly.

"Where was I -- ?"

"Mama."

"Oh, yes. I'll evade this Walter Richardson as long as possible. I'll be in D.C., working my ass off, staying at an address nobody knows. I'll join the Congressional team going to Egypt. I'll attend the hearings of committees I'm not even on. I'll go to a fundraiser in California for one of my colleagues. I'll be very, very busy. But you'll go back to Fort Wayne and cooperate."

"Why?"

"To make sure the investigator looks at everybody but us."

"Like whom?"

"Tarik, Chase, Mimi, Kayla's ex-boyfriend, her nosy landlord, her roommate, the Jespersons themselves."

"The girl's parents?" Cordelia asked in shock.

"Of course. In fact, they're the first suspects anybody would look at."

"I knew you were ruthless, but really, Tad . . . . What about you? How do I know you didn't do away with that silly girl?"

"You don't."

"I wish I'd never married you."

"Too late," he snapped. "Millicent's plan will work so long as you either have nothing to hide or convincingly deny any involvement."

"Mama said that?"

Tad nodded.

"So she doubts me too."

"Millicent didn't say that." He laughed grimly. "The kind of mother she is, if you really did something to Kayla, she'd claim you didn't do it, it was self-defense, somebody made you do it, and you'll never do it again."

"And what would you say?"

Tad stood up and dumped bourbon-stained ice cubes onto the roots of the avocado tree. "Don't test me, Cordelia. So . . . what's it going to be? Are we a team or not?"

She said nothing.

"Well?" he asked as he opened the door. "It's late and I'm tired and I'm going to bed. I need to know before I leave the house at six tomorrow morning."

"I won't be joining you, Tad. Neither upstairs tonight or on the plane tomorrow."

"I didn't expect you would."

"You'll have my answer in the morning," she whispered. "But if I were you, I'd lock the door to your bedroom tonight. I might mistake you for an intruder."

43

Halloween
Friday, November 1, 2013

The Halloween party -- which was held a whole day after All Souls Night so guests wouldn't be forced to recover on a weekday -- was in full swing. Bridget didn't feel like partying, not with Kayla still missing, but Suze, the Academy's art teacher, talked her into it. "It'll be fun. Buck and I have done this every year since we got married and people rave about it. Ask anyone."

"I don't like wearing a costume," Bridget said. "Or a mask."

"No worries there because we don't either," Suze said in her characteristically chirpy way. "Just wear something in the spirit of the thing -- dark and drapey or white and gauzy -- and a little Halloween makeup."

"I'm not good at makeup."

"Come over early and I'll do it for you. I have a million ideas."

"Should I bring something?"

"Food that looks like a body part or tastes slimy. We shine black light on the dining table and make people guess what they're eating. And for entertainment I'm having a psychic named Mama Bee come. Last year she read Tarot cards, but it took too long for everybody to get a reading, so this year she's going to gaze."

"Gaze?"

"Into a crystal ball. She's amazing. I signed up for a gaze just to see her in action but didn't tell her why I was there. Even so, she looked into the ball and immediately saw me at a Halloween party. Imagine! That's why I was there -- to see if I wanted to hire her again for this year's Halloween party."

I don't think that was an amazing insight for Mama Bee, but okay. "Who all is coming?"

"Oh, Bridget. The question is, who isn't coming? You might meet the man of your dreams. That's how Buck and I met years ago. I had Princess Leia's hairdo and was wearing white; Buck was carrying Darth Vader's lightsaber and wearing black -- that simple. But it was natural for us to pair up, given such a massive coincidence. We hadn't even met before the party but we both instantly knew we'd be together forever after. That was nine years ago. So you see? You have to come. It might change your life."

Bridget concealed her doubt about the likelihood of meeting the man of her dreams. "May I bring a friend?"

"Of course you can!" Suze trilled, ducking her head conspiratorially. "You sly thing, do you have a boyfriend I don't know about?"

"No, no. Nothing like that. Just a friend -- a guy -- so I don't have to show up alone."

Chase was reluctant when she called to ask him to accompany her to the party. "I go to so many social functions with Tad, I don't think I can stand another party. And I hate costumes."

"Just one night," Bridget pleaded. "I don't want to go alone. We don't have to wear costumes. I'll dress in white, you in black. If we go a little early, Suze said she'd do our makeup, something simple, suggestive of Halloween. That's all."

"You had me at 'I don't want to go alone.' I don't want to be alone either, not when I can go somewhere with you."

Bridget stared at the phone, her heart flipping at the knowledge that Chase wanted to be with her so much that he'd go to a party to make her happy.

When they emerged from Suze's bedroom, Bridget had a third eye painted on her forehead, fortuitously covering a massive zit, and her hair was waxed into long twisted spikes. Chase had the hairline and eyes of a werewolf. "God, I feel stupid," he whispered.

"You look amazing, though," Bridget said. "Do you want a crystal ball reading? Only two other people in line so we won't have to wait long."

"Why not?" he sighed. "In for a penny, in for a pound."

Too late, she caught the eye of the man across the room: Justin, his face painted in camouflage and wearing a shirt that was shredded and tattered and stained, as if he'd just crawled out of the grave. He was with Julieta, who resembled Cruella Deville and was carrying a toy dog. When he nodded at her, Bridget nodded back but turned away so there'd be no excuse to meet or chat.

"Ah," Bridget murmured, tugging on Chase's arm, "The psychic is ready for us."

They sat down in front of Mama Bee, waiting for her to open her eyes and say something. She was wearing a turban sprinkled with glittery silver stars, masses of silver beads, and a flowing navy gown.

Finally, she adjusted her reading glasses and studied them. "You aren't a couple, are you?"

Bridget was taken aback. "Wh- what do . . . ?"

Chase spoke up. "We're friends. Very good friends."

"And what is on your mind?"

Chase glanced at Bridget, gesturing for her to take the lead. "Our friend is missing. Is she okay? Where is she? Why -- why has she disappeared?"

Mama Bee waved her hands over the crystal ball, then with bejeweled fingers flicked imaginary clouds away. She closed her eyes and after a few seconds picked up a silver bell and rang it. Eyes once again open, she leaned forward, her gaze fixed on the ball. Then she sat back as if shrinking from something. "All is darkness."

Another long pause. Bridget's heart began to pound.

"Ah, wait," Mama Bee said, leaning forward again. "She's wearing a crown of some sort. Leaves. Yes, leaves, as if she were a woodland princess. And a yellow dress."

"That's what she wore to the fundraiser!" Bridget exclaimed. "The yellow dress, I mean. Not the leaves. Why did she leave us?"

"She choked on an apple."

"Choked?" Bridget cried. She turned to Chase. "Did she choke on something at the hotel?"

He whispered, "No."

"Where is she?" Bridget asked.

Mama Bee tilted her head in surprise at something she saw in the crystal ball. "She's dropped out of sight."

"I know that," Bridget said, frustrated. "But where? What's she doing?"

Once again, Mama Bee waved her hands over the ball, rang the silver bell, then sat back, riveting Bridget with dark, penetrating eyes. "That's for you to discover for yourself. Thank you." She looked over Bridget's shoulder and signaled to the pair of girls behind them. "I'm ready for you."

"I'm hungry," Chase said as he got to his feet and took Bridget's hand. "Let's go eat some eyeballs and intestines. And those little casket cakes look good. How about it?"

When they were well away from Mama Bee, Bridget asked, "So what did you think about what that strange woman said?"

"She's full of shit, pardon my French."

"But she called Kayla a princess. That's what her father calls her. And the yellow dress!"

"Lucky guess. Lots of girls are little princesses, at least to their fathers. And Kayla was also wearing a black raincoat -- ."

"Which is mine, by the way," Bridget interjected.

"-- and bright blue stilettos. Mama Bee never mentioned those, did she?"

"You're right. And she couldn't say where Kayla is either."

"She didn't choke on anything either. There wasn't an apple in sight at the hotel. Now I have a question for you, Bridget. Did you notice who's here?"

She looked around at the crowd. "Lots of people but the only ones I know are friends from the Academy."

"Your friend Justin. I just caught a glimpse of him."

"I did too awhile ago. No surprise that Suze invited him."

"But did you see who he's with?"

She nodded. "The same woman he was with at Piere's the

night you and Kayla were at the fundraiser."

"Oh, really. You never told me that before. But what surprises me, for such a buttoned-up dude, is the look of his date. Pretty hot, don't you think? Let's go over and find out about her."

Bridget tugged on his arm. "No."

"Why? You don't want him to know we're dating?"

Are we dating? she asked herself in astonishment. "Not -- not that. Not at all. But I see Justin every day at work and in a few weeks I'm going to be with him every day in D.C., so that's enough. In fact, let's go somewhere else. The look of that food makes me gag."

He kissed her forehead. "Oh, sorry. I just smeared your third eye."

"It probably looks better, right?"

"No, actually, it doesn't, but you still look good, Peanut."

Peanut? You have a pet name for me? Bridget couldn't speak.

"Let's go somewhere where you can stand to look at the food. And tell me what you're going to be doing in D.C. Maybe I'll be out there at the same time and I can show you around."

"That would be heavenly," she said, her breath catching.

44

The Cottage
Saturday, November 2, 2013

"What is this place?" Bridget asked as she jumped out of the Jeep. Though it was a strangely warm day for Fort Wayne in November, at Chase's suggestion they were wearing jeans, long-sleeved t-shirts, and ankle boots.

"Let me spray you with this stuff first," he said. "Lots of critters still buzzing around. By the way, that ponytail is cute."

"You like it better than the spiky curls Suze gave me last night?" she asked with a little laugh.

"That was a great look but this one's better for everyday," he deadpanned.

She looked at the gray shingled cottage nestled in an ancient apple orchard. A huge outdoor chimney dominated the north side, poking above a steeply pitched roofline. The open porch was just big enough to hold two Adirondack chairs. A long row of rough stepping stones fashioned from shale led from the end of the dirt drive to the front door.

"You think Kayla is here?"

"No I don't think she's here," Chase answered reassuringly, "but I want you to see the place. Besides, there's no harm in checking since we don't know where Kayla's hiding and this is one place she'd be safe."

"I've driven by here before but never knew there was a cottage like this so far back from the road."

"This is Tad's private retreat," Chase said. "It's a bit primitive and not very big. Which is understandable because his great-grandfather built it over a century ago. Now it's a refuge for Tad from the madding crowds. Sometimes he brings his advisors out here for a weekend, sometimes -- well, sometimes other people."

"What other people?"

"His special assistants if they look like Kayla. In a few weeks, he'll bring out a few supporters who like to hunt pheasant."

"Never mind the advisors and the hunters. You said 'special assistants,' plural. Does that mean Kayla's not the first . . . ?"

"The first AP?" Chase finished for her. "No. And she isn't likely to be the last either."

"I'm shocked."

"Why, Bridget?" he said, putting his arm around her and pulling her close. He brushed a stray hair away from her eyes. "You're in the real world now. Need I remind you, powerful men can have whatever -- whomever -- they want. Tad is very powerful and he can have whatever he wants, including dozens of young women."

"Who else knows about that . . . that side of him?"

"Nobody but me and a few others who work for him. And his wife, of course. He's very good at keeping his private life under wraps. I'm good at it too. In fact, that's a hefty part of my job." He looked deep into her eyes. "So what I'm showing you, what I'm telling you, is just between us. Right?"

"Right," she whispered, feeling shame that her heart was pounding, not just out of anxiety for Kayla, but attraction to Chase. She liked his voice, his intelligent eyes, the clean scent of him.

"Kayla was in love -- ."

"*Was*?" she asked in a trembly voice.

He shook his head. "*Is*. I meant she *is* in love with Tad. The past tense was a slip of the tongue because it applies to Tad. He *was* in love with her, at least for awhile."

"He isn't now?"

"Not sure. Probably not. Cordelia's terrible words to Kayla Saturday night at the hotel might have had Tad's approval. Cordelia has always ended Tad's little flings for him, very quietly, and he never objected because he was ready to move on anyway."

"What happened to those women -- the other APs, I mean?"

He shrugged. "They got some cash and Cordelia found them another job. That's all."

Bridget closed her eyes. "What a strange marriage they must have."

"Not strange for political couples flying as high as the Bristolls. The women make allowances."

"So Kayla's been out here?" Bridget asked.

"Several times. I'll show you the cottage if I can get inside." But he couldn't, despite repeated pounding on the door and ringing of the bell. No one appeared. Then he lifted up the mat, but there was nothing under it.

"What are you looking for?" Bridget asked.

"Sometimes Tad leaves a key under the mat, but there's nothing here. So the next thing we'll do is take a walk through the woods behind the house, all the way to the creek."

Bridget blanched. "Why? What are you expecting to find?"

"Nothing," he said, giving her a reassuring smile.

"Wait," she said. "Tell me the truth, Chase. Do you think Tad might have done something to Kayla? Is that why we're out here?"

His eyes flickered from hers to the house, then back to hers. "No. But I want to look around, just to be certain that I haven't overlooked anything. Just to be sure that Tad's the man I believe he is."

They spent the next hour walking about six feet apart, from one end of the property to the other, back and forth, their eyes sweeping the ground. Walking was perilous, for the blanket of leaves concealed pine cones, fallen apples, and other woodland debris that could turn an ankle. Chase closely examined a brushy spot under a low-hanging evergreen that he said was a deer nest and then another spot where the ground looked strangely mounded but was so compacted he decided it was of no interest. Near the creek they found an empty underground fox den.

As they returned to the house, Bridget suddenly slipped on rotten windfall apples, lost her balance, then stumbled forward onto something that creaked and flexed beneath her weight. She fell to her knees and rolled away with a little shriek. "What did I just step on?" she cried.

Chase rushed to grab her arms and pull her away. "Damn. I should have paid more attention. There's an old well under there. The lid's rotten, but thankfully it didn't give way."

"Oh," she cried. "One of my worst fears -- falling down a well, screaming into the void, dying in the dark."

He laughed. "What an imagination you have. Nobody's ever fallen into this well. Besides, there are cleats on the inside, so you could climb back up. Back in the day when there were prairie fires, the family would climb down the well so they weren't incinerated, wait for the fire to burn out, then climb back up, all safe and sound. Here, let me show you." He lifted the lid.

Bridget backed away, windmilling her arms. "No way. I'm not going near that. I can see the cleats from here."

As Chase got down on all fours to take a closer look, he said, "I'll remind Tad again to replace this lid." He raised his head and snorted. "Whew! Old wells stink. But there's nothing down there but water."

"Somehow those cleats are not very reassuring," Bridget whispered.

"You're right. I'll roll this big stone onto the lid to make sure no one else makes the mistake you did. The pheasant hunters will be out soon. We don't want one of them going missing."

When Chase got back to his feet, he suddenly froze, straining to listen. He slowly turned to look at the cottage. "Do you feel something?" he asked in a low voice.

"What?" Bridget whispered, goosebumps rising on her arms.

"We're being watched." His eyes raked the horizon. "Don't turn around."

Bridget tugged at his sleeve, desperately wanting to turn around. "Who's watching us?"

He took his time to respond, then shook himself. "Forget it. I just had one of those moments out of a Dean Koontz book." He wiped his face with his shirt sleeve. "Twice in the Rangers I felt that and it saved my life." He took her hand. "I'm sorry. I probably upset you. This time it's nothing, but I *am* glad we're together out here." He cupped her chin. "Let's look on the bright side. Our friend isn't hiding in the cottage, but she's not dead either, at least not here."

"I never thought she was!" Bridget exclaimed.

"All I mean is that no bad news is very good news. Kayla's still got her phone and is using it."

"But I haven't heard from her for a week, so how can we be sure she's okay?"

"Just something I feel." Laughing, he took her hand. "And this feeling is right. We're going to find Kayla, don't you worry about that."

"Maybe the private investigator Dr. Jesperson recommended will get somewhere," she said. "Have you talked to him yet?"

"No. But I will on Monday. He's coming in to talk to Tad and me and Tarik and Mimi -- everybody. Tad thinks it's probably a waste of time, but we're going to cooperate because . . ."

"Because what? Because you don't want the cops or media getting hold of this?"

He opened the Jeep door for her. "I'm not going to lie. As Tad's press aide, the last thing I want to deal with is a missing employee. My life, professionally speaking, would be interesting, of course, but Tad's would be hell. It's his welfare I'm responsible for. Mostly, though, we're going to cooperate because we want to find Kayla alive and well."

Before he closed the door, he took her hand. "Cheer up, my lovely friend. I'm starving and you probably are too, so let's go eat something. You choose the place. And we'll think happy, positive thoughts. What do you say?"

"Happy, positive thoughts," she repeated.

"Which'll be easy because we're a team." He leaned in for a kiss. "A really special team, don't you think?"

She nodded, words having fled. The kiss was just right for a first kiss -- gentle but warm, stirring unfamiliar emotions.

45

Gossip
Monday, November 4, 2013

Chase glanced at his watch. It was almost noon. If he didn't leave the office in the next thirty minutes, he'd miss his flight to Washington. Tad was waiting for him there, impatient to talk privately about how to deal with Kayla's disappearance and Walter Richardson's investigation. But Chase didn't need instruction. He knew what needed to be done.

Chase had spent the morning, first talking to Walter about how he couldn't find Kayla downtown after the fundraiser, though he'd driven around and around the streets. Then he sat in on the interviews with Tarik and Mimi. Mimi's was droning to a conclusion.

With his pudgy cheeks and flyaway white hair, soft voice, and old-world manners, Walter wasn't much of a threat to the Congressman after all, Chase decided. He might even turn out to have been a better choice than Sly Poolow because of his stellar credentials and reputation. Walter would find no one in Tad's universe who had anything to do with Kayla's disappearance, and because he was so credible, the story would die a natural death, as it should.

When Mimi left Tad's office, where the interviews were conducted, Walter did not pack up his briefcase and prepare to leave as Chase expected. Instead, he sat back and said, "You look very comfortable in your boss's chair, Chase. Quite natural."

"I love politics. When Tad retires, I hope to take his place."

"Does he know that?"

"Oh, yes. Behind the scenes, he's grooming me to take his place. I'm very lucky. From the first time I heard Tad speak, I knew I wanted to be him."

"What is it about politics that guns your motor?"

"Guns my motor?" Chase said with a smile. He looked out the window for a second. "The importance of what we do, I suppose. The chance to govern a nation, to change the world."

"Change it how?"

"Make it better. Do things for the people they don't even know they need."

"For example?"

Chase glanced at his watch. "I could give you dozens of examples, but if I don't leave now, I'm going to miss my flight to D.C. I have a lot to do there."

"Is that where the Congressman is?"

"Yes, at least for a few days. He's got a killer schedule, though, so he's going to be all over the place until Thanksgiving."

"I need to talk to him."

"I know that. Believe me, I'll do my best to find a date and place that work for him."

"Your title is press aide, but it seems to me you function more as a chief of staff."

Chase humbly ducked his head, then shot Walter a diffident smile. "I've told him that myself, but only in jest. I like my job just as it is."

"So you have the power to help me a lot in this investigation."

"Of course."

"And you want to protect your boss as much as possible."

"Both of us want to protect the integrity of the office, but if you're implying something, we'll be straight with you. We have nothing to hide."

"Tell me again about your relationship with Kayla Jesperson."

"I already told you. We're friends. We work well together.

And I like her a lot."

"But you aren't dating."

"No."

"Mimi thinks you are," Walter said. "She says you send Kayla flowers from time to time and go out with her."

Chase sighed. "Mimi's a romantic, so she makes a lot out of a bunch of flowers and the occasional box of candy. It's true Kayla and I have been out with friends but we don't pair up. Kayla's simply not my type -- a little too flighty, too hooked on superficial things like clothes and parties. Sometimes, as I already told you, she drinks too much. The girl I'm seeing now -- Kayla's roommate actually -- is more my type."

"What's her name again?"

"Bridget Deel. She teaches at Summit Academy."

"When is the Congressman's wife returning to Fort Wayne?"

"Tomorrow, I think, but I don't know for sure. She's in Boston with her mother, who's recovering from surgery, so it's a sacrifice for her to come back just now, but she wants to help too. I'll try to find out today and let you know."

"You said she had a fight with the missing girl the night of the fundraiser. What was the fight about?"

"I told you," Chase said, squelching his irritation, "it was an argument, not a fight. I was standing a few feet away, Cordelia was speaking very quietly, and people around me were chattering, so the only word I heard was 'whore.' But Mrs. Bristoll's tone was definitely angry and Kayla started to cry. That's all I really know."

"Is Mrs. Bristoll the jealous type?"

Chase was shocked. "Absolutely not. She's the perfect wife."

"Why would Mrs. Bristoll call Kayla a whore?"

"She must have been angry about something."

"Is Kayla having an affair with the Congressman?"

"You'd have to ask them."

"I'm asking you, Chase."

"The one thing I never want to talk about is somebody else's love life."

"I see," Walter said. "The Congressman must encounter a lot of temptations along those lines."

"All powerful men do." Chase tapped his knuckles on Tad's desk blotter. "No disrespect, but I think your line of questioning about Kayla's love life, or lack of it, is off the mark."

"You do?"

"I do," Chase said. "The last person to see Kayla was her old college boyfriend, Asher Stroheim. Mimi told you about that scene he made here soon after she started work. He was crazy wild and violent the way he tore that necklace off her neck. I'd give him a close look."

Walter looked amused. "But isn't that the same line of inquiry -- her love life or lack of it, as you put it -- that you think I shouldn't pursue?"

"What I mean is, her love life *at work*, if she had any, is less relevant than what went before she got here. Kayla's only worked in this office a couple of months, but she dated Asher for a couple of years, so there's a lot more history there. And then there's her landlord, a nasty little guy who is so obsessed that he" -- making air quotes around the next two words-- "*just happened* to see her get out of the Congressman's car before the fundraiser at the hotel. If you talk to my girlfriend, she'll tell you a story about how the weasel checked window locks in their rented house and left the ones in Kayla's bedroom unlocked. The guy has a screw loose."

"So is that your best guess about what happened to Kayla -- either Asher or the landlord abducted her?"

"That or some random stranger saw a beautiful woman, a little drunk, walking alone late at night on a deserted downtown street in a storm and decided to take advantage of her. Maybe he offered her a ride, thinking she was a prostitute, and things went south from there."

Walter clicked his aluminum briefcase closed and moved to the edge of his chair.

"I almost hate to say this," Chase said, "but before you go, there's one more thing I just thought of. Kayla said her mother is very angry that she isn't living within her means. If she ever found out that her father is still paying Kayla's bills, her mother would go postal."

"To your knowledge, does Mrs. Jesperson know that her daughter is still cadging money from her father?"

"That I don't know for sure, but I think so," Chase said.

"Have you met Kayla's mother?" Walter asked.

"No, but I heard a lot about her from Kayla. Janice -- that's her name -- has a history of . . . how do I put this? A history of GWEP." He caught Walter's inquiring look "Gut-wrenching emotional problems. Sorry, I like acronyms. Janice was even institutionalized for a few months when Kayla was little and, according to Kayla, lives on a complex regimen of pills. Have you talked to the Jespersons yet?"

"I have," Walter said.

"I didn't know that. Then I suppose you already know all this."

Walter shrugged noncommittally.

"Maybe I shouldn't have told you that, Walter, because it sounds like the kind of gossip I hate. I don't believe either one of the Jespersons would actually do anything to their own daughter. . . . But I thought you ought to know the facts."

"Quite right, Chase. Facts are key. You've been very helpful." He glanced at his watch. "I hope you make your flight."

"I'll walk you to the elevator," Chase said politely.

"No need, but thank you," Walter said, equally politely. He paused at the door without turning around. "Do you think Kayla's still alive?"

Chase was caught by surprise. "Don't you?"

Walter turned and fixed his eyes on Chase but said nothing.

"I - I don't know," Chase said. "It's been over a week since she disappeared, and I suppose" -- looking off into space -- "the odds of finding her . . . her whole and healthy aren't good, are they? But she texts Bridget, so she must be alive . . . somewhere. I hope she's okay."

"Any idea where that somewhere is?"

"No. No idea at all. I wish I did."

46

Headline
Monday, November 4, 2013

When Bridget drove into her driveway late Monday afternoon, she saw someone sitting on the front steps of the bungalow. Big nose, long hair, windbreaker, plaid shirt, ripped jeans. He was smoking something. Asher.

Heart pounding, she was about to back out to the street when he strode over to the car. He slapped both hands on the roof and then signaled to roll down the window.

Reluctantly, she did, but only a few inches, simultaneously making sure the door was locked. He flapped a rolled-up newspaper at her. "You see this?"

She shook her head. She didn't want to speak to him.

"The *News-Sentinel*. See the headline?"

"Hold it still," she snapped. "I can't read it with you waving it around like that."

"I'll read it to you," he said. "'Politician's Assistant Missing.' It's about Kayla. How come you never told me she was missing? That she never came back?"

Bridget closed her eyes and took a long breath. Her missing roommate was finally front-page news. She knew it might come to this, but like everyone else in Kayla's life, she hoped by some magic the media wouldn't get involved. As Chase had emphasized more than once, the worst possible spin would be put on the story, forcing everyone in the victim's world to defend themselves against the suspicion of being a culprit, especially if she didn't return soon.

Asher jiggled the door handle. "Come out of there, Bridget. Talk to me. I'm not the boogeyman, you know. I'm human. I love Kayla. I'm not going to hurt you."

At a noise, she looked toward Mac's house. He was just walking over. For the first time in her life, she was glad to see her landlord.

"What are you doing here?" Mac asked with a challenging glare at Asher.

"Have you seen tonight's paper?"

"No," Mac responded.

"God, people, don't you read the newspaper? I don't even live here and I see it every day. Kayla's missing. I want to find out what you know." He bent down to Bridget's window. "Are you getting out or not?"

Asher looked so genuinely distraught she felt sorry for him. When she unlocked the door, he pulled it open. "See?" he said. "You're perfectly safe. Now talk to me. Where's Kayla?"

"I've got to let Doug out and then feed him before taking him for a walk, so I don't have time to stand around out here. I haven't seen the paper and I don't know anything anyway."

"Well, do that," Asher said, "and come back out. Or let us come in. You can read the article then."

She reluctantly invited both men into the bungalow and let Doug out into the backyard.

"You have a Coke or a Red Bull or something?" Asher asked. Without waiting for an invitation, he took a chair at the little dining table. "I'm thirsty. Mind if I smoke?"

"No Red Bull and no smoking, but I'll get you a Coke."

She took three little cans of Coke out of the refrigerator and found a bag of potato chips, which she dumped into a bowl. She was thirsty too and Mac never wanted to be left out of anything.

"The article," Asher said, "says I was the last to see her Saturday night. How do they know that?"

"Who wrote the article?" Bridget asked, pulling the paper

toward her and smoothing it out. "Oh!" she gasped. "Josh."

Asher looked at the byline. "Joshua M. Rosen, it says. Who's that?"

"Never mind," she said, gulping back her dismay. She had no desire to reveal that it was her sister's fiancé. How in the world would he know enough to write an article about Kayla's disappearance? She told Kate about Kayla's not returning Saturday night but little else. Chase had done everything he could to keep the story from becoming public. Now, the very reporter who made it public was associated with her. What would Chase think? That she had deliberately flouted his wishes? That she was not to be trusted?

When Asher started to talk again, she waved her hand and said, "Stop, Asher. Let me read the damn thing."

"Read it aloud," Mac said.

So she did. When she got to the line that read, "Mac Bevan, Kayla's landlord, reportedly went looking for her that night too but claims he didn't find her, though he admitted that hours earlier he fortuitously managed to be at the hotel just as she ran inside," Mac shot out of his chair and practically shouted, "What does that asshole mean, 'claims'? I didn't see her and that's the God's truth." He ducked his head and asked in a small voice, "What's fortuitously mean? Is that a bad word?"

For a second, Bridget almost laughed. "No, Mac. It means accidentally."

"It *was* accidental. That's how I saw her in the rain. I was just passing by."

She shot him a skeptical look. "Really?"

Mac turned red. "Sort of. I just wanted to see her all dressed up and see who she was with and the car that she rode in and all that kind of stuff. So I followed the car to the hotel. That's all. I wanted to see what the swells were doing. But I wouldn't hurt Kayla for the world."

"Speaking of the God's truth," Asher said, "it's also true that she didn't get into my car either, yet it says I was the last to see her as if that means something bad. She's been gone over a week.

Somebody must be holding her somewhere. If that's right, then I *wasn't* the last to see her. Stands to reason, right?"

"Did either of you speak to Josh?" Bridget asked.

"No," they exclaimed in chorus.

"I never seen the man," Mac said.

"Me neither," Asher seconded.

"Did you talk to anybody on the phone? Maybe somebody who sounded authoritative and demanded answers to questions."

"No," again in chorus.

Bridget got up to let Doug back in. She poured some kibble in a bowl and refreshed his water bowl. The two men watched her every move as if she had explanations for the hateful publicity that had suddenly ensnared them but just stubbornly meant to keep them in the dark.

"Well?" Asher asked when she resumed her seat at the table.

"Well what, Asher?"

"Was Kayla having an affair with her boss?"

Bridget shot a look that made him shrink. "She's missing, Asher. That's all you have to know."

"Okay, okay, calm down. Just asking. The paper sort of hints that Kayla might be hiding out somewhere for awhile because she wants to and will come back when she's ready. You think that's true?"

"I don't know," Bridget said.

"Or do you think somebody's done something bad to her? Not me, that's for sure. But somebody."

"I don't know that either, Asher."

"So now what?"

She put her head in her hands. "I'm as lost as you are. I can't think any more. Kayla, Kayla, Kayla. That's all I think about. She's in my every waking thought and most of my dreams. I can hardly even gather my thoughts so that I can teach properly. I'm going mad myself."

"At least you're only mentioned as Kayla's roommate," Mac said.

Asher glared at him. "What a stupid thing to say." He scooted his chair close to Bridget's and put his arm around her. "Poor girl. It's worse for you."

For a second, she allowed herself the small comfort of Asher's hug. Then she got to her feet. "Please. I need to make some calls. I'm sorry, but you've both got to go."

47

Deep Throat
Monday, November 4, 2013

After the men left, Doug whined and pawed at the front door, his eyes flicking meaningfully from his leash hanging on a hook to Bridget and back to the door.

"Oh, I know, Doug, you need a walk, but I'm sorry, you'll have to wait."

Trembling, Bridget sat down again at the dining table and punched in her sister Kate's number.

"Bridget. How -- ?"

Bridget was in no mood for niceties. "Kate, have you seen Josh's article in tonight's newspaper?"

"Yes. What about it?"

"What about it?" Bridget yelled. "I told you and Josh about Kayla in confidence. The last thing I ever expected was that Josh would betray me like this."

"Calm down, Bridget. Josh didn't betray you, but why don't you speak to him personally? He's right beside me."

Bridget could hear muffled sounds of conversation. "Josh here. Kate says you sound upset about the article."

"Upset doesn't begin to cover it, Josh. I'm furious and embarrassed. Why did you go public with something so personal, something I told you in confidence? The Congressman is doing everything he can to avoid publicity. Kayla's family too. They've hired a private investigator to find her. And now this! You blew everything wide open."

"It's a story worthy of attention," Josh said dryly. "A politician's assistant goes missing for more than a week. She's texting you but won't say where she is. What do you want me to do? Pretend nothing happened? Let some other reporter get the scoop?"

"What do I want? . . . I want . . . oh, God, what do I want? I want the story to go away is what I want because Bristoll's office is going to think I'm your source and Chase will never speak to me again."

"Put your mind at ease," Josh said. "I first heard the story from you, but I couldn't publish anything based solely on what you told me, especially because so much of it was hearsay. Believe me, someone else also knew about the argument in the lobby and Kayla walking out in the rain and all those guys driving around town looking for her after the fundraiser and the texts you've been receiving. I wouldn't have written the piece if the only source were you."

"So who's your source?"

Bridget could hear Josh take a deep breath. "Sorry, Bridget. Media ethics. I won't reveal my sources. And if a court tried to make me, I'd go to jail first."

"Is the source male or female?"

"No can do," he said.

"Was it Dr. Jesperson or his wife? Maybe they decided publicity would help locate their daughter."

"Nice try," Josh said.

"Somebody from Summit Academy? When I was asked a question about Kayla, I had to tell Sheila and Justin, who's head of security, that Kayla hadn't come home. I can't believe one of them would say anything, but maybe you tricked them."

"You're neither hot nor cold."

"Somebody from the hotel? Or someone in Congressman Bristoll's office, like his secretary or driver?"

"No point in asking, Bridget. I won't even give you a hint."

"Both Asher and Mac deny they talked to anybody. Are they

telling the truth?"

"Whether you believe them, that's for you to decide. I can't help you."

"So is this like that Deep Throat thing with Nixon?"

"You know your history, don't you?"

In a fury, Bridget pushed the off button, wishing she'd used the land line so she could slam down the receiver.

48

Assumptions
Monday, November 4, 2013

Monday night in Washington, Tad and Chase were huddled in the Congressman's office. Tad's wife had just gotten off the phone about the article in the *News-Sentinel*.

"Who the hell is Joshua Rosen?" Tad asked. "Nosy little bastard. I'd like to kill him."

Chase shifted uncomfortably. "He's Kayla's roommate's sister's fiancé."

"I don't follow."

"Kayla's roommate is Bridget Deel, who teaches at Summit Academy. You met her in the summer when Sheila Powers talked to you about private school accreditation."

"I remember Sheila at the meeting, of course, as well as my wife, but not the girl."

"She's a brunette, pretty, very smart. But then you also saw Kayla that day, so why would you remember Bridget?" Before Tad could respond to the sarcasm, he said, "Anyway, Bridget's sister is Kate Deel, who works for Lexie Wright. You know who that is, right?"

"The scrapyard queen, the one who's nagging me about the abuse she's getting from federal agencies. She thinks there's a conspiracy to punish her."

"There might well be, but that's another matter. Kate Deel

is engaged to Josh Rosen. He's a freelance writer working on a master's degree at IPFW."

"You know him?"

"I've met him."

"Recently?" Tad asked.

"A few weeks ago. I'm sort of seeing Bridget, so the four of us had a drink one night."

"Sort of seeing her? What's that mean, Chase?"

"Bridget and I go out now and then. Nothing serious yet, but it could be. Time will tell."

"You know, as I think back, Kayla said something about how Bridget had a crush on you."

"Really!" Chase said with a smile. "And here I thought I was chasing her."

Tad sat forward and offered his aide a cigar. Smoking in the Capitol was a treasured privilege Congress denied to the public but reserved for themselves. The pause to sniff the cigars, cut the ends, and light up was welcome to both men, allowing Tad to collect his thoughts and Chase to gauge the atmosphere.

"So," Tad said after puffing out a smoke ring, "did your girlfriend talk to this Josh-boy-reporter?"

"No." Recognizing the edgy tone, the anger seething below the surface, Chase kept his answer short. It was like being dropped in a savanna near a pride of hungry lions that smelled blood. If only a deep moat would open up between them.

"No? You sure?"

"Yes. Bridget's discreet. She knows how important it is to avoid bad publicity."

The silence that followed was so uncomfortable that Chase spoke up again, though he knew he shouldn't. "As it happens, Bridget's a lot like Cordelia. Maybe that's why I like her so much. No matter what happens, she's loyal to the team."

Tad pinched the sides of his mouth in thought. "Cordelia. She worries me."

Chase froze. Tad never talked about the women in his life, especially his feelings about them. The subject was much too dangerous. Where was this going?

"I wonder...," Tad mused in a voice so low that Chase had to lean forward to hear him.

"You wonder what?"

"Never mind," Tad said, waving his hand. "What do you really think of this Walter Richardson, superman investigator?"

"He's smart. I think we should do some prepping before you make yourself available."

"Why?"

"The questions are going to focus on your relationship with Kayla. You need to decide how much you're going to tell."

"Isn't that your cell ringing?" Tad asked.

Chase extracted his phone, checked the screen, mouthed the word "Bridget," and punched Talk. "Peanut. What's up?"

He patiently listened to a long, somewhat hysterical recitation about the *News-Sentinel* article, Bridget's tearful promise that she had nothing to do with it, and her conversation with Josh about not naming his sources.

Chase had a hard time calming her down and assuring her that he already knew about the article. It took awhile to convince her that he suspected no betrayal from her.

When he finally hung up, he took his time to check other messages, then returned his attention to his boss. "That was Bridget."

Tad nodded.

"She talked to Josh. He won't tell her who his sources are but said he wasn't relying on anything she'd first said to him and Kate about Kayla's not coming home that night."

"I suppose it was natural for her to tell her sister what happened," Tad mused, refreshing their bourbons and pushing Chase's toward the far edge of the desk. "Paranoia kind of goes with the territory -- a professional hazard -- but when I'm in my right mind I know not everybody is nasty. So who do you think these unnamed sources are?"

Stalling for time, Chase sipped the bourbon, then picked up his cigar and took a puff. "An enemy. Somebody who's not happy with you."

Tad laughed derisively. "Who does that eliminate? 'Enemy' probably even includes some of my donors, like Lexie Wright -- and Sheila Powers if she's found out I'm supporting Common Core and mandatory teacher certification even for private schools."

"One thing I hate to ask, Tad, but is there anybody you personally suspect might have done something to Kayla? Somebody close to you."

"How close?" Tad asked, his narrowed eyes glittering with malice.

"You tell me. I have to know how to prep you. And I have to know the facts if I'm going to protect you from tabloid reporters."

"Tabloids?" Tad growled.

"A fact of life I can't do anything about."

"What you're really asking, Chase, is whether *I* did something to her."

Chase didn't move a muscle.

"Well, that's between me and God, isn't it? But assume I didn't. And assume Cordelia didn't either. But don't let your assumptions get in the way of doing whatever you have to do to keep my résumé clean."

49

Bridget's Journal
Monday, November 4, 2013

I'm still shaking. I can't believe Josh wrote that article. I can't believe Chase didn't suspect me of being his source.

I finally took Doug for a walk, even though it was dark and I don't like the dark. When I walked past Mac's house, I saw him in the window, watching me. He waved. I waved back. He makes me nervous.

I was grading papers at ten when my cell buzzed. Another text from Kayla:

Silly girl, why would I be at the cottage? 8 - D

That's the whole text. Why the emoticon? Why not say she's laughing her ass off at me?

I assume the cottage she's referring to is Tad's private retreat. So somehow she knows I went to the cottage on Saturday. How does she know that? Where is she? Who's she talking to?

And then I remembered how Chase suddenly froze after he rolled a rock onto the lid of the old well. He said he felt we were being watched. Then he dismissed the idea.

Maybe he shouldn't have. Maybe we were being watched. The very idea is the stuff of nightmares. Who else was out there?

I forwarded K's message to both the Jespersons and Chase, with a note that my call to her went to voice mail again. Now I'll have to explain to her parents what the cottage is, what Chase said about Kayla being there at least once before she disappeared, and what I was doing there.

What was I doing there?

I miss Chase.

50

Wolverine Mother
Tuesday, November 5, 2013

On Tuesday Bridget arrived an hour early at the academy because she couldn't sleep and didn't want to be alone. Justin signaled her. "How are you holding up?"

"Not well," Bridget said. "I'm having nightmares."

"Sorry to hear that. Mrs. Powers wants to see you immediately in her office."

"About what?" Bridget asked, almost in a wail. She hadn't been on her best teaching game since Kayla disappeared. Had Sheila noticed? She hadn't yet turned in her ideas for promoting the Academy. Was she about to get reprimanded?

"She has a visitor who's been in there" -- checking his watch -- "at least twenty minutes. That's who really wants to talk to you."

"Man or woman?"

"Woman. Mrs. Jesperson. She looks . . . well, you'll see for yourself."

Bridget closed her eyes in despair, pivoted on her heel, and trudged down the hall.

The once-pretty woman pacing in Sheila's office looked like she hadn't slept in days, which she probably hadn't. She was wearing an inside-out sweatshirt over baggy jeans. Her skin was blotchy, her blond hair stiff and uncombed.

She looked like Kayla's avatar, middle-aged and crazy.

"Bridget," Sheila said, "this is Janice Jesperson, Kayla's mother. She wants to talk to you. I'm told you two haven't met before."

"No, we haven't," Bridget murmured. She wondered more than once why Mrs. Jesperson hadn't accompanied Dr. Ed to the bungalow that night or at least called to talk about Kayla. Perhaps the poor woman needed a hug, but when Bridget took a step in her direction, she backed against a wall.

"I'm Janice," the woman said unnecessarily. "I'm Kayla's mother. I don't like to be touched. Don't look at my clothes. I haven't washed anything in a week, not even myself." Her voice was that of a robot, raspy, without inflection.

"I'm glad to meet you, Mrs. Jesperson. It must be so hard for you," Bridget said, regretting her lack of eloquence. "Why don't we sit down?"

"Where's Kayla?" Janice asked, not moving from the wall. Her large round eyes showed so much white she looked like she was about to have a seizure. "Where is my daughter?"

"I wish I knew, Mrs. Jesperson."

"Last night Kayla mentioned a cottage. What's she talking about?"

Bridget glanced at Sheila, who spoke up. "Do you want me to stay, Janice? I can leave you two alone if --."

"No," Janice answered without taking her wild eyes from Bridget. "Stay here. The more the merrier." The laugh that followed chilled both Bridget and Sheila. It was like listening in on a psych ward.

"I've had to take a leave of absence from my job, you know," Janice continued. "I have to take so many pills I can barely choke them down. Pills to sleep, pills to wake up, pills for blood pressure, pills for anxiety. This can't go on. She's my only daughter. I want her back."

"We all do," Bridget murmured.

"You know what the worst thing is?"

Bridget and Sheila waited for the answer.

"Not knowing what has happened. Imagining terrible things. Feeling helpless. Waiting without hope."

"I'm so sorry," Bridget said.

"So. What cottage is she talking about?"

"I'm not sure, but it might be a little cottage her boss owns near the Ohio state line. It's an old family place, occupied mainly on weekends. I went out there Saturday with a guy who works for Congressman Bristoll and we looked around."

"Why?"

"Chase just said he wanted me to see the place because Kayla ... Kayla had been out there and maybe she felt safe there."

"Chase?"

"Yes," Bridget said. "Chase Sumner, Congressman Bristoll's spokesman."

"Kayla claimed she was dating Chase. But she never brought him to the house so I didn't believe her."

"You're right. Kayla isn't dating him. She works with him, that's all. They're friends."

"Are you saying she lied to me?"

You just said so yourself! "Maybe you misunderstood her."

"I never misunderstand my daughter. She's flesh of my flesh, blood of my blood, bone of my bone. Kayla said you're smart, so you know why she lied." Janice stared at Bridget, waiting for her to say something. When she didn't, Janice supplied the answer. "She was dating someone all right, someone she didn't want to name."

Bridget looked at Sheila for help. Sheila palmed her cellphone, stood up, and walked slowly toward Janice. "Please, have a seat on the sofa, Janice. You'll be more comfortable. Have you eaten this morning?"

Janice shook her head.

"Then I'll get you a cup of coffee and something to eat. Would you like pastry or fruit?"

"Pastry," Janice said in a mechanical voice. "Yes, pastry. Coffee with sugar. No fruit."

While Sheila slipped away, Janice sat down at one end of the sofa and began digging for something in her fanny pack. When Bridget started to sit down next to her, Janice gestured at the far end. "Not here. Sit over there. I need my space."

After more digging, Janice said, "Here it is." She dangled Kayla's gold chain with the pendant intertwining the initials K and T.

Bridget averted her eyes. Suddenly she noticed that Janice was wearing her husband's carpet slippers but no rings on her left hand. Her nails were raggedy and dirty.

"Have you seen this, Mrs. Powers?" Janice asked when Sheila returned.

Sheila shook her head.

"It's a necklace. Bridget told my husband that the T stands for her old boyfriend's first name, but I know Asher didn't buy her this." She glared at Bridget. "Did he?"

"I don't know," Bridget whispered.

"This is her boss's initial, isn't it? He's Theodore. He's married."

"His name is Theodore, yes. And he's married."

"He's rich enough to buy gold. Asher isn't."

Silence.

"He seduced my daughter, didn't he?" Janice asked.

"Please, Mrs. Jesperson, don't ask me these questions."

"I know what your cowardice means. Kayla and her boss were having an affair. Did he get tired of her? Did he kidnap her? Is she at the cottage? Is that why she's safe?"

"No one was in the cottage," Bridget said. "It was locked. No one answered the bell."

Janice's smile was frightening. "So did he kill her? Is her body in there?"

Bridget gasped. "Don't say that. She's not dead. She's still got her phone."

"In that text you got last night, why did she tell you she wouldn't be at the cottage?"

Bridget shook her head, out of answers.

"Is she pregnant?"

Bridget hid her face in her hands. "I don't know." And that, at least, was the truth.

"Look at me, Bridget. Do not insult me by crying. I'm the

only who can cry over this. Nobody else. I'm Kayla's mother, she's my only daughter."

Bridget blinked away tears and lifted her eyes to Janice's, which were bulging with emotion.

"You think I'm crazy. Everybody does. Even my husband. But I'm not. Why did Chase take you to Theodore's cottage?"

"I'm not sure other than what I already said. He wanted me to see the place."

"What did you do there?" Janice asked.

"We walked around."

"Why?"

"I don't really know that either."

"Did you two take a picnic there?" Janice asked sarcastically. "Shoot a little film?"

"No."

"Chase was looking for Kayla. He thinks Theodore did something to my precious Kayla, doesn't he? That's why he went out there."

"He says he doesn't suspect his boss of anything. Besides, we're all sure Kayla's alive."

"What did you find at the cottage?" Janice asked.

"Nothing."

"But Bristoll did do something. Something bad to the flesh of my flesh, the blood of my blood, the bone of my bone. Chase knows that. Why else did he visit the damn cottage? I know it in my gut. That sewer rat Bristoll got tired of my daughter and threw her away like an old rag. Or his wife did."

"Oh, Mrs. Jesperson, be careful what you say. There's no proof of anything so horrible. The Congressman won't take kindly to any public accusations."

Janice laughed maniacally. "I'm a mother. I have instincts. I should have been a wolverine mother because nothing will stop me from finding Kayla and hunting down her enemy. When I find him I'll tear him apart with my bare hands." She flexed her hands into claws. "I don't need proof of anything. I know about men like Bristoll. I can say what I want to say about him to anybody I want because every mother in the world will know I'm right. And if I don't shout what I know to the rooftops, nothing will happen."

When the office door opened, Janice looked up, expecting a pastry and coffee. But it was her husband, in surgical blues, standing in the doorway. "Time to take you home, my dear," Ed said. "You need your rest. And you left so early, I think you skipped a couple of your pills this morning."

He nodded imperceptibly at Sheila, who returned the gesture.

51

A New Friend
Wednesday, November 6, 2013

Cordelia sat alone in her beloved conservatory, only one table lamp on. She had busied herself with orchids for hours, checking moisture levels, adding food to some, repotting two planted in bark, checking for disease. But the pleasures of horticulture had mysteriously fled as her energy waned.

Now she was lying on a cushioned lounge, a decanter of Spanish sherry on the French moderne side table. In her hand was a tiny etched glass from her grandmother's set of crystal -- a set once once owned by Marie Antoinette. It had already been refilled many times. When friends teased her about the tiny glasses she insisted on drinking from, she retorted that it was the ladylike thing to do. She was upholding age-old standards.

Her mind moved upstairs. Porter was in his bedroom, supposedly asleep but probably still on his computer or even sneaking a marijuana cigarette on his balcony. Mrs. Brighton was ensconced in the en suite guest bedroom reserved for her, supposedly asleep but probably watching yet another episode of *Castle*. Her housekeeper, Mrs. Tooley, who suffered from a thyroid condition, was on the third floor, possibly the only person in the whole house who was actually asleep.

And Tad was still in D.C. doing God knows what with whom. She hated being alone. She'd arranged her life from the age of twenty-one, when she married Tad, to have people around her every minute of the day. A husband and children underfoot, as many servants as she could afford, friends dancing attendance whenever she needed company, her parents a block away. Very briefly, as a silly teenager, she'd actually entertained visions of becoming a circus performer traveling in a railroad car, night after night, with dozens of other free spirits, all living in a noisy, chaotic metal tube, playing cards and telling stories as they happily rattled along the rails to yet another destination. But she willed the fantasy away, of course, for she was far too practical to deny herself the luxuries that life had led her to expect.

Now nothing was as she had planned. Her two daughters were married, one living in London, the other in Los Angeles. She rarely saw either one and then only if she traveled to visit them. Porter, the treasured baby boy, was sullen and silent, given to slamming doors, wanting nothing to do with either of his parents. Her widowed mother had sold the house in D.C. and returned to her childhood home in Boston and, besides, how much longer could she live? Most of her best friends were scattered across the globe and those that remained were second-best.

Cordelia focused her disappointment on the husband she once adored. In the early days of their romance, she forgave his sins before he even thought of them. She loved his sinewy body, his optimism and ambition, his lively if devious mind. He shown so brightly that his mere presence overcame her innate disdain of his lack of breeding.

Only a man of no breeding would fall for a flighty girl like Kayla Jesperson the way he had -- and in a mere seven weeks. And only a man of no breeding would deliberately flout his wife's wishes, which in the political arena were very few, quietly advanced, and always reasonable. What in the world was Tad thinking to doublecross her on the subject of education? Didn't he care that her pet project, Summit Academy, would be damaged severely and that as a middling student there Porter would not gain the academic foundation he so sorely needed?

And then there was Walter Richardson. She liked the man

very much. He had the grace and manners that she grew up with. He was intelligent without parading his perspicacity, soft-spoken without sounding like a frightened rabbit. Yes, Walter, master of the art of conversation, was a gentleman down to his toes.

She didn't know that, of course, when she met him in Tad's office. She'd steeled herself to answer as minimally as possible, to reveal nothing of herself, to take umbrage if he stepped over the line, which he was sure to do. She prepared for probing questions about Tad's history with other special assistants, the state of her marriage, her unfortunate argument with Kayla in the hotel lobby.

But the unprepossessing little man with the kind smile had asked nothing along those lines. All he wanted to know at first was about Tad's politics. His relationships with donors and supporters and staff. The identity of his closest advisors and the supporters at the fundraiser. The nature of the reelection campaign that lay ahead of him. The opponents he was facing in the May 2014 primary. His duties as Chairman of the Ways and Means Committee. His most deeply cherished political views. His alliances in the House.

Then he turned the conversation to her but the subject wasn't her marriage or Kayla Jesperson. Instead, Walter encouraged her to talk about her own political views, especially on education. He openly enjoyed her stories about the family she came from. He talked knowingly about the charities she supported and the clubs she belonged to. Disclosing that he and his wife had moved almost every year before retirement, raising three children in the process, he commiserated with her about the difficulties of maintaining homes in both Fort Wayne and Washington while raising three children and keeping a close eye on her mother.

The interview was not an interrogation but the chance meeting of two strangers who instantly liked each other.

Then, as she drained another glass of sherry, the cold fog of truth slithered from her feet to her head, evoking a violent shiver. Walter wasn't her friend. He couldn't be. Everyone knew he was a very skillful soul-searcher, an interrogator who had spent a lifetime ferreting out the secrets of spies and traitors and terrorists. It was almost certain that he learned something significant that she never meant to disclose.

What in hell was it?

52

Tabloids
Monday, November 11, 2013

Mimi threw *The National Enquirer* on Chase's desk. He frowned. It wasn't a newspaper he ever bought. Every week, after Mimi left, he retrieved it from her wastebasket and read it at home. For a press spokesman employed by a politician like Bristoll, it was an unhappy necessity.

"I blame you," she said.

"For what?" Chase asked with a jaunty smile that masked alarm.

"Your job is to keep the Congressman out of trash like this. You failed."

Chase picked up the paper, which had been folded to an inner page. "If this thing is trash, why do you read it, Mimi?"

She harrumphed and stalked back to her desk.

Chase took another gulp of coffee while glancing at the headline. "Pol's Gal Pal Takes a Walk." The article with pictures took up two pages.

The first few paragraphs about Kayla weren't bad. She was described as a recent IU graduate, where she majored in political science and was vice-president of her sorority. A young woman from a good family, she was the daughter of a Fort Wayne physician and his wife, a medical technician. She had one brother. A former high school beauty queen, she had a backside rivaling Pippa

Middleton's. A black-and-white picture showed her from the rear entering a D.C. bar; another showed her sipping champagne at the French Embassy. In September she was hired by Congressman Theodore Bristoll as a special assistant, reportedly as much for her charm and beauty as her brains.

Then the tone became a little darker. A member of the House for twenty-five years, Congressman Bristoll was described as the charismatic and much-feared Chairman of the Ways and Means Committee. He had risen to spectacular heights in the nation's capital despite an old scandal about academic plagiarism that surfaced from time to time. Popular on the Georgetown cocktail circuit, Bristoll was famous for his Cuban cigars, Kentucky bourbon, colorful language, and back room deals so fierce his enemies described them as barroom brawls.

Married for thirty years to the elegant, rich, and aristocratic Cordelia Tilley of the Mayflower Tilleys and the father of three children, "Tad" (as he was known to intimates) was nevertheless known to have an eye for beauty queens. Kayla was just the latest in a long line of sexy assistants rumored to have been unusually close to their boss.

The condo he owned in Dupont Circle was "a love nest" bought by the very wealthy Sheldon Steinmacher, an investor and alternative-fuel baron rumored to have made Bristoll rich through insider trading. A third black-and-white picture showed the front of the Dupont Circle condo building, a fourth showed the Bristoll family a decade earlier posed in front of a Christmas tree, and a fifth showed Sheldon at a shareholder meeting, looking malign. Though Bristoll did not come from wealth and had only worked in the private sector for a few years before his first run for Congress, he was now the twenty-ninth richest member of the House, worth over twelve million dollars.

Then the focus switched to recent events. Kayla had not been seen since Friday night, October 26, after leaving a fundraiser in Fort Wayne, Indiana. At the dinner she'd entertained the guests at her boss's table with gossipy stories about D.C. Then, out of the blue, she'd been the subject of a vicious attack in the hotel lobby by Cordelia (pictured in her conservatory holding an orchid). Though it wasn't known if the attack was only verbal or, as claimed by one observer, involved a slap across the face, Kayla was so hurt that she cried for an hour and was comforted by Bristoll in the hotel lounge. They were pictured sitting on adjoining chairs as he dabbed at her face with a handkerchief.

Then the timeline switched again to show the affair wasn't merely rumor. In late September Kayla was caught on camera emerging from Bristoll's love nest, wearing a gold pendant intertwining the initials K and T. A closeup of the pendant was thoughtfully offered as proof that Kayla and her boss were having a very romantic affair. The lovebirds dined out at the best restaurants and attended parties together, including one at the French Embassy. A grainy shot of a crowd on Congressman Doyle's yacht purported to include Bristoll and his latest mistress.

Finally, unnamed sources took center stage. Kayla reportedly told a friend that Tad was getting a divorce and soon they'd announce their engagement. She hinted to her friend that she was pregnant. They were planning a beach wedding in the Bahamas. They'd even been house hunting in Georgetown.

A long-time friend said Cordelia understands the temptations her husband has been subjected to by unscrupulous women coveting his money and status. She views Kayla as a "daffy duck who won't leave Tad alone. She follows him everywhere, quacking at his heels. So pathetic." Mrs. Bristoll has been overheard saying she hoped the affair would end before someone got hurt. Yes, the friend admitted, even Cordelia's admirers privately lament her inexplicable tolerance for Tad's many affairs because it's so old-fashioned to stand by your man. But Cordelia's favorite retort was, "I was married before God and by God I'll stay married."

A different unnamed source "close to Bristoll" hotly denied that any of the rumors about divorce are true. "The Congressman has no intention of leaving his wife. He's a family man." But the same source acknowledges that the affair with Miss Jesperson is common knowledge among the Congressman's inner circle. "We're concerned that he's facing a very hot primary next year. If people find out about the affair, the campaign money will dry up."

Well, too late for that, Chase thought, before he read the last couple of paragraphs.

The article concluded with pure speculation. Kayla is in the Bahamas planning a wedding. Kayla has been sent across the country for an abortion. Kayla is hiding out in Sheldon Steinmacher's Florida beach house. Kayla is entertaining a Saudi Arabian prince. Kayla has been kidnapped by sex traffickers and flown to Thailand.

Then Chase picked up the *Washington Post*, a newspaper that in the past treated Representative Theodore Bristoll with some respect because he often bucked his own party. But the article about Kayla's disappearance and Bristoll's history with his special assistants was even more devastating, for it was mainly factual and quoted both his friends and enemies by name.

Chase got up and stood at the window, looking down on Calhoun Street. The press release he had to draft required words that hadn't even been invented yet.

His phone began ringing. And ringing. The torrent of comments and questions, well-wishes and threats did not stop. Political backers, personal friends, donors, opponents, supporters, advisors, family members, reporters -- the deluge, he thought, rivaled Noah's flood.

53

Bridget's Journal
Monday, November 11, 2013

Suze showed me the tabloid article about Kayla. When I got to the line about an unnamed friend who said Kayla and Tad were going to announce their engagement and hinted that Kayla was pregnant, I almost fainted. Who was the unnamed friend? It wasn't me.

But I knew Chase would be suspicious. And I was right. He didn't get mad about the News-Sentinel article, but the National Enquirer set him off. We had our first argument a few hours ago.

I never told a soul about how when Kayla was packing for another trip to D.C. she said that she and Tad would have an announcement soon, a big surprise that couldn't be hidden. That was the middle of October. I don't know how long they'd been sleeping together, but she couldn't have been more than a month pregnant at the time. Would she even have known?

Maybe. Maybe that's what she was hinting. I should have checked her bathroom for pregnancy tests, but I didn't.

Even if I knew for sure what Kayla meant, I would never tell anyone, not even her parents, much less some sleazy tabloid reporter.

When Chase called at seven, he was hoarse. I could tell from the way he clipped his words he was tired and frustrated, pumped up on caffeine, probably suffering from low blood sugar. He was angry at the world.

He's never taken such an aggressive tone with me before. All I could do was deny that I'm the unnamed friend who talked to the reporter. I told him over and over that I have no idea who that treacherous friend is.

To my chagrin, I finally started crying. At that point, he softened his tone but didn't say he was sorry for doubting me. Neither did he come right out and say he believes me. I wish he had.

Walter Richardson has been very nice to me. He's doing something with what he calls triangulation to find out where Kayla's texts are coming from. I'm sworn to secrecy about that.

Locating Kayla's phone is the only bright spot right now. Maybe she'll be found soon.

I have to keep looking at the photos of her in my journal to remember exactly what she looks like.

54

Vigil
Wednesday, November 13, 2013

Wednesday night as she was eating dinner, Bridget gradually became aware of an unusual noise outside. Pushing aside a curtain in the living room, she was startled to see a few people standing on the sidewalk, gesturing at the bungalow. Others were approaching from down the block. The crowd swelled, occupying the entire sidewalk, the driveway, and half the front lawn. They held candles. Some placed flowers and teddy bears around the stump of the fallen oak tree.

As the crowd swelled, she became anxious. This might be a well-intentioned vigil for Kayla, but Mac would be furious. Even in ordinary circumstances, he was fanatic about strangers, all of whom he assumed to be trespassers. Like a rabid guard dog, he challenged everyone -- the postman and delivery drivers and solicitors and even guests -- if he didn't recognize them. He would be furious at people trampling his carefully tended lawn.

Why hadn't anybody warned her? What should she do?

She went around the house turning out the lights and shutting curtains. After locking Doug in her bedroom with his favorite toy so he'd quit barking, she sat down on the wicker lounge in the living room to watch through a gap in the curtains. She realized the crowd was friendly but felt apprehensive all the same.

Then she thought of Chase. He was apparently still mad at her, but she needed him. And he needed to know what was happening. With trembling fingers, she texted the news of the spontaneous vigil to him.

And then, to her alarm, she spotted Mac in the driveway. What was he going to do? What fury would he unleash?

When he approached a knot of girls holding flowers and stuffed animals, she steeled herself for the riot to come.

But all was kumbaya. In fact, that's what the crowd began to sing. As they sang, Mac mingled, talking to one person, hugging another, helping arrange the little offerings around the oak stump.

Cautiously, she slipped outside just as a television crew appeared. When a male reporter began walking toward her, she cringed, but Mac intercepted him and signaled the crowd for quiet. Once the mic and lights were adjusted, he began to speak. "Thank you for being here for Kayla. I promise I won't stop searching for our beautiful girl. She's alive somewhere, we know that. But if God forbid something bad happens to her, the pervert will have to answer to me. We can't have animals like that roaming the streets. So, pervert, if you're listening, listen hard. Take my warning to heart. Return Kayla now. I will find you if you don't. I will tear you limb from limb. I'm a veteran, I have guns — legal ones -- so don't mess with me."

Someone from the crowd tried to push him aside, but Mac was having none of it. Bridget had never seen him so animated before. He was the ringmaster at a circus, relishing the spotlight.

Then, just as another television crew showed up, she spotted Chase elbowing his way through the crowd, not toward Mac but toward her.

"How did this happen?" he asked, putting his arm around her and pulling her close.

"I have no idea."

"Do you recognize anybody?"

"Just Mac and a few neighbors."

"Who called the TV stations?"

"I didn't. Maybe Mac. Or someone in the crowd."

"Tad's going to go ASC."

"Go what?"

"Ape-shit crazy."

"Where is he?"

Chase bent down to whisper in her ear. "Not for public consumption, but he slipped back into town a few hours ago to take care of some matters at home. He's with Cordelia. But in a few hours, he's flying to California for a colleague's fundraiser."

Chase returned his attention to Mac, who was still prattling on about how outraged he was at Kayla's disappearance. Tomorrow, he said, everyone should gather at a nearby park to begin combing the area for the missing woman.

"What's that fool thinking?" Chase sneered. "He knows more than the police? In a case like this, he's the one the cops are going to look at. The nosy guy feigning outrage, vowing to find the missing woman, pretending he's the hero. He protests too much, don't you think? Remember how he went looking for her but claims he never found her? I wonder. . . . Good job letting me know what's happening."

Chase then stepped up to the array of mics, pushed Mac aside, and, without preparation, uttered a heartfelt statement portraying the Congressman as a deeply caring family man who thought of Kayla as a daughter who was terribly missed. "If you can hear this, Kayla, contact me right away. Everyone in the office loves and misses you and wants nothing more than your safe return."

Only a few seconds of Mac's diatribe appeared on the nightly news, but every word Chase uttered did.

55

Bridget's Journal
Wednesday, November 13, 2013

I asked Chase to stay awhile after the people drifted off and the television crews pulled away. The quiet that descended on the neighborhood was eerie. Some of the candles in glass vases were still burning.

I put Doug on a leash so that we could take a closer look at all the little offerings around the oak stump. The thing that caught my eye was a plaster statue of the Virgin Mary holding a sign reading "Kayla." Ironic, I thought. Before I saw what he was doing, Doug lifted his leg on a giant teddy bear missing an eye. I didn't like the mangy thing anyway.

I blew out the candles before coming back in.

Chase said he wanted to stay longer but had too much to do. He said nothing about our earlier tiff, but I suppose his actions speak louder than words. Though I didn't get another kiss, at least he said "good job" and gave me a hug. We're friends again.

And then, an hour later, I got another text from Kayla. I could barely make myself read it.

Don't get caught up in the chase. : - XX

I am so frustrated. Why is she angry? What does she mean? That we shouldn't try to find her? That can't be.

And then it hit me. She has access to a television. She saw the vigil. That means she isn't a prisoner in some pervert's dungeon. So is she in a hotel? A hospital? The home of one of Tad's friends?

I immediately forwarded the message to Chase.

Chase called back right away and offered to come over. But I said no. I have to work tomorrow. I need my sleep. The only thing that sounds good now is my nice soft pillow and Doug at my feet.

56

Last Call
Wednesday, November 13, 2013

With mounting fury, Tad Bristoll watched the late night television news about the vigil for Kayla. He was alone in his den, hiding like a criminal. He wasn't a criminal. He was a man like any other.

The plantation shutters were closed and the drapes drawn. The television was finally off and there was no light except for a little table lamp. Cordelia and Porter were upstairs, as were the servants.

Tarik had offered to stay with him, but what could he do? They had nothing to talk about. "Then I check locks and cameras," Tarik said. "What else, boss?"

"Check everything. I'll leave for the airport in an hour."

Even though the vigil honored Kayla, he was brimful of scorn. He despised sentimental demonstrations, especially by strangers wanting to parade their virtue. Now they had their fifteen minutes of fame. He eyed the teddy bears and candles with contempt as childish and superstitious. The off-key rendition of Kumbaya made him crazy. The original Gullah spiritual appealing to the Lord for help had been so corrupted by popular culture that to his ears it sounded naïve and stupid, fizzing with hypocrisy.

Still, it reminded him how much he missed her. And how much he stood to lose.

How had it come to this?

He'd led a double life for over thirty years without being found out -- at least not by anybody willing to punish him. His thesis advisor accused him of plagiarism but after a little rewriting he was awarded his Master's degree anyway, largely due to his father's connections. When the youthful scandal was unearthed a few years later during his third reelection campaign, a powerful Washington law firm hired by his father-in-law quelled the furor with payoffs and threats of lawsuits. His alma mater held nothing against him. In fact, two years ago it awarded him an honorary doctorate and paid him handsomely to speak at graduation.

He wondered if there was precedent for taking a degree back.

His fortune was definitely shady, but there was nothing unusual about that in Washington. He and his fellow Congressmen exempted themselves from insider trading laws on the bogus theory that disclosure of their financial transactions posed a national risk, though the risk was solely to their private bank accounts. Among themselves members whispered about each other's fortunes but said nothing publicly. They were cannibals who wisely never dined on their own tribal members.

This time there might be an investigation into his affairs, one that might even uncover his off-shore accounts. He'd be bankrupted by the investigation. He might even go to jail.

Cordelia knew about his affairs but she never threatened him with divorce or ordered him to end them. Their love was real and their marriage meant everything to her -- until now. She accepted his excuse that since age eleven he'd been caught up in a hormonal vortex that grew worse when he was constantly surrounded by nubile girls on the make. His need for sex was no different than his need for money and power.

But now his private life had been hung out to dry like filthy, tattered washing.

His political career, if examined under a microscope, was a mess. Publicly he advocated family values and fiscal responsibility. He championed small government and small business. But he also prided himself on working across the aisle, negotiating win-win strategies, and accepting the consequences of elections.

It didn't take him long in the Capital to learn that small businesses may be the foundation of the nation's economy but they can't fund expensive political campaigns. Low taxes force sensible economies but they also eliminate the earmarks that win elections. Small government offers freedom but it's too weak to accomplish big things. And defending principle is noble but it doesn't win the chairmanship of a powerful committee.

For most of his career he was heralded as a centrist, a moderate, a consensus builder. He was a statesman who got big things done in the name of bipartisanship. Now he would be portrayed as a greedy, unscrupulous opportunist who could be bought, a man no one could trust.

He had no supporters left. For years Sheldon couldn't do enough for him. But Sheldon was furious at being mentioned in a scruffy tabloid and pictured with a Nixonian five o'clock shadow. Cordelia, who was of the old school -- ladies' names should appear in the paper only when they're born, get married, and die -- was more furious. Chase gave him the bad news about the campaign pledges that were being rescinded, one after another.

And then came the call that no Member of the House ever wants to get from the Speaker. It was time for him to step aside on the Ways and Means Committee, maybe even resign his seat in the House. The Governor of Indiana would replace him with someone who'd continue voting with the majority, so his resignation would not be a critical loss for the party.

All along, Tad thought he was indispensable. But now he was merely garbage, all because Kayla was missing and his life had been opened up like a can of worms.

He poured himself another bourbon and relit his half-burned cigar.

What happened to her should not have happened. He actually loved her. She had already picked out baby names. When he gently broached the idea of an abortion, she was horrified. Whatever happened between them, she was having the baby and it would bear his name. He didn't care much about the baby, but he cared about her. Though he hadn't yet come to a final decision, he found himself scheming to divorce the wife of his youth and marry the concubine of his middle age without sacrificing his reputation, career, or fortune.

Now he could see no way to save anything that he valued.

Even loyal Chase Sumner hinted that this time defiance and denial were losing strategies. The police and reporters, not to mention political opponents, would continue dogging him and everyone associated with him. His campaign coffers would dry up. He'd be shunned by the Georgetown socialites. He'd be ridiculed by his colleagues and rendered powerless. His name would forever be linked with tabloid scandal.

But resignation, however dignified, was the last thing his pride would allow.

He opened a desk drawer. There lay the Luger his father had given him many years ago. It had a clip in it. He laid it on the desk.

He closed the drawer and sat down to write a note.

Then he lay back in the recliner, the gun in his right hand. It was like last call for a close vote in the House. Before he arrived in the chamber, he'd better have made up his mind whether to call Aye or Nay. He pictured himself running through a maze of unfamiliar marble corridors, all leading to dead ends.

He lay there a long time before deciding.

Part Three

"It's easier to fool people than to convince them
that they have been fooled."

Mark Twain

"I want to die in harness,
doing my duty as a public servant."

Congressman Theodore M. Bristoll

57

Revenge of a Sort
Wednesday, November 13, 2013

Crouching under the bushes outside Congressman Bristoll's den, Asher heard the shot, muffled but still recognizable. It wasn't a door slam or a TV noise. It wasn't a firecracker or a car backfire because it definitely came from inside. It was a gunshot, he was sure of it.

Who in the house had fired a gun? He waited for a second shot or return fire, but there was only silence.

Hooking his chin on the window sill, he peeked in. He found a gap between two louvers and a sightline into the room where the drapes didn't meet.

The room was dark except for a bit of light thrown by a lamp he couldn't see. He squinted. There was something white across the room. Ah, yes, a white shirt. And then, in the white shirt, he made out the shape of a man sprawled in a dark recliner. Was the guy in the recliner the big shot Congressman who looked like an actor and called him an asswipe? The guy wasn't moving. Had he been shot? Who the hell did it? No one else was in sight.

Asher moved his head around, trying for a wider view into the room, but that was futile. And then he saw Tarik, the bowling-ball driver with the slitty eyes, suddenly standing at the foot of the recliner, blocking his view. When Tarik turned, phone in hand, Asher ducked below the sill. And waited. What the hell had happened in there? What was going to happen now? Was Tarik calling the cops?

With his back to the house, Asher let himself slide down to his haunches. Heart beating a little faster than usual, he waited, his eyes on the street, not sure what to do. Should he run or should he stay? What should he do with the bag of rocks?

He'd staked out the effing house for a week. Finally, just a few hours ago, he saw the Congressman driven into his garage. Fifteen minutes later he saw a light come on in Tarik's apartment over the garage. He then waited a long time in his hiding place back of the bushes to be sure there was no other activity. When it was all clear, he would leave a bag of crack cocaine rocks on the doorstep of the house, ring the bell, run away, and make an anonymous call to the cops. But the unexpected sound of a gunshot stopped him in his tracks. Shit! He was only minutes away from getting revenge. Maybe something even better was happening. Or worse.

Despite the night chill, he was sweating. Nothing he ever did went as planned. Nothing.

He crouched behind the bushes for another fifteen minutes after seeing Tarik. Finally, he saw a Jeep pull into the driveway. A tall guy carrying a briefcase got out and rang the garage bell. When the garage door went up, a light came on. He recognized the tall smooth dude from the Congressman's office. A few minutes later lights went on in the window above his head.

Chin hooked on window sill, Asher resumed his vantage point. The tall guy entered the room, followed soon after by a woman in a robe. He watched for awhile without understanding what the three of them were doing.

As the people moved around, he caught another glimpse of the guy sprawled in the recliner. He hadn't moved an inch. Was he dead? Who shot him?

Asher shook his head. If the arrogant Congressman really was dead, it was, he supposed, revenge of a sort. But it wasn't satisfying.

58

The Note
Wednesday, November 13, 2013

When Cordelia entered the den, she was surprised to see Tarik and Chase.

She'd expected to be alone with her husband. Upstairs in her room, she'd had time to think about the scandal. She missed her husband. She needed her marriage. Even if Tad was not contrite, she was ready to apologize and start hatching a plan to save his reputation. They were a team. They were fighters. The life they'd created was bigger than either one's ego.

In the upstairs hall, just as she peeked into Porter's room, she heard an unusual sound from the front of the house but assumed something had fallen over or been dropped. She never imagined what actually happened.

When she saw her husband sprawled in his recliner, blood streaming from his temple, the Luger on the floor under his limp hand, her heart nearly stopped. Not this! Not suicide! How had her warrior hero come to such an end?

She knelt by the chair and touched Tad's cheek, which was still warm. She checked the pulse in his limp hand, though she knew she'd find nothing. She gently tried to close his eyes but they wouldn't close completely. She wanted to wipe the blood away.

No one else should see him like this.

Transfixed by the scene, the men watched her rise and slowly turn on them. In a steely voice, she ordered them to leave.

"Okay, but don't touch anything," Chase said.

"I'll touch anything I want. Don't call anyone. Close the door. I'll let you know when you can come back."

Cordelia knelt again. She took her husband's limp hand in hers and kissed it. She touched his cheek again.

When she looked around the room, she saw the handwritten note on his desk, a gold Cross pen lying across his office letterhead. She sat down to read it, careful not to touch it.

Cordelia ~

I'm so sorry. I never meant for any of this to happen. I wish I could take it back.

Now I find myself in a dark tunnel, no air, no light at the end -- if there is an end. I've never been this lost.

It was a good run while it lasted though. Wasn't it?

I have lot of explaining to do, I suppose, but not here. You'll have to wait for that.

You'll find a way out, old girl. You always do.

Tad

Her face burned with humiliation. No "My Dearest Cordelia" or "With Undying Love, Tad." No explanation for this savage, cowardly act of betrayal.

She stared at the last lines. "You'll find a way out, old girl. You always do."

What in heaven's name did that mean? Find her way out of what? He once asked if she had anything to hide about Kayla. Had he doubted her heated denial? Had he shot himself because he feared that she was guilty of something criminal? That she'd have to find her way out of terrible trouble of her own making, in the process taking him down too?

She sat at his desk a long time. Should she destroy the note? Every fiber of her being said yes because it hinted at such dark, incriminating things. Was it a confession or a denial? Of what?

But a cautionary voice said no, leave it where it is. She might become a suspect if there was no suicide note.

She turned around to gaze at the body of the husband she once adored. She was tempted to slap his face or spit on him. Instead, she put her head back and wailed a promise so pitiful it surely encircled the globe and reached the ears of Venus in her ruined temple. "I'll never love again."

Upon hearing the wail, Chase and Tarik burst into the room. When Chase tried to put his arms around her, she pushed him so hard he stumbled backward. The touch of a man was poison.

Finally, she left the room she now thought of as her husband's tomb. Not quite resigned to her fate, she was nevertheless willing to let happen whatever would happen.

59

Whirlwind
Monday, November 18, 2013

For the next five days Chase's life was a whirlwind. There were press releases to be written, reporters of all stripes either to be answered or shunned, talk shows to appear on, Tad's Twitter account and Facebook to be updated. There were endless meetings and phone calls. He was assured through the grapevine that the Governor would appoint him to take Tad's place pending the 2014 election. Tad's cronies, including Sheldon Steinmacher, pledged their support for him to run for the primary.

The excitement about replacing The Honorable Theodore M. Bristoll was a macabre mixture of regret and relief.

And, of course, there was Tad's funeral. Chase had no part in that, however, for Cordelia consulted only her mother about the event. Because Tad had committed suicide, Millicent insisted on certain conditions: a long and detailed obituary notice extolling Tad's career and the illustrious history of his wife's family but omitting any hint of the manner of death; no viewing of the body; service in Fort Wayne to keep the Washington crowd away; short and simple rites; a family-only cortège to the cemetery.

Pleading ill health, Millicent herself did not attend. Nor did the Bristoll daughter living in London. She could not possibly leave her new job as a public relations executive.

Nothing that Millicent or Cordelia did could stop the press

coverage, however. The next day as she ransacked her husband's den for his will and insurance policies, Cordelia found a little blue clutch containing Kayla's credit card and lipstick. It was sealed in a manila envelope under a ream of paper in the bottom desk drawer.

Cordelia intended to keep the purse a secret -- maybe dump it in the river or burn it in the fireplace -- but Chase persuaded her to turn it over to the police. At the police station, Janice Jesperson and Bridget Deel both positively identified the purse and lipstick as Kayla's. The Jespersons disclosed that her credit card had not been used since her disappearance. But everyone was puzzled about the missing cellphone.

The implications were confusing. How had Tad come to have the clutch if he had not done something to its owner? If it had come into his possession innocently, then why hide it?

And what about the missing cellphone? Was Kayla alive and using it? Or had he taken that too, perhaps sending texts to Kayla's roommate to foster the illusion that she was alive and had voluntarily disappeared. And where was the cellphone now? A search of the Bristoll house and grounds found neither the cellphone nor any sign of Kayla. Had Bristoll hidden or disposed of the phone before killing himself?

But there was one known fact about Kayla's cellphone. The triangulation of cell tower signals indicated that all of the texts transmitted from her phone after she disappeared had been transmitted from the vicinity of the Bristoll house in Fort Wayne except for one sent on November 4, when Tad was in Washington, D.C. Kayla's cellphone stopped pinging the night Tad killed himself.

So, though the implications were confusing, the tabloid press concluded that Tad had killed his young and beautiful inamorata. He kept the little clutch as a souvenir. He sent the cellphone texts to Bridget Deel to throw her and everyone else off the trail of murder. He then took his own life as a gesture of something despicable: guilt, shame, cowardice, fear of being caught. He took the secret of Kayla's whereabouts to his grave, thus denying the Jespersons of even the small comfort of burying her.

Chase did not think his boss's motive for ending his life was despicable. In the circumstances, it was the honorable thing to do. But he wisely declined to say anything about that to anyone, especially to Cordelia.

At the same time, he felt Tad's loss keenly. He needed a mentor, especially now. But the man who could have assured his appointment to the vacant seat and plan an election campaign was now gone.

60

Keepsakes
Monday, November 18, 2013

Ed and Janice Jesperson agreed that Walter Richardson must be kept on the case but disagreed about his task. Despite the speculation in the press that Congressman Bristoll had killed his lover and hidden her body, Ed was sure his daughter was still alive and could be found. Janice, however, who believed the worst of the Congressman, was convinced that Kayla was dead and her body had to be recovered.

Walter warned the Jespersons of the very great likelihood that they would be disappointed no matter what he did. "I don't have access to the Bristoll family. The police are circumscribed in what they can tell me about their investigation. It's rumored that the FBI might be called in. If that happens, even the local authorities will be shouldered aside."

"That filthy man killed her," Janice said in her robotic voice. She was sitting on the sofa in her living room, clutching a book of nursery rhymes that was her daughter's favorite when she was a toddler. She had begun carrying the book everywhere. "He threw her away like a used tissue. I can't punish him now. But I want her back."

"I know you do," Walter murmured. "Of course you do. But there are forces out there . . . ."

"Forces," Ed repeated. "Like what?"

"Big ones. Family interests. Political secrets. Government stonewalling. Loss of public interest. For instance, when Bristoll's aide, Chase Sumner, called me in, he said he had no authority to keep me on the payroll. Neither Bristoll's family nor supporters feel an obligation to fund an investigation that probably leads nowhere. Or worse -- though, of course, they don't admit it -- leads right back to the Congressman himself. In their minds, the case is solved. Their part is done. If the authorities want to continue looking for Kayla, then that's what they'll do and they alone have the resources to do it. With the publicity that's developed, the police are flooded with tips, but until there's evidence of foul play, they aren't likely to devote a lot of time to the effort, especially because the Bristolls don't want them to."

"So cold," Janice said. "Kayla's cold too. I feel it."

"Is there a way for us to check out that cottage in the country?" Ed asked. "You know, the one Bristoll used as a private retreat."

"You think I'll find something there?" Walter asked.

"I don't know," Ed mused. "But Kayla's message about how she wouldn't be there got me to thinking."

"Thinking the opposite?" Walter asked.

"Exactly. If somebody else sent it, then it was to throw us off the scent."

"You aren't the only ones who want a look at the cottage, but I'm told there's some complication about ownership of the property, so a search warrant hasn't been obtained yet. It might be a waste of time anyway. Remember, Bridget said she and Chase knocked on the door and rang the bell but no one answered."

"How could my daughter answer?" Janice asked at the top of her voice, rigid with indignation. "If Kayla's dead in there, stuffed in some locked closet or under the floorboards, she can't answer the door. She can't hear the bell. She can't do anything."

"Is that where you sense she is?" Walter asked softly.

Janice shrank against the cushions, hugging herself. She shivered violently. "Somewhere like that.... I don't know. I don't know anything any more. But she's in the dark and she's cold and all alone and I want her back."

Ed got up to place a knitted throw over his wife's shoulders. When he tried to sit down next to her, she pushed him away. "No. Sit over there. I need my space."

The three of them sat in silence for awhile. Janice stared at the fireplace, Ed fixed his gaze on the ceiling, and Walter watched both of them. He was looking at a secondary tragedy, for parents who lost a child from unnatural circumstances had an increased risk of divorce and bereaved mothers an increased risk of psychiatric problems. If Kayla was dead, as seemed likely, the suffering didn't end with her.

Finally Janice broke the silence. "Why were those texts sent to the roommate instead of us?"

"What?" Ed asked.

She turned to glare at her husband and spoke slowly, as if he were a moron. "Why did Kayla send texts only to Bridget? Whenever she's in trouble, she tells you first, then me. She knows you'll do anything for her and I always give in. She's known us all her life. She's known Bridget only a few weeks. Communicating only with her roommate is like a lost sheep bleating into the empty air. We're the rock in her life. No one else. It makes no sense."

Walter leaned forward. "You're right, Janice. It makes no sense."

"You know what else?" Janice continued. "She never used all those silly little signs and doodles when she texted us. I hate them."

"You mean the emoticons," Walter said.

"Is that what they're called?"

"Yes." Walter's glance fell upon Ed's cellphone lying on the coffee table, then upon the tattered book of nursery rhymes clutched in Janice's hand. "Tell you what. I need to know your daughter much better than I do. Have you preserved any of the texts she sent you before she disappeared?"

"Yes," Janice said. "Everything since she graduated from college."

"How about the little stories and poems and cards she wrote at school? Perhaps a high school book report or a term paper in college."

Ed looked puzzled but Janice immediately came alive. "You mean keepsakes? Everything she ever did or owned or loved I kept. It's all in a beautiful big box. Stories, poems, notes, book reports, essays, term papers. Report cards too. Invitations to parties and the ballet shoes she outgrew. The diary she started when she was six. It's really special because she pasted in coins and dried flowers and stamps and made little drawings of birds and insects. She collected heart-shaped rocks. She made things too. A plaster cast of her hand. A tongue depressor Christmas ornament. A safety-pin necklace. Cute things like that. Come with me. I'll show you everything."

I only want to see her writings, Walter thought, *but no need to tell you that. I'll look at everything.*

61

Bridget's Journal
Monday, November 18, 2013

Tomorrow we leave for D.C. Sheila decided we'll travel by tour bus, with an overnight in Gettysburg on the way east and in Shanksville on the way back home. I'm all packed. I can't imagine sleeping tonight. Doug will stay next door with Mac.

Chase says our tour of the Capitol is still on. He'll be in Tad's office and will take the kids to the Rotunda and Statuary Hall.

We've only spoken a couple of times since Congressman Bristoll killed himself. I thought I'd see Chase at the funeral, but I wasn't invited. The few times I've heard from Chase he sounds different -- distracted, remote. All he talks about is what's happening to him. It looks like he's really going to take Bristoll's seat. That's good. It's what he's always wanted and he'll do a fine job, even though he's so young. In a way, at least in his mind, he's already left Fort Wayne and is happily ensconced in the Capital.

He never mentions Kayla. And of course she never texts me any more -- if she ever did. I hate to think the rumors are right -- that Bristoll did something terrible to

her and used her phone so I would keep thinking she's alive.
 Walter called. He wants to talk to me again when I get back from Washington.

62

Style
Tuesday, November 19, 2013

Cordelia was surprisingly cooperative. She invited Walter to her house for lunch in the conservatory. She first gave him a half-hour tour of her prize orchids, an unexpectedly lively and informative diversion. The chicken salad and sherry were excellent.

And then she led him to Tad's den. "That was his favorite chair. It's ruined, of course, so I have to have it hauled away but I can't bring myself to do it just yet."

"Grief is a strange thing, isn't it?" Walter said. "A friend of mine died a few years ago. He'd been happily married for thirty-eight years and we were worried about his wife. But within a month of his passing, she had sold the house and all its contents, plus his boat and his car, and moved to Florida to start over, as she put it."

"I wish starting over were that easy, but for me it isn't. Here's Tad's phone. I haven't deleted anything. Look through the texts as you will."

"Thank you. I'm not looking for content. I'm looking for style."

"Why?"

"The first assumption about Kayla's texts was that it was she who sent them. Her roommate, Bridget Deel, thought so, at least for awhile. It's called a 'truth bias.' We want to be believe what we read is true. But, with the help of the Jespersons and Bridget, I've been able to take a look at Kayla's texts and the diary she kept. The texts she supposedly sent her roommate after she disappeared aren't in her style at all. Kayla was an open book, very chatty, letting her thoughts and emotions hang out. She capitalized words she wanted to emphasize. She didn't use emoticons. As her roommate pointed out to me, she was smart but not clever, though the post-disappearance texts read like clever little brain-teasers.

"So if Kayla didn't write them, I ask myself, who did? The default assumption, popular in the press, seems to be that your husband sent the texts to promote the illusion that Kayla was alive and well. That way, he could delay an investigation that would implicate him in kidnapping or murder. I want to test that assumption."

"So what are you looking for?"

"As I said, his texting style. Have you ever heard of statement analysis?"

Cordelia shook her head.

"It's a law enforcement technique for ferreting out deception by analyzing a person's words. Ah, here's an example from your husband: 'Hate to tell you this, but still at office. May be home before midnight.'"

"What do you get out of that?" she asked.

"Your husband omits personal pronouns. He's distancing himself. The 'hate to tell you this' phrase means he just doesn't want to tell you in person. Without using the pronoun 'I,' he indicates he 'may be' home at a certain time without committing to a definite time. He's hiding something about where he is, what he's doing, and when he really plans to get home."

She chuckled derisively. "You're telling me he was being deceptive. As a politician, Tad was very practiced in that game and I accepted it as integral to the job. But it's true he had commitment issues. And he did distance himself from me."

"I'm not trying to analyze your husband or your relationship. But Kayla's texts, both the real ones and the disputed ones, and the entries in her diary are very personal. She uses the first person pronoun a lot. In the disputed texts she won't say where she is, which is not like her, but of course whoever sent them (if it wasn't Kayla) wouldn't want that known.

"Here's another of your husband's texts. 'Believe me, I don't want to disappoint you about the private school bill, but the issue is complicated and there are at least three sides to it. You know that's true. Stay with me on this one.' A person who says 'believe me' is often lying. By repeating himself your husband is letting you know how important the matter is to him. The disputed Kayla texts don't do that. They skip from point to point without saying anything definitive. I notice also that your husband doesn't use emoticons, but the disputed texts do."

"No, thank God, Tad didn't use them. I don't either. But my daughter in London does. I find it annoying and childish."

"If you don't mind, I'd like to read a few more of your husband's texts."

"Before you do that, I'd like to ask a question. After you talked to me in Tad's office, I realized I must have given something away that I didn't even realize because you're so low-key. What was it?"

Walter smiled. "You confirmed my hunch that Kayla's disappearance had nothing to do with sex and everything to do with politics. Beyond that, I'm not quite ready to elaborate."

"Ah," Cordelia said. "May I get you a coffee?"

"Yes, please."

While Walter scrolled through Tad's phone and sipped his coffee, Cordelia sat on the sofa and dipped into Mark Steyn's *Passing Parade*. Witty obituaries were such fun. She could write a doozy about her own husband. It might be purgative, but she wouldn't publish it, of course.

At last, Walter hit the off button. "Interesting."

"What is your conclusion, Walter?"

"Neither Kayla nor your husband sent those texts. Nor did you."

"You're sure about Tad?"

"I'm sure. The real Kayla was personal, chatty, emotional, telling all, hiding nothing, sometimes pointless. Your husband wrote impersonally and unemotionally, always with a reason, brimming with deception. Your texts are personal and open but not chatty. So the disputed Kayla texts were written by someone else."

"You have a lot of suspects to choose from. So who sent them?"

"Someone who has a lot to hide but can't refrain from looking clever."

"What do you mean?"

"A lot of serial killers -- BTK, Zodiac, the Unabomber -- taunt the police. They don't consciously want to get caught, but they can't restrain their need for recognition as a clever killer smarter than the authorities. That may be what's going on here."

"You think the girl's dead then?"

"Given the time she's been missing, the fake texts, and the purse you found right in this room, it's likely. Your husband's suicide adds to the suspicion, even if he didn't do anything to her -- which I believe he didn't."

"You have a name for this culprit?"

Walter smiled enigmatically.

63

The Riddler

Thursday, November 21, 2013

"The kids were very impressed with you this morning," Bridget said. "Seeing you in the Congressman's chair. Listening to your talk in Statuary Hall. You look like what they imagine a big-time politician should look like: tall, handsome, strong. And you sound that way too. If they knew you were a member of Mensa and served in Afghanistan with the Rangers, they'd fall at your feet. A politician like that stands out."

"Please. Not a politician, Bridget. I reject the moniker. I'm a CPS."

"A CPS?"

"A committed public servant. That's what I am in every fiber of my being from the hairs on my head down to -- ."

"The hair on your toes?" she giggled.

"Bridget! Be serious.... Now I've lost my train of thought. Oh yeah, thanks for telling me what the kids said. I did my best." Chase squeezed her hand. "I'm so glad we can spend the afternoon together."

"Me too." She had the afternoon off while Justin took the seniors to the Air and Space Museum. Chase suggested they stroll through the residential section of Georgetown. Every now and then they stopped to admire a particularly magnificent house.

"Will you get Tad's office once you're sworn in?" she asked.

"Not a chance," he laughed. "As a junior junior member, I'll be in one of the House office buildings because Tad's office suite in the Capitol building is highly coveted and will be claimed by someone very senior. But someday I'll work my way back to the palace."

"The palace? You mean the Capitol building?"

"The look on your face is priceless," he teased. "It's a palace to me. Thanks to old George, we don't have a king or a House of Lords. We don't have royals with distinguished titles. But we do have a ruling class, thank God, and we deserve to rule from an imposing edifice that looks like a palace. Admit it. Everything good in this country emanates from our nation's capital, the beacon of light on the edge of the Potomac, the center of the political universe. The architecture reflects that."

"Chase!"

He smiled down at her. "Just kidding. Sort of. Anyway, I love Capitol Hill, the White House, the Mall, the Smithsonian, the Lincoln Memorial. The bigger, the better."

Bridget was in no mood for a philosophical debate about how imposing the capital of a republican (small 'r'), democratic (small 'd') government should be. "I've missed you, Chase. I haven't seen you since . . . since your boss died. And I think you only called me twice before today."

He stopped in his tracks. "As Tad used to say, politics is a cruel mistress. My time isn't my own. But I promise to do better." He glanced around, then put his hands on either side of her face and kissed her. "I don't go in for PDA," he said huskily, "but there's a time and place for everything."

Opening her eyes to drink in his handsome face, Bridget whispered, "That was better than our first kiss."

If Chase noticed the subtle rebuke, he said nothing. "And the next one, when we're all alone, will rock your world, I promise." He put his hands on her shoulders and turned her to face the property on the other side of the fence. Through the trees they could just glimpse a long white house in the Italianate style. "Do you know what this is?"

"Let's see," she giggled. "A wrought-iron fence. A big lawn. A huge house. Altogether, I'd call it an estate."

"Not just any estate. Guess who owns this?"

She shook her head. "Somebody rich. Maybe that publishing family. The Grahams was it? The ones who owned the *Washington Post* and gave cocktail parties everyone wanted to be invited to. I think they're both dead now, but maybe the family owns it."

Chase looked astonished. "You know about the Grahams?" He hugged her. "That's not a bad guess, Peanut. You're a woman who knows her politics. You'll make a great Beltway insider. But guess again."

"I have no clue," she protested. "I've got nothing."

"Then let me give you a riddle. You like riddles?"

"Not really."

"I do, so bear with me. The owner of this estate is an animal that changes in a croak room."

"A *croak* room?"

Chase nodded, mimicking the sound.

"Frogs croak, don't they?"

Chase rotated his hand. "Keep going. What does a frog change from?"

Bridget looked off into space for the answer. "A tadpole."

"So?" he asked.

She stared at him in dawning comprehension. "Tad. Tad owns this place."

"He does. Well, he did. Cordelia owns it now. But someday I'm going to own it." His eyes gleamed. "We'll live here, the power couple from Indiana. I'll be Speaker, third in line to the most powerful office in the world. You'll be the hostess with the mostes'. We won't stop there, of course. Eventually Air Force One will be ours. We'll travel all over the world. You'll pick your favorite cause and promote it globally. We'll give parties at the White House that are so coveted by the high and mighty they'll sell their children to be invited." Once again he fixed his attention on the imposing estate behind the wrought iron fence. "But before we get to the White House, we'll live here in this beautiful, historic house. Rich, powerful people will enter through these gates, just to be within grabbing distance of our coattails. Can't you see it?"

Bridget caught her breath. The two of them would live here? As a married couple? Where had that come from? "I think you're getting a little ahead of yourself, Chase."

"No," he said emphatically. "No, I'm not getting ahead of myself. If you don't dream it, it won't happen. Everything I ever dreamed of is coming true. In a few weeks, I'll be The Honorable Chase Sumner. With the help of Sheldon Steinmacher and your boss and Lexie Wright and a whole bunch of other patriots, I'll win the primary and then the election. I'll move in with you in Fort Wayne so for my first term I can afford to rent an apartment near Capitol Hill. You can pick it out. Sheldon will make sure I have transportation fitting for a Representative. Best of all," he said, enfolding her in an embrace while still gazing at Tad's house, "I have you, the perfect woman for a CPS."

"How -- how am I the perfect woman for -- for a committed public servant?" she mumbled into his suit jacket. "You hardly know me."

"I know you well enough. I once told Tad you're like Cordelia."

"Cordelia?" Bridget asked. "I barely know her."

"She's wonderful, the perfect wife, always behind the scenes, never out front. Smart but doesn't show off. She's loyal. Her manners are impeccable and she knows how to give a party. She loved Tad with all her heart, but she was wise enough to make allowances for his little indiscretions."

Bridget pulled away. "You mean his affairs."

"Indiscretions," Chase insisted. "They never meant anything. In his way, Tad was completely loyal to Cordelia."

"Chase, you're making no sense. Think about it. By any definition a man who has multiple affairs cannot be deemed to be completely loyal to his wife.... But we're not really talking about the Bristolls, are we? We're talking about us. And I'm confused. Are you telling me you'd expect me to look the other way if you had a ... a dalliance?"

"Well. Wouldn't you?"

"No!" she cried.

He grinned ruefully. "Just kidding. I'd never cheat on you. I'm just saying, the wives of CPSs don't always agree with their husbands about everything, but they have to keep up a united front. It makes all the difference. A man with a rebellious wife is like a racehorse carrying a fat jockey."

Bridget laughed. "That image is so awful, Chase. Let's go find a coffeehouse. I need a mocha latte and some pound cake.... But why are we talking about husbands and wives? We've only known each other a few months. We've only been on a couple of real dates. We've never traveled together or met each other's families. I don't even know your favorite color or middle name."

"My favorite color is green and I don't have a middle name."

"You're kidding."

"No, I'm not, Bridget. Mom said she and Dad couldn't agree on one and she was too tired to think up something that he'd accept. He was always contrary."

"Speaking of your father, you once hinted you didn't agree with him about clothes."

"I don't agree with the son of a bitch about anything."

"So, that's the way it is. I've hardly ever heard you swear before, so he must be something."

"I have nothing more to say on that subject. But as to us not knowing each other.... I know all I need to know about you."

"How?"

"Well, for one thing, we've spent quite a bit of time together. I looked you up on line. I check out your Facebook all the time. Kayla talked about you. I've met your sister so if she's anything to go by, you're solid."

"Solid!" Bridget cried. "What a romantic thing to say."

"Okay, so I'm not a romantic guy. Does a guy have to be romantic to know what he wants for his future?"

"No. But there is such a thing as love."

"So let's fall in love," he said.

"What?"

"I'm serious, Bridget," he said, taking her hand. "Let's fall in love."

She cocked her head in disbelief. "Things don't work that way."

"We're halfway there already, so the rest will be easy. Just keep your eye on the prize."

"And the prize is ...?"

"The prize is me." He winked as if joking. "A scintillating career in the center of the universe. Power, prestige, every material need satisfied and more."

"And serving the public, of course," she said.

"Of course," Chase said, oblivious to the sarcasm. "I'm serious about that. Tad got off course, but I won't. That's why his supporters are backing me. I'll be true to my principles."

"Which are what?"

He shook his head. "I'll sit down with you any time to talk about my principles. And I'll listen to yours too."

"But if I don't agree with you ... ," she trailed off.

"You'll pretend you do," he said, smiling. "Riddle me this, Bridget. How does a cannibal choose his girlfriend?"

"Eew, Chase, that's gross! What made you think of that?"

"I repeat, how does a cannibal choose his girlfriend?"

Bridget looked away, fearing Chase could actually hear her brain whirring like a pinball machine. "Quickly -- before she's overdone?"

"Now you're being gross. And you just spoiled the punch line."

"Tell me anyway, Chase."

"He chooses the one who suits his taste."

She didn't bother to hide her disgust, though she did conceal her pleasure at spoiling the punch line. "I hate riddles, especially that one."

64

Motive

Thursday, November 21, 2013

They walked another few blocks in silence before reaching a coffee shop. Like the gentleman he was, Chase ordered mocha lattes and lemon pound cake for the both of them while Bridget chose a table.

As she cut the cakes into squares, Bridget said, almost in a whisper, "You've hardly mentioned poor Tad. You must be devastated, the way he . . . ."

"The way he took his own life?" Chase reached for a piece of pound cake. "This isn't the way I wanted to get into government. Tad retires and I take his place because I'm ready -- okay with me. Tad kills himself and I take his place by default -- not so much. But it seems he was just overwhelmed with guilt."

"So you think the tabloids are right. He did something to Kayla."

"Don't you?" he asked. "Even the police think so."

"Didn't they ever suspect you? You said you tried to find her that night, but they might think you lied."

"They did try out that theory. I'm sure they tried out a lot of theories. I didn't hear what they asked Mac and Asher and Cordelia, but I'll bet they got grilled too. The police checked public cameras and interviewed hotel employees and ran down every lead, but what did they come up with? Zip."

"So the cops believe you and all the others are innocent."

"I wouldn't go that far, but Tad looks pretty guilty now, so I think the only thing left for the authorities to do is to find the body."

"What motive would Tad have had to harm Kayla?"

Chase glanced around the room, then leaned in. "Kayla thought he'd leave Cordelia, but I knew that would never happen. This wasn't Tad's first rodeo, you know. All the other women were pushed out quietly, but Kayla was hanging in there. And she wasn't going to be pushed out without a very noisy, very public fight."

"That doesn't sound like Kayla at all. She loved Tad but she kept it a secret even from her parents. I think I'm the only one who knew they were going to make a big announcement right about now -- had they lived."

"What announcement?"

"She didn't say. She said it was big, though, and it couldn't be hidden. At the time, I had no clue what she was talking about, but as I thought about it, a few things came to mind. Maybe Tad wasn't going to run again. Maybe she was pregnant. Maybe they were going to get married."

"You were speculating."

Bridget paused, deciding whether to go on. "I'm not proud of this, Chase, but last week I decided to read her diary. She wrote every day, sometimes pages and pages, so I'm only part way through. I thought it might give me a clue about why she left and where she is."

"And?"

"I've probably said too much already. It was her life to disclose, her secrets to keep. Let's just say, I'm convinced from what she wrote that Tad was about to retire." She was startled at the change in Chase's expression.

"You mean, all this was unnecessary?"

"All what, Chase?"

The wordsmith struggled with words. "The stunt Kayla pulled. Or if it wasn't a stunt, the stupid thing that Tad did."

"I'm not following."

"Here's what I think happened. Tad tried to comfort Kayla after Cordelia berated her in the hotel lobby. After the fundraiser he could only stay an hour because he had to maintain the fiction that they weren't romantically involved, but he promised her to come back to talk things out. He got a ride home with a friend, as previously planned, but he drove right back downtown. She waited for him somewhere outside where she wouldn't be noticed getting into his car. Then she demanded he leave Cordelia. He said he wouldn't. They argued. Tad's temper got the best of him and he lost control. Tad never meant to go as far as he did, I'm sure of that. Maybe he backhanded her and she fell against the door and split her head open. Maybe he tried to stop her yelling and accidentally suffocated her. When he couldn't revive her, he had to hide the body."

Bridget nodded. "He kept her purse as a sentimental souvenir and he used her phone so people would think she'd just taken a little break to think things over. The longer it took for the police to get involved, the less likely it was that Kayla's body would be discovered."

"Exactly," Chase said, draining his coffee cup.

Bridget shook her head. "That's not a bad story you put together, and it certainly explains why you never found her that night, but it doesn't sound like Kayla. But let's assume it's true. Why didn't Tad make her texts sound more like her?"

"What do you mean? They sound exactly like a girl with secrets."

"No, they don't, Chase. They're much too clever. Kayla was smart and unconsciously funny but she wasn't clever. . . . In fact, you could have written them."

He looked shocked. "Me? No. They don't sound like me at all. I never had access to her phone. Besides, I had nothing to do with whatever happened to her. I'm not a murderer."

"I never thought you were."

"Good," he said sarcastically. "My bet is that, given his suicide, Tad did the dirty deed and sent those texts as cover. His proudest achievement was graduating from Harvard; it made him think he was among the intellectual elite. And he was a practiced deceiver, a guy who was so slick people never knew what he was really thinking. It was in his nature to concoct brain-teasers sprinkled with clues for anyone clever enough to solve them. If no one solves them, then the body stays hidden forever.... So, Peanut, have you solved Tad's brain-teaser?"

"No," she said. "Have you? Do you know where Tad hid her body?"

"Jeez, Bridget, if I knew that, I'd have told the police. Don't you think?"

"But you're a Mensa guy. You're good at riddles."

"Maybe in time I'll solve this one, but don't hold your breath. Tad's gone. Kayla's gone too. What difference does it make now where she is?"

"Did you like Kayla?" she asked.

"What a question! Of course I liked her. But probably not as much as you did. More important, she didn't like me. I overheard her tell Tad that I was too young to take his place if he ever retired. At heart she was a mean girl. If I advised Tad one way, Kayla advised the opposite. If I said the sky was blue, she said it was green. She kept her secrets. If you're right that Tad was about to retire, why didn't she tell me? She knew what his retirement would mean to me." He shook his head. "No. Kayla wasn't an LTP."

"A what?"

"A loyal team player." Chase reached across the table to take her hands in his. "Look at me, Peanut."

She did. The strange thing was that his eyes looked unfocused, as if an invisible barrier stood between them. His wasn't the penetrating gaze of a lover but the indistinct gaze of a speechmaker.

"That's why I like you so much," he finished. "You're nothing like Kayla. You're like Cordelia. A loyal team player."

65

Bridget's Journal
Thursday, November 21, 2013

Chase asked me to join him for cocktails with a lobbyist tonight, but I begged off, saying we're taking the kids to an historic tavern in Old Town Alexandria once visited by George Washington and besides I didn't bring the right clothes. Both excuses are true.

The real reason, though, is I'm stunned by what happened this afternoon in Georgetown. He didn't propose but he's planning our life without asking me what I want.

The kiss was strange, right there in public. Maybe because it was in public I didn't really feel as much as I pretended. Or maybe the chemistry isn't what I imagined it to be. It felt rehearsed.

And then that riddle about the cannibal was revolting. One time I watched a cable program about a photographer who lured over fifty women to their deaths with promises of getting them modeling jobs. One of the girls who didn't go with him was asked why she said no. She said she felt a foreboding when she was near him.

I didn't exactly feel a foreboding when Chase hugged me in front of the Bristolls' house or when he told the cannibal riddle, but I did feel manipulated. I definitely don't want to be the fat jockey on her thoroughbred husband's back.

When did everyone in Kayla's life slip from the hope of finding her alive to the hope of finding her body?

66

The Human Heart
Sunday, November 24, 2013

After leaving Washington, on the way to Shanksville, Justin sat down beside Bridget. The bus was dark and quiet. Most of the seniors were awake but preoccupied with electronics. Most of the adults were asleep.

"I've hardly gotten to talk to you this week," he said. "What do you think of our Capital?"

"It's imposing. More ornate than I expected. I've never been to Rome, but all those pillars and pediments, the statues and temples, the long mall made me think of it. What about you?"

"You'll think I'm just being agreeable, but I had the same impression. The buildings are beautiful but not human scale. I guess they're intended to make us feel how important government is. Speaking of scale, you missed a great afternoon at the Air and Space Museum. The Mercury Friendship 7 that John Glenn rode into space for three orbits of the earth is so small you can't believe he fit in it. The kids were knocked out."

"What did you do on your afternoon off?" she asked.

"I joined a kayak tour of the Potomac." He chuckled. "You know me. If there's water, I have to be on it. How about you?"

"I took a walking tour through Georgetown with Chase."

"He must be on cloud nine if the rumors are true that the Governor is going to appoint him to take Bristoll's place."

"I think so." She stared out the window, unwilling to meet his eyes. "May I ask you a strange question?"

"The stranger the better. Talking to you is never dull."

She was suddenly aware that their arms were touching. The heat of his flesh was welcome. Everything about the situation -- the dark bus hurtling through an unfamiliar landscape, the closeness of his solid body, the need to unburden herself to someone familiar -- caused her natural reticence to vanish. "How long do you think two people should know each other before the guy proposes? Have you ever been in love? How did you know? Is a shared interest enough for marriage?"

"Whoa!" he whispered. "Where do I start?"

"Start with you and your girlfriend, if that's not too nosy of me. She's beautiful, by the way."

"Who are you talking about?"

"Julieta. The woman you were with at Piere's and Suze's Halloween party."

"Good heavens, Bridget. She's not my girlfriend. I tried to tell you that before. She's my younger brother's wife. A month after they got married, he was shipped off to Afghanistan with the Rangers. My older brother and I and one of my cousins switch on and off taking her to fun places so she doesn't get depressed. She's from California, so we're the only family she has here. She's so afraid of being alone she lives with my folks and likes it."

"Oh, dear," Bridget murmured. "I thought . . . ."

"What did you think?" he whispered.

She looked out the window again. She felt like Jericho, all her walls falling to the ground, not at the blast of a trumpet but at the sound of one man's whisper. "She's so hot, so demonstrative, I thought I'd misjudged you. You once said you like strong women like Freya. I looked up the name on the Internet and read all about her. Julieta's not my image of Freya."

"She's doing the best she can, but you're right, she's not Freya. Let's put it like that. Besides, she's my brother's wife, and even if she wasn't, she's not my type. But tell me something. Why all these questions about love and marriage? Has something happened in your life?"

"Yes."

He laid his hand on hers. "You want to talk about it?"

"I probably shouldn't, but it's weighing on me. Chase stopped in front of the house the Bristolls own in Georgetown and said we'd live there someday, a power couple. He didn't propose exactly. But he says I'd make a great wife because I'm an LTP for a CPS -- a loyal team player for a committed public servant. He's planning our future."

Justin laughed quietly. "Sounds like he's considering you for a BIJ."

She gave him a quizzical look.

"Big important job."

It was her turn to laugh. "That's the way it came across."

"Do you want the job?"

She shook her head. "I don't think so."

"Why not?" he asked.

"Something I felt. A bad feeling. Which is strange, because I was attracted to Chase the moment I met him. In fact, I've had a little crush on him for months."

"That was obvious."

"It was?" she asked.

He nodded. "Every time we were all together, I noticed."

"I was always a little mean to you, Justin. Kayla said so that night we were at the yacht club."

"She was right."

Her laugh was barely audible. "I'm sorry."

"Apology accepted."

"I've been wrong about a lot of things. For starters, I should never have waited so long to tell the Jespersons that Kayla didn't come home from the fundraiser when she was supposed to."

"If Tad really did something to her," he said, "it probably wouldn't have made any difference."

"Do you think the papers are right? That he killed her and hid her body?"

"From all I've read, he was a tough son of a bitch who looked out for himself every way he could, but murder is a whole other matter. So without knowing all the facts, I'm skeptical. Four, maybe five men had the opportunity that night. Her old boyfriend and your landlord. Chase and Tad's driver. Plus any stranger who happened to see her on the street in a storm. And let's not forget Cordelia."

"If it was Mac or Asher or a stranger, how did Kayla's purse end up in the Bristolls' house?"

"Good point. So we narrow it down to people with access to that house. Tad and Cordelia, of course, plus Chase and Bristoll's driver."

"I can't think that any of them had a motive horrendous enough for murder."

"All of them had the opportunity and the means. And I'll bet if we look hard enough, they all had motive too."

"Such as?"

"Take Cordelia first," Justin said. "Maybe Kayla was a threat to her marriage."

"More than you know," Bridget said. "From what I read in Kayla's diary, I think Tad might really have been contemplating divorce."

"I didn't know that, but there you go," Justin said. "Then there's Tad himself if you're wrong about his intentions and he really was trying to get rid of her."

"Which I don't think was the case."

"Now we come to the driver."

"Tarik," Bridget said.

"Tarik. I never met him, but from what I read in the papers, he immigrated from one of the lawless 'stans' where violence flourishes like poisonous toadstools in mountain hideouts. Maybe Tarik thought he was doing his boss a favor. Or maybe he made a pass at her, she rejected him, and he struck out. Or maybe Bristoll hired him to get rid of Kayla."

"Tad didn't hire him to get rid of Kayla, that I'm sure of. Tad loved Kayla. As I said, I think he was considering marrying her. So that leaves Chase."

"Not quite," Justin said. "We haven't eliminated Tarik."

Bridget sighed. "I just don't know enough about him. But I don't think he's the culprit because how would he know enough English to write clever texts?"

"Another good point. So back to Chase. I'm going to sound spiteful," Justin said, "if I say anything about the guy who's planning your future."

"Say it anyway."

"He's a lot more complicated than anybody else in this mess. Let's just say hypothetically he wanted Kayla out of the picture, knowing it would bring bad publicity to his boss, who would then be forced to retire early, thus allowing Chase to ascend to the position he aspired to all along. To get her out of the picture permanently, he had to kill her."

"He couldn't have known Tad would kill himself."

"No. But the suicide wasn't necessary to his plan, just extra convenient."

"I hate to think that. But Thursday afternoon when I told Chase I thought Tad really was going to retire soon, based on what I read in Kayla's diary, he responded in a very strange way. 'You mean, all this was unnecessary?' he asked."

"What did he mean by 'all this?'" Justin asked.

"When I asked that very question, it took him awhile to answer. He said something about Kayla's stunt or Tad's stupid action."

"But there's a different explanation, isn't there? He might mean what he did to Kayla was unnecessary because he was going to inherit the job soon without that."

"I can't bring myself to believe that," Bridget murmured.

"Because you're in love with him?"

"No. I thought that might happen in time, but the controlling way Chase acted Thursday -- ." She shook her head, struggling with words. "Well, I won't go into detail, but no, I'm not in love with him and I don't think I ever could be. But I can't believe Chase is evil, or Tad either. Tad was unfaithful and Chase is ambitious, but that doesn't make either one a murderer."

"No, of course not, Bridget. But it doesn't eliminate either one from a police lineup, does it?"

"Well, under the circumstances, Tad is eliminated, isn't he?" she quipped.

Justin chuckled at the black humor. "So one man with access to the Bristoll house in Fort Wayne is left standing. And he's a strange one."

"What do you mean?"

"He was never in the Army. In other circumstances, I wouldn't have told you that."

She caught her breath in shock. "Are you sure?"

"Very sure."

"So he's a liar," she said sadly. "How do you know that?"

"I got curious at your Labor Day party. Chase just struck as me as a little soft, the way he was so upset over a little dog hair on his pants. Then that day on the sailboat at the Lake, he didn't seem comfortable in his own skin, like a novice grifter pulling a con on you. A con he hadn't practiced."

"A con on me?"

"Yes, on you. How many times did he offer you dramamine or a life vest or more suntan lotion? He was romancing you the way a prince would seduce the lowly, naïve kitchen maid -- not that you're any of those things. And then at dinner he bragged about Ranger school. So, if you remember, I questioned him about his training. My brother's a Ranger, so I know what's involved, and his answers were way off the mark. I checked several sites. There's no record of Chase Sumner in any military record."

"Strangely, I do remember that night at the club. I even wrote about it in my diary, the way you were challenging him and the way he was flustered. But again, inflating his résumé doesn't make him a murderer."

Bridget, who was looking out the window, missed Justin's shake of the head. "The human heart is such a mysterious thing, isn't it?" she mused. "You never know what someone is hiding. It makes life very chancy. It certainly did for Kayla."

"Speaking of the mysteries of the human heart and chancy

things," he said, letting go of Bridget's hand and pointing out the window, "we're on the outskirts of Pittsburgh. Only an hour drive in the morning to Shanksville. I can barely imagine what the terrorists were thinking to do what they did, let alone what the innocent passengers thought when they realized they'd been forced into a suicide mission."

Bridget shivered. "What a world."

67

Good Instincts
Tuesday, November 26, 2013

Walter Richardson was sitting in his car outside the bungalow when Bridget arrived home from the Academy Tuesday night.

After letting Doug out the back door, she arranged some cheese and crackers on a plate and asked Walter what he wanted to drink. "Water is fine. Unless you have bourbon."

"I do have bourbon, a leftover from our Labor Day party. I forget who brought it. I'll have a glass of wine myself."

"How was your trip to the Capital?"

"Very interesting. And very tiring. It was hard to go to work today. Thank goodness our Thanksgiving vacation starts tomorrow. Do you want soda with the bourbon?"

"No thanks. Ice if you have it and a little splash of water."

She set their glasses on the dining table and took a chair. "The Academy seniors are great, very well behaved, but you know how much energy kids that age have. They can run all day and all night if you let them. Do you have children?"

"Three, all grown up and married now," he said. "Plus two grandchildren."

"I'd like two children myself someday, but that's a long way off. First, I have to find a husband."

"Somehow I don't think that will be hard for you, Bridget. You're like my daughter, Stephanie. Pretty, well-spoken, and accomplished. Any man would be lucky to win you."

"Thank you." She liked Walter's friendly face, his fatherly air. In his company, she felt comfortable saying anything on her mind. "Actually, something happened in D.C. that suggests you're right."

"What was that?"

"Chase sort of proposed. Not directly, but he said I'd make a good political wife because I'm an LTP -- a loyal team player."

"That's an unusual approach to romance."

"I thought so too. It took me by surprise. We know each other, but not that way. When I mentioned love, he said, 'Let's fall in love then.'"

"And what did you say?"

"It doesn't work like that." She sipped her wine. "Does it?"

He chuckled. "Not for me. You can't force it, but given time and proximity, it can happen. My wife worked in a clerical position when I started at the CIA. First we were just workmates, then friends. Then we started eating lunch together. One day, when she was absent, I realized I couldn't wait to see her again. I'd forgotten she was on vacation, so I had to wait a week before she returned. I asked her out the first day she got back. We were married a year later."

"That makes sense. But that can't happen with Chase because he's going to be in D.C. as much as he can."

"The reason I wanted to talk to you is something about your roommate."

"What?" Bridget asked, her eyes wide. "You know where she is?"

"No. I wish I did. But we've made progress. The texts you received from Kayla after she disappeared weren't written by her or Theodore Bristoll or Mrs. Bristoll."

"How do you know Kayla didn't write them?"

"She didn't typically use emoticons. The words in the texts you received are not like her because they're terse and opaque, impersonal and oddly clever."

"Remember, the first time you and I talked, I told you the

texts seemed too clever."

"You did, Bridget. Once I found out more about Kayla, I agreed."

"So who sent them?"

"I hesitate to say this, but Chase is the candidate at the top of my list." Walter opened his briefcase and extracted a folder. "This is a dossier I prepared on him. He was never in the Army, never a Ranger, and never in Afghanistan."

"Justin told me the same thing."

"He isn't a member of Mensa either."

"Really?" she said. "He lied about that too?"

"I'd say so. But he is clever. Not only is the style of the texts something Chase could come up with, but logistics put him in the right place. The cell tower signals from Kayla's cellphone indicate all the messages were sent from Tad's house in Fort Wayne or somewhere very near it except for one sent from D.C. on November 4 when he was out there. Assuming neither Tad nor Cordelia sent the messages, and assuming Tarik the driver isn't fluent in English -- ."

Bridget nodded. "I think that too."

"Then that leaves Chase. He could have sat outside the Bristolls' house in his car to send them and he was in Washington with Bristol on November 4. The question is whether he was covering for Bristol or himself. We can't rule Bristol out as the person responsible for Kayla's disappearance, but we can't rule out Chase either. Do you think Chase is capable of murder?"

Bridget looked away. "That's Doug at the door. Let me feed him before I answer."

A few minutes later, she said, "Yes, but only because I think anyone is capable of it in the right circumstances. Chase is ambitious and presumptuous and something about him in D.C. put me off. But I don't want to think he's evil."

"What put you off?"

"Nothing specific. Just a feeling I got when he hugged me while we were standing in front of the Bristolls' house in Georgetown. Like a warning from an angel I couldn't see."

"Women's intuition. Never underestimate it," Walter said. "It's saved many a woman's life. Where is Chase tonight?"

"Still in D.C.," she said. "He's overseeing the movers who are packing up Bristoll's office."

"Is he coming back for Thanksgiving?"

"No," Bridget said. "Some friends invited him over for a turkey dinner and, besides, he says he wants to get a jump on things over the recess."

"I take it that you haven't told him whether you're ready to be his team player for keeps."

Bridget looked ashamed. "There hasn't been any need for me to say anything one way or the other. Chase just assumes that we'll keep seeing each other. I don't know what the future holds."

"Are you going out after I leave?"

"I'm driving over to my sister's apartment. Just to talk, that's all. I need some company. Why?"

"Nothing. You have good instincts, so keep listening to them."

"Now you're the one talking in riddles, Walter."

★ ★ ★ ★ ★

Before pulling away from the curb, Walter watched Bridget and her dog get into her car. He was tempted to sit there until she returned, just to be sure she was safe, but he wasn't her guardian angel. And he had a wife waiting for him.

68

Timeline
Tuesday, November 26, 2013

Before Bridget left for Kate's apartment, she scanned the timeline she'd prepared. Did anything in it suggest Chase was the ghost in Kayla's cellphone?

October 26 (night of the fundraiser)

Kayla: Back TMR. : -)
 (smiley face)

Bridget: Where are you? What are you doing?

Kayla: Nosy. X-P
 (sticking tongue out)

October 27 (night after the fundraiser)

Kayla: Don't worry. I have a lot to think about, want to crawl under a rock. : $

Bridget: What's : $ mean?

Kayla: Embarrassed. Now I'm really embarrassed. Do I have to spell out everything?

Bridget: Where are you?

Kayla: Things are upside down, but just know I'm well.

Bridget: You're making me crazy.

Kayla: I'm still a tease. :-)
 (smiley face)

Chase after he saw Kayla's messages: Just what I thought. :-))
 (double smiley face)

October 28 (night after Chase and I called Jespersons)

Kayla: With what fruit do you poison a princess? :' (
 (crying)

*November 1 (Halloween party, psychic's words from memory)

Mama Bee: All is darkness. She's wearing a crown of leaves, like a woodland princess, and a yellow dress. She choked on an apple and dropped out of sight.

Chase's comment: Princess and yellow dress were lucky guesses; Kayla was also wearing black coat and blue shoes. No apples at the hotel. No statement about where she is or what she's doing.

November 4 (after Chase and I walked the grounds of Tad's cottage)

Kayla: Silly girl, why would I be at the cottage? 8-D
 (laughing her ass off)

November 13 (night of the candlelight vigil)

Kayla: Don't get caught up in the chase. :- X X (angry)

69

Apparition
Tuesday, November 26, 2013

When Bridget arrived back at the bungalow after visiting with her sister Kate, Mac was waiting on the front steps. She no longer thought it was likely that he had anything to do with Kayla's disappearance, but still she hated meeting him alone in the dark. Fortunately, Doug was with her. He was now five months old and much bigger and stronger than as the runt of the litter he was expected to be. Though Doug liked Mac, Bridget was his pack leader and he'd protect her with his life. Doug's presence gave her courage.

"Where'd you go?" Mac asked.

Bridget made a face. "That's not a polite question, Mac. What are you doing out here so late?"

"Somebody was sneaking around in the bushes, so I came out to see what's what, but whoever it was got away."

"Was there a car on the street that shouldn't have been here?"

"No."

"You get a look at the person? Male or female?"

"Can't tell you that for sure, but I just got the sense it was a guy. Dark clothes."

"It's dark and the person's clothes were dark. So how in the world did you see this apparition?"

"What's that?"

"Apparition. The person you couldn't quite see but somehow sensed was out here."

"Oh, that. There was a flashlight moving around, but as soon as I came out, it disappeared. I could hear heavy breathing and somebody moving through the bushes."

"Did you call the cops?"

"Never thought a that."

"Great. So what do you think this app -- this invisible person was doing? Trying to peep in my windows? Planning to break into my house? What?"

"I don't know. Just make sure you lock up real good. You want me to come in and check the windows and door locks?"

"No. I'll do it myself. But thanks."

"I'm going to stand out here till you get inside and I hear the lock click. You and Doug here check out the house, all the closets, the basement, Kayla's bedroom. Close all the curtains. If everything's okay, flick the kitchen light twice. Okay?"

"Okay," Bridget said, on the verge of hysteria, poised between screaming with alarm and laughing at the absurdity.

Ten minutes later, she flicked the kitchen light twice.

70

Stones

Wednesday, November 27, 2013

A whisper. A rustle. A mysterious sibilance. A quantum change in the atmosphere.

At the end of the bed Doug raised his head, sat up, growled softly, then stood to attention. Ears cocked and nose twitching, he faced the front of the house and stared into the dark. Then still growling, he leapt off the bed.

"What?" Bridget asked, raising her head from her pillow. Head down and ears back, Doug raced out of the room. Throwing on a robe and grabbing a flashlight, Bridget followed.

Still growling softly, Doug leapt up on the wicker lounge in the living room and nosed the curtain aside. And then he barked so sharply Bridget jumped with fright. "Who's out there?" she whispered.

Doug jumped down and trotted to the front door, where he crouched to sniff the air at the bottom. He sniffed and snorted and pawed at the kickplate.

Bridget peered through the peephole but could see nothing. She crept to the living room window, cautiously moving the curtain a fraction of an inch. It was just enough. Out of nowhere, a blinding light hit her full in the face. It appeared to be attached to a moving vehicle. The light made it impossible to see the shape of the vehicle.

Doug began to leap at the door and bark. And bark and bark.

"Shh, Doug." Leaving the chain attached, she switched on the porch light -- why hadn't she switched it on before she went to bed? -- and opened the door a few inches. There was something on the top step. It looked like a simple box.

Puzzled, Bridget slammed the door and leaned against it. Why a box? Who put it there? Was the secret deliverer still outside? Or had he left in the car with the spotlight? Did she dare to see what was inside?

She listened for what felt like an hour. Perhaps the prowler Mac warned her about had returned. She could hear nothing but the beat of her heart in her ears.

"Okay, Doug," she said, undoing the chain. "I'm going to open the door." Panting, in full-body rock and roll, Doug muscled past her, found a scent, and began racing around the yard.

The object on the step was a small cardboard box. She nudged it with her toe and stepped back. It didn't move or explode. She bent down to open the interlocking flaps with the tips of her fingers, then shone her flashlight on the contents.

Stones. Just stones. She picked one up. Flat, like a skipping stone, but sharp-edged and rough to the touch. She let it drop back and picked up the box.

"Doug," she hissed. "Come back in."

Head down, he was running back and forth along the curb, sniffing like a scent hound. "Doug. Now," she said, blowing the dog whistle.

He immediately trotted back to the house.

In the dining alcove, Bridget removed the stones and laid them on the table. There were thirteen of them. Roughly similar in size and shape, the stones were clean, not a speck of dirt on them. Bits of mica sparkled under the ceiling light. Nothing was inscribed on them. Did the number thirteen mean anything, or was it random?

Who left the stones on her doorstep? And why?

She shivered. Irrational though it was, she felt the stones were a torment, a creepy way to test her deductive abilities. But why did she need the test?

She turned off the light and stood at the kitchen window awhile, looking at Mac's house. Perhaps he made up the story about a prowler and put the stones on the porch to scare her, to make her more dependent on his protection.

Or had Asher done it as some kind of weird prank?

Did she have a stalker she didn't know about?

Or was Chase involved? By a process of elimination, he was now the prime suspect in Kayla's disappearance. But if he wanted her to become his wife, why would he torment her with the mysterious stones? And how did he arrange this surprise from D.C.?

After once again checking that the back door was locked, she removed the key and hung it on the wall. And then a terrible new thought struck her.

Before Kayla left for the fundraiser, she checked her evening purse and said she had four items in it: her phone, a lipstick, a credit card, and her house key. But her house key was not in the little clutch that had been found in the Bristoll house and which she and Mrs. Jesperson had examined at the police station. Where was the key?

It was too late to call Mrs. Jesperson to see what she remembered.

Perhaps the key had simply been lost. But what if Cordelia had kept it, or Tarik got his hands on it? Or what if the person who made Kayla disappear kept it? If that person was Chase, as Walter seemed to think, then she was safe for the moment, for tonight he was six hundred miles away in Washington.

The bungalow in which she felt safe suddenly felt like a cage made of rubber instead of steel, no protection at all against sharks.

Panicked, she double-checked the lock and chain on the front door. She jammed a dining chair under the knob of the kitchen door and made another inspection of the window locks. She locked the interior door to the basement.

What else could she do? Tomorrow she would call a locksmith.

Though it was two in the morning, she sent Chase a text:

"Somebody just left thirteen stones in a box on my front porch. I'm more puzzled than scared, but still I wish you were here instead of six hundred miles away. Only a Mensa guy like you can tell me what they mean."

71

Wake Up Call
Wednesday, November 27, 2013

Bridget woke Wednesday morning, the day before Thanksgiving and the start of a five-day holiday, without any thanksgiving in her heart. As she let Doug out to the backyard, she was greeted by a leaden sky that reflected her mood. Her outdoor thermometer read twenty-six degrees and light snow was falling. The wind was sharp.

As she waited for Doug to finish his business, she recalled the nightmare that troubled her and wrote it down.

She was standing in a valley gazing up at a sprawling castle hidden from the world by giant trees. The trees were home to wild roosting birds and hanging fruit crawling with worms. Carefully stepping from slippery flagstone to slippery flagstone, she stopped at a drawbridge arching over a crevasse, afraid to step onto it because of the troll living underneath. She could not see the troll but she could smell him and hear his demented ravings. Though she crept along the bridge on her tiptoes, her footsteps reverberated like drum shots, enraging the troll. She could hear his frenzied thrashing below her. Only yards from the castle, just as she reached the middle of the drawbridge, it sprang open and she lost her balance, falling into the gap, tumbling down and down into a deep well that stank of mold and decay. When she screamed, the troll, laughing maniacally, rolled a giant stone over the well, blocking out the light and all hope of escape.

Bridget studied her notes and once again scanned the timeline of the "Kayla" texts, to which she had added the mysterious appearance of thirteen stones.

On impulse, she walked out the front door and counted the stepping stones between her porch and the sidewalk. Eighteen. So the stones delivered to her last night had nothing to do with the bungalow.

And then it came to her, whole and complete. She knew where Kayla was.

But intuitive certainty arising out of a nightmare was not proof. She was not a psychic, after all. She was not a witness or a trained investigator. Her story would sound foolish.

Chase had not responded to last night's text, so she called him on the pretext of getting his read on the thirteen stones. Really what she wanted to confirm was his whereabouts.

"Hey, Peanut," he said groggily. "What time is it?"

"Seven-thirty. Did I wake you?"

"Yeah, but that's okay. Happy Thanksgiving -- almost. What's up?"

"Did you get my text last night?"

"I did. Sorry I didn't get back to you. I was still in Tad's office till two in the morning. It's been like emptying out a warehouse, there's so much stuff, so many papers to sort through. You okay?"

"Of course. I'm just sitting here, drinking my morning coffee and looking at thirteen stones delivered to me last night. Any thoughts?"

Chase chuckled. "Somebody's pranking you, that's all. Probably some teenager who's secretly in love with his teacher but is too awkward to do anything sensible."

"But why leave stones? Why thirteen of them?"

Bridget could hear Chase sigh deeply. "The stones are just plain quartz or feldspar, I take it."

"I don't know. Why would you think that?"

"Just working with probabilities because quartz and feldspar are the two most abundant minerals on earth. My point is, there's nothing special about them, right?"

"They're pointed and flat with a rough surface, a mottled gray-brown. They're sort of like miniatures of the flagstones in front of this bungalow."

"Nothing special there. What comes to mind is this. There's an old tradition of leaving stones on graves to make the soul stay put. Thirteen is an unlucky number in most cultures. So I'd say you're being warned by somebody to leave the Kayla thing alone -- let her stay wherever she is, let her soul stay at rest -- or you'll be unlucky."

"The Kayla thing?" she asked.

"I don't mean to sound flippant or morbid about it, but let's face it. She's dead . . . most likely. So, to be safe, you should stop worrying about Kayla and get on with your life -- our life. . . . Anyway, you asked what I think and that's my best guess."

"You're brilliant, Chase. I wouldn't have thought of that explanation in a thousand years. So how do I signal to the person who delivered the stones that I'm leaving the Kayla thing alone?"

"Stop talking about it," he said. "Distance yourself from that Richardson guy who thinks he's so brilliant."

"Who do you think gave me the warning of the stones?"

A long pause. "I hate to say this over the phone, Bridget, but one of the Bristoll operatives. Tarik maybe. Or even Cordelia, not personally, but someone who works for her. You ever tell anyone I said that, I'll deny it. But you're dealing with forces far more powerful than you can imagine, so take heed."

It was Bridget's turn to sigh. "You're right. . . . It's a cold, ugly day in Fort Wayne. It snowed a little bit, just a dusting this morning, but it's stopped now. What's it like out there?"

"Hold on, Peanut. I'm still in bed. Let me check." A long pause. "It's raining and in the sixties. Sorry to hear about your weather. Are you working today?"

"No. We're off at the Academy until Monday."

"What are you going to do with all that free time?" he asked.

"Nothing much. Take Doug for a walk. Read a book. Spend some time with Kate. Tomorrow we're all going to the farm for

Thanksgiving dinner with the rest of the family, so I've also got to think of something to take. That's about it. How about you?"

"Office work."

"When are you planning on being back in Fort Wayne?" she asked.

"Not till next week. So you miss me, do you?"

"Of course," she said, straining to sound truthful. "And you miss me too?"

"I'm counting the hours."

After the call, she looked at Doug. "Is Chase really in Washington or not?"

Doug wagged his tail.

"Whether he is or not, he doesn't know where we're going, so we'll be okay. You want a ride in the car?"

Doug wagged his tail harder. He loved the car.

72

Sixth Sense
Wednesday, November 27, 2013

Bridget drew a rough plan of the property, sketching as many important features as she could recall.

Then she got dressed. Long underwear, a down vest, a dark nylon jumpsuit, a knit cap, and walking boots. She assembled survival gear -- cellphone, flashlight, rope, gloves, matches, an all-purpose Sheffield tool with knives, and bottled water, among other things -- into a backpack. At the last minute she remembered the dog whistle, silent to human ears but a signal to Doug to come immediately.

Though she was eager to test her theory about Kayla's whereabouts, she was afraid too. She paced. She studied her notes again. She checked her backpack again. She considered whether to call Walter or Justin or even the police. It was long after lunch before she summoned the will to leave.

The long dirt drive was more rutted than she remembered. She headed her old green Bug into a thicket of switchgrass and buckthorn hidden from the road and from the cottage as well. "Okay, Doug. Here's your chance to chase rabbits and squirrels." Doug leapt out and began running in circles, pursuing enticing scents. In seconds, he had disappeared.

Bridget walked to the shingled cottage, which looked forlorn under the gray dome of the sky. The orchard reminded her of one of Kayla's texts: With what *fruit* do you poison a princess? An apple, of course. And Mama Bee's words too: She *choked* on an apple and *dropped* out of sight.

The slate stepping stones -- yes, thirteen, just as she suspected -- were slick and treacherous with just a slight dusting of snow. She didn't bother trying the front door, instead heading into the woods. The atmosphere was thick with menace, as if Hansel had ditched her and she alone had stumbled upon a gumdrop cottage and was being watched by the hungry witch next to a hot oven.

Just before entering the woods, she stopped to remove her binoculars from their case, looked in all directions, then trained them on the road. No movement. Stock still, she strained her ears but heard nothing other than the occasional scolding of a crow and the rustle of switchgrass. She steeled her nerves. No one knew she was here. Not even Chase.

The apple trees had lost all their leaves, which now formed a thick, soggy blanket on the ground. She strode first to the deer nest and then to the fox den. Nothing, just as she expected.

Heart racing, she then headed for the old well, where she knelt to brush the leaves into a pile before rolling the heavy stone away and grasping the thick pull handle. She wrestled the rotten lid to the side and flattened herself on the wet ground. When she shone the flashlight straight down, she gasped at the smell and the flash of yellow far below. Kayla was wearing a yellow dress the night she disappeared.

Bridget studied the shadowy form and yellow scrap. Was it Kayla? Did she fall in? Or was she pushed? She couldn't be sure but it looked like Kayla had gone in head first.

The gorge rising in her throat, Kayla's message --Things are upside down, but just know I'm well. -- came back to her.

Fighting back the urge to vomit, she suddenly felt her whole body turn to goosebumps. A sixth sense told her someone else was on the property. She froze, listening for human sounds. Slowly, she pushed herself backwards and raised her head. Her vision was blocked by grasses. Afraid that she was being watched, she didn't try to replace the lid on the well but instead rolled away and lay there a few seconds longer, straining to hear a sound other than the wild thump of her heart.

Slowly, soundlessly, she crawled into a thicket under an old apple tree she remembered from her visit with Chase. It was a tree made for climbing, the kind her survival training taught her to notice. She crawled to the back side and began climbing, one limb at a time, flattened against the rough trunk.

When she reached the midway point, she used the binoculars to scan the creek on the east end of the property and the road on the west. As she panned to the house, she almost screamed.

A dark figure rounded the side of the house and halted like a sentry near the back porch. He was wearing a ski mask and carrying a shotgun.

She scrambled to the ground in a flash, adjusted her backpack, and keeping as much thick brush between her and the dark figure began to walk in a wide circle in the direction of the thicket where she'd hidden her car. She wouldn't call Doug until she got there.

73

Secrets
Wednesday, November 27, 2013

But she would not reach her car. She was still a hundred yards away when she came to a little clearing. She could either keep walking as if she had nothing to hide or crawl on her hands and knees. But if he spotted her sneaking through the brush, he would know she had no innocent reason for being on the property.

The Kayla texts mocking the visit to the cottage and angrily ordering her not to get caught up in the *chase* flashed before her mind's eye like neon signs.

So she made the most important decision of her short life. She waved and cried out, "Chase. What are you doing here?" He stood stock still as she changed direction and made her way toward him. He was wearing a dark jacket and jeans. He pushed his ski mask up, revealing tight jaw muscles and tense, stony eyes. Bridget spoke first from a distance of several yards. "You caught me."

"Caught you doing what?" His voice was colder than the wind.

She willed herself to sound jaunty and casual, not a care in the world. "You know how I hate to work out, but ever since that week in Virginia with Kayla, I like testing my survival skills. Running zigzag courses, climbing trees, locating emergency shelter. Keeps me in shape. What are you doing with that gun?"

"Thought I'd shoot a few crows. Do you realize you're

trespassing?" he asked menacingly.

"So are you." Jokingly, soothingly. "At least I'm not planning to kill anything. But I don't think the Bristolls would mind either one of us being here, do you? Ever since you brought me out here, I've wanted to return. That was such a good day. Remember how beautiful it was? The first time you kissed me was out here."

"You remember that?"

"How could I not?" She sat down on the top step of the porch and patted the space beside her. "That gun makes me nervous."

He sat down too and laid the shotgun beside him. She took his hand. "I expected to be very lonely today, but thank goodness you're really here." She looked up at the dull pewter sky and shivered. "It's hard to be alone on a holiday, especially when the weather's so grim."

"You don't seem surprised to see me, Bridget. What tipped you off?"

"I'm surprised to see you here, but I thought you might not be in D.C. It took you a long time to tell me what the weather was out there. Did you look it up on your phone?"

"You're smarter than I thought." His face softened almost imperceptibly, his eyes lost just a touch of wariness. "I suppose you wonder why I lied to you on the phone."

"No." Bridget shook her head vigorously. "No, I don't."

"Why not? Why aren't you mad?" He intertwined his fingers with hers.

"A politician has his secrets," she said, trying to keep her voice steady. "You taught me that and I listened. I completely understand, Chase. I really do. I'm sure there are people who would harm you if they always knew where you were."

"You have no idea. Every day I get death threats from opponents, from the crazies in the blogosphere. I'm too young, I'm an opportunist, I've been anointed, I haven't earned the privilege, I have no principles."

"But none of that is true, Chase. You're the future of the nation."

"So we're a team?" he asked. His vulnerability was suddenly

laid out like a sacrifice on an altar.

"I think we can be," she murmured. "If we're open with each other. You're a secretive guy, so it's been hard for me to feel like I'm your partner. You don't tell me where you are, you don't tell me when I'll see you next, sometimes you go days without calling or texting me. And I know nothing of your background -- where you went to school, what your father does for a living, why you got into politics in the first place."

"That's going to take awhile, Bridget. There are things I don't like to talk about."

"Me too. But if we're both reserved, what kind of relationship will we have?"

"So where do we start?" he asked, avoiding her gaze.

She too stared in the same direction as Chase, gathering her courage. "You did your best to protect Tad, but won't there come a time when you have to come clean and tell somebody -- at least the Jespersons -- where Kayla is? They need closure, you know."

"Closure!" he barked. "There's no such thing."

"Not closure in the emotional sense. They'll mourn her forever. But at least they can put an end to speculation about what happened to her, and they'll have a body to honor."

"How would I tell them without revealing that I'm the source?"

Bridget shook her head. "I don't know, but together we'll figure that out."

He pulled his hand away from hers. He was silent a long time, his stillness broken only by the twitching of his hands. And then the dam broke.

"I picked her up a few blocks from the hotel. I told her Tad was waiting for her here at the cottage. On the drive from the City, we argued about the way she was slandering me to Tad, saying I wasn't fit to succeed him. She was stubborn. The cottage was dark. When we got inside, she realized Tad wasn't here. She got suspicious. When she tried to call Tad, I wrestled her phone away. She threatened to tell him that I tried to rape her. So I pretended to give in, to make up with her. I said I was sorry for tricking her, that

I didn't really even want Tad's job. I promised to take her home. When she let me hug her as a sign that bygones were bygones, all was forgiven, I found myself choking her. Very strange. It was like I'd left my body and was watching myself from a distance. I couldn't believe I was doing it. I had no control over my hands. I never meant to kill her, though. It was an accident, a momentary break in the order of the universe, like the moon stopping in its course. And then, when she stopped struggling, the moon resumed its course and I had to get rid of her. When that was done, I went home to change clothes and then drove to your house."

"So you sent the texts, pretending you were Kayla."

"I made sure I was near Tad when I sent them so he'd be the logical source. I needed time to think."

"Why send them to me?"

"I had to send them to somebody. If you didn't figure out what was going on, nobody would."

"And you planted her purse in Tad's house."

He nodded. "Not until the night Tarik called me over, though."

"Did you keep the key to my house?"

He looked startled. "How do you know that?" he asked.

"It's not important. But why did you keep it?"

"No reason," he said unconvincingly. "I never used it."

"Did you know Tad would commit suicide?"

"No!" he said, raising his voice. "No. I never wanted that. I just wanted him to resign, that's all."

"Unintended consequences?" she asked.

"That's the one thing I really regret. His suicide. He had his father-in-law for a mentor during the early years. I need Tad now for the same reason. He shouldn't have left me high and dry like that."

"Were you the source of the newspaper articles that broke the story?"

"I had no choice. Unless Tad felt the pressure of public scrutiny, he wasn't going to resign. Or at least that's what I thought until you told me he was probably going to resign anyway."

"So you were Josh's Deep Throat?"

"Is that what he called me?" Chase chuckled. "Yeah, I was Deep Throat. Not just for him."

"Well," Bridget said, willing her pulse to slow down, "that's a start."

"On what?" he asked, putting his arm around her and pulling her close.

She glanced at the hand cupping her shoulder. What if that hand -- the one he had no control of -- moved to her neck? Every atom of her body wanted to run. "On being frank and open with each other."

"You don't hate me for what I did?"

"No," she said shakily, her breath catching. How could he confess to murder and sound so plaintive at the same time? When she involuntarily jerked a hairsbreadth, he pulled her even closer. She felt pinioned. "How could I judge you? But for the grace of God . . . ."

"So you'll keep my secret?"

"Of course," she whispered.

"When did you spot the clues in the texts I sent in Kayla's name?"

"A few hours ago," she said. "Before I called you."

"How did you put them together?"

"The words. The images. Rock, well, upside down, poison fruit, princess, cottage, chase. And the things Mama Bee said too. Crown of leaves, princess, yellow dress, choked on an apple, dropped out of sight. And then the capstone was the box of stones and your explanation about keeping a soul in its place and me quiet. It started with a dream last night, and then this morning -- another look at the texts and your explanation of the stones -- there was the answer, fully formed, like a voice from the heavens speaking something formless into existence."

"So you came out here not for exercise but to find Kayla."

She shuddered. That was one truth she couldn't admit to. "No. I came just to look at the place I dreamed about last night, just to be sure it's real. But how did you know I'd be here?"

"Those questions you asked me about the weather turned my radar on, so I drove over to your street to see if you left and where you were really going."

After a long silence, Chase asked "Do you want me to show you exactly where Kayla is?"

Bridget could not get her breath. "No." *I didn't replace the lid on the well. You'll know I saw her. You'll know I lied about why I'm here. I don't want to be in that well.*

"Why not?" he asked.

Her mind raced. "I can guess but I don't need to know everything. Not every last detail."

"I don't believe you. You said the Jespersons need to know where she is so they can have closure. I'll bet you feel the same way."

"No. And the Jespersons don't need to hear it from me. Better that I don't know exactly where she is in case someone ever questions me. It's our secret she's out here somewhere."

He got to his feet and loomed over her. "How do you know for sure she's out here?"

Bridget caught her breath. "I don't. Not for sure." She began to babble. "I might have put the clues together wrong. My dream means nothing. Besides, it's logical to believe if you killed her out here, you hid her somewhere close. Though, come to think about it, I can't imagine where because that day we were out here and walked the whole property you checked everything and she wasn't here." She got to her feet and turned. "Is she is in the house?"

"If I hadn't been here," he said menacingly, "you'd be prattling to the police right now, wouldn't you?"

"No. No."

"I can hear the lie in your voice. You know where she is, don't you?"

"I don't want to know," she said.

"Let's take a walk," he said, taking her arm a little too firmly.

Again, she looked at his hands as if they were wild animals. "Wh - where are we going?"

"Why do you sound like that?" he asked.

"Wh - what do I sound like?"

"Frightened."

She shook her head. "I'm not frightened. I'm with you. I want to be with you forever. But I'm getting cold and hungry. Let's go somewhere where we can warm up and get something to eat."

"Later," he said, his voice tight with suspicion. He picked up the shotgun.

"Stop," she said. "I need to pee. Let me go inside a minute."

"Go behind that oak tree. I won't look."

"But it's outside."

"The tree or nothing," he said.

Once behind the tree, she tried to calculate an escape route, but there was none that he couldn't see. And he had a shotgun. So she opened her backpack, took out the dog whistle, and blew. Chase couldn't hear the sound and he couldn't see what she was doing, so she felt relatively safe. Then she palmed the Sheffield all-purpose tool.

★ ★ ★ ★ ★

Doug cocked his head, locating the sound. He was torn. Near the creek he'd treed a squirrel and was panting for it to come down. But then came two more short blasts of the dog whistle, which focused his mind. That meant, COME NOW, no more dilly-dallying. He sniffed and snorted and began to run in the direction of his Pack Leader.

74

Closure
Wednesday, November 27, 2013

Chase and Bridget marched in silence in the direction of the creek. It wasn't a companionable walk, as it had been the first time they visited the cottage. Shotgun in his left hand, Chase used his right to keep a firm grip on her arm. She glanced at his profile. It looked like something carved out of stone. She barely recognized him.

It was now almost fully dark. Darkness was Chase's friend, not hers. The open well they were fast approaching was her watery grave.

Bridget tried to stuff down her panic, but her mind was awhirl.

I will not die like this. I won't. I have to get away. Never let an attacker take you where he can rape or kill you. But right now he's so focused on protecting himself, which means getting rid of me, that diverting him will be hard. I've already appealed to his softer side, the part that once cared for me. Or did he ever really care for me? No point in trying to talk him out of what he's going to do. I can see death in his face. I must act -- and act now. Did Doug hear the whistle? Will he obey? If he finds us, will Chase shoot him? I should never have come out here. Nobody knows I'm here. How stupid of me!

And then she saw the crow, big and black, watching them from the top of the very apple tree she had climbed. Silent and impassive with unblinking eyes, it cared nothing whether she lived or died. Its menacing presence embodied every fear that shattered her assumptions about a benign world.

Good people weren't murdered.

Ordinary people weren't murderers.

Innocent mistakes weren't fatal.

The wild beauty of the land was a mockery, an illusion. A secret poisonous river raging just beneath the apple orchard had found a blow-hole and was about to send her skyward into hot, sulfurous oblivion.

The scream that rolled out of her mouth and echoed off the clouds shocked even her. For just a moment, Chase, startled, loosened his grip on her arm. She flung herself to the ground, stabbed his calf, rolled away, shot to her feet, and began to run in the direction of the well. She prayed that Chase would follow directly in her path without shooting her.

And with a limp he did follow. But not directly, for he turned his head a fraction when he heard Doug barking behind him. Head down, eyes fierce, teeth bared, Doug pounded through the brush, intent on his prey, the Man Who Doesn't Like Dogs.

Keeping one eye on the hound behind him, Chase stayed on the path taken by Bridget but didn't comprehend why she suddenly made a great leap across something he couldn't see until it was too late.

He could not avoid the open well. At the last second, he tried to halt and, arms flailing, scramble away, but it was too late. With a roar, he disappeared out of sight.

Doug stood on the edge of the well, looking down, sniffing and panting and barking until he was hoarse.

Bridget finally persuaded him to be quiet so she could call for help.

Epilogue
Survival
Monday, December 30, 2013

The group from Summit Academy gathered around the fireplace in Ignace Lodge, a long, two-story log cabin on a bluff above Lake Michigan in the Upper Peninsula. The fireplace was big enough to roast a boar. Through the huge glass windows on either side of the fireplace Bridget could see big globs of snow falling like gravel from a dump truck. It was good to be inside.

Christmas trees and poinsettias decorated the gathering room. Holiday garlands hung from the antlers of the deer heads mounted on the walls.

The group was ready for rest, mulled wine, and light chatter before going into a gourmet dinner of venison and roasted winter vegetables. They'd changed out of camouflage, down jackets, and heavy boots into bright holiday clothes. The mood was light-hearted, almost giddy. Tomorrow they would leave for home, happily bonded, feeling both exhausted and elated, virtuous and coddled.

The holiday excursion was Bridget's idea, though Sheila Powers and Justin Creed were vital to its execution. Offer the parents and their teenage students a wilderness trip between Christmas and New Year's and they would jump at it if it combined light survival training and perhaps a little skiing during the day with five-star accommodations and parties at night. It was a fusion of hardship and luxury only Americans living the American Dream could fully appreciate. Bridget promised it would generate money and good will in copious amounts. And it had.

She sat on a stone ledge with her back to the fire, sipping mulled wine, focused on staying in the moment. If she let her guard down even for a second, her mind drifted into dark places -- the murder of Kayla Jesperson and her unborn baby boy, the suicide of The Honorable Theodore M. Bristoll, the perfidy and death of Chase Sumner. In those moments, she felt profoundly alone, haunted by unseen menace, distrustful of everyone and especially of herself.

But this was not the season or the place for dark thoughts. She wasn't alone. She was safe. With pleasure, she watched Justin, wearing a dark blue crewneck sweater and a big smile, cross the room toward her. He sat down beside her.

"You've let your hair grow," she said. "It's wavy. And redder than I thought."

He ran his hand over his head. "I'm not in the military any more, so I thought I'd soften my image."

"Don't soften it too much," she said. "It's a reassuring look. I like to think that if anything bad happened, you'd protect all of us. The crowd loved the days in the woods. They think they're ready now for whatever disaster they might encounter."

"You were right about this little adventure," he said. "All I hear is how much people enjoyed themselves. Half a dozen have already told me we have to do it again next year. And Sheila's bragging about you."

She laughed. "Every muscle in my body is screaming for rest and I'm still just warming up and I'm starving, so I can't bear to think about another week of survival training right now, even if it's a year away."

"We make a great team, you know. You really are Freya."

She made a face and said lightly but with an edge, "Don't ever say that to me again."

He laughed in confusion. "What? Why? You don't like

Freya?"

"No. She's okay. But I don't like 'team player.' That's what Chase called me. A loyal team player. LTP. The term has bad connotations now."

"Objection noted."

"Did I ever tell you the question Sheila -- or was it Lexie -- asked me when I interviewed with them?"

Justin shook his head.

"They asked me if I'd ever misjudged anyone and what I did about it."

"Great question," he said.

"Prophetic, right? I misjudged Chase completely."

"Don't kick yourself about that," Justin said. "Pretty much everyone else did too. Do you miss him?"

Bridget looked down at her mulled wine. "I miss what I thought he was. That's all."

Justin grew serious. "How close were you to him? Did you ever . . . with Chase . . . did you ever . . . ?"

"No."

He raised his eyebrows. "How do you know what I'm asking?"

Bridget giggled. "What else would you be asking? He kissed me twice. That's it. I'm not that kind of girl."

"Meaning what?"

She blushed. "I have to think there's a future before anything goes that far, that's what I mean."

"So what are *we*?" he asked. "Brother soldiers? Comrades in arms? Fellow adventurers?"

"No. We're friends, Justin. I like that word. A lot. Friends. It's a cozy word, very hard to taint. Friends can last a lifetime."

He raised his glass in a toast. "How about we become MTFs?"

"What?" she asked, giggling at the acronym while raising her own glass. Mocking the past was one way to put it to rest.

"More than friends. MTFs. What do you think?" he asked. "Any possibility?"

"It all depends."

"On what?" he asked.

"Can you dance?" she asked, unable to take her eyes off his handsome face. She leaned in. "What is that scent you're wearing, by the way?"

"Calvin Klein Black. Don't get off the subject." He scanned the room, saw that nobody was looking their way, kissed her cheek, and whispered, "I dance like Fred Astaire only straight. I'll show you New Year's Eve."

"Are you asking for a date?"

"I am. You also owe me an evening watching the Vikings because you lost that bet about who was on the Congressman's boat on my birthday."

"I hoped you'd forgotten that."

"I forget nothing. Anyway, do you have a prior engagement for New Year's Eve?"

"No."

"So?"

"I accept. I'll be Ginger Rogers only not blond and I can't dance backwards for long," she whispered in return, inching her hand toward his until their fingers were intertwined. "I hope nobody's looking at us."

"Somebody is," he said, not moving his lips.

"Who?" she breathed, searching the room.

"Sheila," he said. "She just gave me a nod and a smile. She's looking your way."

"Oh, Sheila." She caught her boss's eye and raised her glass. Out of the corner of her mouth, Bridget said, "We owe her. She predicted this."

"Predicted what?"

"It's complicated. I'll explain later."

ABOUT THE AUTHOR

Margarite St. John is the pen name of Margaret Yoder and Johnine Brown, two sisters who were born in Iowa and now live in Fort Wayne, Indiana.

Margaret, the Storyteller, is a fan of true-crime stories and forensics programs. Formerly a school teacher and hospital administrator with a B.A. in Education from Indiana Purdue at Fort Wayne (IPFW), she enjoys crossword puzzles, Bible study, visits with her three children, and travel with her husband, a local surgeon.

Johnine, the Scribe, is a retired attorney, college professor, and editor with a Ph.D. and Master's in English Language and Literature, a J.D. from the University of Chicago, and a Bachelor's in Psychology. She has two children and five grandchildren.

We both love beautiful shoes and dogs, the Nick and Nora movies, Joe Kenda Homicide Hunter, and BBC series like *Downton Abbey*. And we like to travel, especially to settings that appear in our books.

Readers seem surprised by our dark, irreverent sense of humor. Sometimes they find themselves strangely attracted to our lovable rogues -- though not, of course, to our very twisted villains. Fortunately for us, our readers look forward to the shocking but credible endings.

photo © Barb Sleminski; aspen42a@juno.com

Our favorite fan comment is, "I couldn't put the book down."

Our books bear the seal "Winner American Author Contest."

We are available to lead workshops for writers interested in crime fiction.

Visit us on our web site at www.margaritestjohn.com or on our blog at www.margaritestjohn.blogspot.com. Our books are available for Kindle and other electronic devices and in paperback

Made in the USA
Coppell, TX
26 March 2022

75602949R00177